FIRST LIFE

PRAISE FOR THE GIFTEDVERSE

This one kept me interested from the very beginning. With a lot of drama, intrigue and some magic, it's fast paced and entertaining.

— DOODLE BUG

…This trilogy is action packed from start to finish with love and loss along the way… From first book to last, the Owens women will keep you fascinated.

— SUNNI

Packed with excitement, danger, adventure and a roller-coaster ride of emotions. I couldn't put it down until I finished it!..

— CYNDEE MARLING

Wow. That is all I can say about this book. It kept me on my toes waiting to find out what came next. It was well-written with a lot of character and world building.

— SARAH COLEMAN

THE GIFTEDVERSE SERIES

In reading Order:

<u>The Owens Chronicles</u>

Prophecy

Destiny

Legacy

<u>The Gifted Chronicles</u>

First Life

Second Chance

Third Eye

<u>Companion Volumes</u>

Annabelle

Etta

Find out more at

www.giftedverse.com

FIRST LIFE

THE GIFTED CHRONICLES
BOOK ONE

AMANDA LYNN PETRIN

For my grandparents and everything they gave me.
Love, support, encouragement...
and for all the stories.

~

CHAPTER ONE

"How bad is it today?" I asked my sister while counting out her pills. One red, two blue, half a green, and a yellow one I put on the nightstand for her to take in a couple of hours. Last night was rough thanks to a stupid cold that was not going away. Sybill couldn't fall asleep until maybe two in the morning, and that was with me running my fingers through her strawberry blond hair for hours. I tried humming, but my voice hovered between so bad you wanted to fall asleep to get away from it, and so off-tune that it jostled you awake. Her runny nose was better this morning, but she was too weak to get out of bed.

"Maybe a three. Or a two."

"You're not supposed to lie to me, Syb," I warned.

"Tiredness is at a twenty, but I feel fine otherwise. Like, if I could sleep right now, I would be great."

"You can sleep." I handed her the pills and a glass of water, but she looked at me like I was asking her to swallow her cell phone. "I know you want to come, and I would love to have you there, but there is no way you're making it like this." I handed her the chocolate pudding she still needed to swallow pills. You would think she'd be used to it by now. They'd been treating each of her symptoms with industrious quantities of pills for over a decade.

"Maybe I was referring to your incessant talking." She threw a pig-shaped stuffed toy at me, but even without her terrible aim, it didn't make it off the bed. Less like a throw and more that it just fell out of her hands. "I need a five-minute power nap, and then I'll be good to go," she assured me.

"Syb…"

"A little makeup and you won't even notice–"

"Why don't I make you something more substantial than chocolate pudding, and we can see how you feel after that?" I glanced down at my watch. I'd told my dad we might cut it close, but it was looking like we would be at least fifteen minutes late for the presentation, if we got there at all.

"How much time do we have?"

"We're good." I put my hand on hers and gave what I hoped was a reassuring smile. But even if her body was weak, her mind was sharp.

"But what time is it?" she pressed.

"It's 9:45," I said after checking again.

"Doesn't it start at ten?"

"Around there."

"What the hell are you still here for?" This time she threw a stuffed frog, which must have been lighter than the pig, because it hit me in the arm.

"I'm not leaving you alone when you're like this."

"If this were a hangover, you would gladly leave me home to suffer. You would open the blinds and put music on."

"They would ground you for underage drinking, and you would deserve it." I knew she wanted me to treat her like a normal fifteen-year-old, but she wasn't.

"Al, I will never forgive myself if you stay home to keep me company and miss your birthday because of it."

"It's still my birthday, even if we stay home and watch movies. We can give up our tickets and go another day."

"You deserve to go out and celebrate it properly. You've already given me my pills, and my pudding. Now I need you to get the hell out of here so I can finally get some sleep without your dreadful singing and yapping and fussing and—"

"I get it." I stopped her from a longer list of things I did that were annoying, ignoring the fact that she was the one who asked me to sing last night.

I rushed to put on a pair of beige capri pants and a plain white t-shirt, leaving my long blond hair loose. I threw on some necklaces and almost looked put together, as opposed to the "fashion mess" Syb always accused me of being.

I put my lips to her forehead before heading out, relieved she didn't have a fever. To be honest, she looked better than she had in days, other than the fact that she'd stayed in bed most of the week and still had bags under her eyes.

"I'm fine, and you're late," she warned without opening them.

"Get some sleep." I gave her another kiss, this one with no ulterior motive, before rushing out.

CHAPTER TWO

I rode my bike to the subway station and made the train without a second to spare, rushing in just as the doors were closing. I let out a breath of relief and took a seat by the door. I tried both of my parents' phones to tell them I was running later than expected, but I would bet a good chunk of money that my father left his phone in the car to be present and not let work distract him from this for me, and my mom's was dead long before my dad picked her up at Massachusetts General Hospital following an overnight shift.

I checked my phone to see if Sybill messaged me, but took my zero messages to mean she got back to sleep, which was good. She needed rest so she could kick this bug and get back to normal. Or at least her normal.

As a self-respecting millennial, I scrolled through Instagram and Facebook before heading to the spam emails that made up most of my inbox. I deleted at least five newsletters for book-stores and clothing sales, then opened an email from my dad. His accounting firm was closed for the summer so we could have our six-week family 'vacation', and so they could renovate the office. I still had two years of university left, but he'd already put my office into the plans and sent me a photographic reminder of what the rest of my life would look like.

I knew how proud and excited he was. He'd worked his way up in a small firm until he was running it. I couldn't remember the first time one of us mentioned me taking business courses so I could join him and bring the firm into the twenty-first century for him. I did, however, know the moment I realized he was serious about it. I was writing an essay for my college application and Sybill made the joke that my greatest challenge was having to live with the shame of not being as awesome as my baby sister. My dad jumped in, telling me to write about how I took it upon myself to manage my sister's pills and all her treatments because it showed familiarity with numbers and a head for business. I was going to tell him I was applying for a double major in archeology and history, but then I saw his face. He was dead serious. All those jokes I thought we were making were actual plans for him. He'd even talked to the old couple who owned the company about it before they retired and left it all to him. To us. I couldn't crush his dream.

I still applied to Archeology, as a back-up, but when the Business Administration program accepted me, I knew what I had to do.

I replied to my dad's picture with a heart and was about to put my phone away when a new email came in. I assumed it was spam, but the headline caught my attention.

Want to make a difference in the world? Take charge of your life and career with a summer internship at the Boston police department. Become a real-life Bones!

It was sent to my school email, addressed to everyone in the archeology department. They usually only sent out department emails about potlucks and networking events, so this seemed out of character. Still, I was bored and trying to avoid social interactions, so I read on.

If you are currently studying archeology, we want you to join us.
Bring comfort to grieving families by helping our team get to the
bottom of unsolved mysteries.
Eight-week commitment.
Priority will be given to second-year students, but all are welcome
to apply!

It was obviously a gross exaggeration of what summer interns would contribute, but my two archeology electives hardly qualified me. Even for a glorified coffee-getter position.

I WAS STILL LOOKING over the pictures when the train reached my stop, so I quickly deleted the email and returned my phone to my pocket. I took the stairs two at a time and ran the three blocks to the lecture hall.

The woman at the entrance was playing on her phone, not expecting anyone to show up forty-five minutes into the hour-long presentation.

"Can I help you?" she asked, her fingers still texting while she looked up at me with a smile.

"I have a ticket under Alison Carmichael," I shared, hoping this wasn't the kind of thing you weren't allowed into once it started.

"Oh…it's almost over and Professor Mallory has very precise timing. Do you want me to see if I can transfer it to another date? She has another talk tomorrow afternoon or Tuesday evening."

"I have people waiting for me inside."

"You'll have to stand once you get in, unless they saved you a seat at the end," she warned, handing me my ticket.

"Thank you."

I wasn't sure if she was judging me or if I was projecting, but I felt like everyone in the room turned to stare at me as I walked in. I considered walking right back out and telling my parents I sat on the upper level, but my dad waved at me from two rows above, saving the last seat on the end for me, with my mom asleep beside him.

"Where's Syb?" he whispered, kissing the top of my head when I got to him.

"She wasn't feeling up to it."

"Do you want us to try this again when you can actually listen to the whole thing?" he offered, and I loved him for being willing to sit through it a second time for me.

"It's okay, I'm sure I can catch up."

"Your mother was in charge of taking notes," he teased.

CHAPTER THREE

"What are we doing to celebrate, Birthday Girl?" Mom asked, taking me in her arms once the talk was over and the clapping woke her up. I appreciated my parents insisting on participating in our interests for our birthdays, but while I would have loved Professor Philomena Mallory's talk on the significance of musical instruments through time, my mom looked like she'd slept through it and wanted nothing more than to go back to sleep.

"I was thinking we could order pizza and maybe watch a movie?" I suggested.

"It's your twentieth birthday, Pumpkin. This is your chance to go to a nice, fancy dinner, see a movie, whatever you want," my dad offered.

"Syb stayed home. It wouldn't be a celebration without her."

"We can pick up donuts from that place with the pink boxes." Mom raised her eyebrows suggestively.

"With an extra order of the espresso-filled ones?" My dad kissed the top of her head.

"That sounds perfect."

They each wrapped an arm around me, so it was slow getting to the car. My mom passed out almost as soon as she buckled her seat belt.

"Give her a power nap and she'll be good as new." My dad looked at me through the rearview mirror with confidence, even though we both knew she needed more than a fifteen-minute nap after an overnight shift. They'd been working opposite shifts since I was little, so someone could always be home for Sybill and I.

"I don't mind if she gets her rest and has cold pizza when she wakes up," I assured him.

She started telling us she liked cold pizza better so we would stop feeling bad for her every time she got home late, but after a decade of overnight shifts at the hospital with microwaves eating into her nap times, I think she got used to it.

"It's your birthday," he reminded me.

"I'm not even twenty-one. That's the fun one."

"Don't be in a hurry to grow up, Pumpkin. Try to enjoy being a kid sometimes," he said, ruffling my hair.

I smiled because I knew it was what he was trying for. I had the most amazing parents in the world, and I loved them to pieces.

SYBILL WAS WAITING on the couch in the living room, ready to throw confetti at me when I walked in. Mom stayed awake long enough to eat a piece of pizza and a donut before she and Sybill were both asleep. It was barely evening, the sun still shining bright outside, just thinking about eventually coming down.

"You can switch it," I told my dad, careful not to let the cream filling from my second donut fall on Syb's hair, as she'd fallen asleep in my lap. We'd chosen a romantic comedy when it was three against one.

"It's your night," he argued.

"I'll have to re-watch it with them anyway."

"History channel?" he suggested.

"At least until eight." That was when the reruns of his police procedurals started. They were always incredibly predictable, but you could watch them in whatever order you wanted, and they solved the mystery by the end of the hour. It was good for when Mom and Syb watched them with us.

My dad smiled at me before we watched a special on medieval pottery. He was a good sport, even waiting until I told him the other show was starting to change the channel, as if he was so enthralled that he'd forgotten.

We watched a couple of episodes, then debated whether real cops and criminals would behave like the ones on TV, and if corner store security cameras could really read license plates from a block away. It was almost eleven by the time he carried my mom up the stairs like she weighed no more than a small child, and I woke Sybill up when I stood. It was a shame she was such a light sleeper because I easily could have carried her the few feet to our bedroom. We'd moved into the den when the stairs became too much for her.

"I got you something," Sybill said, leaning her head against my shoulder as we walked.

"You already got me the books," I reminded her. Granted, I was halfway through them, but that was because she was too excited and gave them to me as soon as they arrived two weeks ago.

"This is a bonus. It cost nothing, but you'll like it."

"I'm sure I will." Her homemade gifts ranged from wild-flowers and macaroni cards to peanut butter cookies and makeovers. Some I enjoyed more than others, but it was the thought that counted.

"Since you missed the talk today, I got you the recording," she said, handing me a USB key.

"It was a live event; they didn't have a recording," I argued.

"It was in a university building that records all their classes."

"You asked the AV people to send it to you?" I was pretty sure the answer would have been no.

"I would have, but then they would know it was me."

"How did you get it?"

"A magician never reveals her tricks." She shrugged innocently, but I kept my eyes on her. "It's not like you would understand if I told you."

"Just because you're a lot better with computers than I am doesn't mean I'm completely illiterate."

"Not completely," she agreed.

I found the frog she'd thrown at me this morning on the floor and threw it at her, careful to miss her head. I had an average knowledge of computers, but she was in a special high school that focused almost entirely on IT. It made life easier when she had to work from home, but also convinced her the world wide web was her oyster to use as she pleased.

"I'm sorry. It sucks that I get to study computers while you're in a program you hate."

"I don't hate it," I argued. "It just wasn't my first choice."

"I'll pretend to believe you."

"Will you watch it with me tomorrow morning?" I asked of Professor Mallory's talk.

"Mom wants to bring me in again to switch the blue pills. She thinks they're what's making me so tired." Sybill was too exhausted to roll her eyes, but I understood. Since no one could figure out what was wrong with her, they gave her pills to manage the symptoms. Some worked while others gave terrible side effects, but Mom was determined to find the perfect combination that would make Sybill feel okay again. Not that Syb and I had given up...we simply believed she would get better once they figured out what was wrong with her, not when they perfected her prescription drug cocktail.

"When you get back?"

"We can revisit this conversation when it's no longer your birthday," she teased before I turned out the lights.

CHAPTER FOUR

I took a deep breath before bringing my hand to the breastplate, running my fingers over the old metal. I could practically feel the blows inflicted upon it and smell the fear of the man who wore it. Almost.

"You can see from the carving in the metal that this piece was used in addition to the standard armor of the period. It would take another hundred years for a breastplate like this to become the standard, which is why earlier historians misidentified it as a simple dish, or as being from the wrong century," I told the sixth graders in my tour group.

Two students in the back garnered a small audience by using their pens for a sword fight, but everyone else seemed interested in my presentation. I loved student groups so much more than the business functions they sometimes brought in. Giving tours of the museum was my favorite part of the after-school job I'd been working since junior high. Well, that and archiving, because nothing can beat the first time you encounter a new piece.

"This indentation probably came from an arrow, and this

line here from a sword attack they were unable to avoid," I added, finding satisfaction when the two opponents in the back row looked up at the mention of swords.

"ANY QUESTIONS?" I asked once the tour was over, passing around the replicas Dr. Richards made my second year working there. Kids were more engaged when you let them manipulate the ancient artifacts, but you didn't want to entrust children with medieval weaponry. Especially not heavy and priceless medieval weaponry that can cause a lot of damage if two people get upset over wanting to hold it at the same time. Thank God Dr. Richards didn't hold it against me; he just made safer replicas. We still used the genuine artifacts to show texture, debris, and color, but only staff members could handle them.

"Yeah, um, did anyone die while wearing that breastplate?" One of the sword fighters asked, nervous laughter coming from the rest of the class.

I anticipated the question since it came up every time, but it always surprised me. It was like none of them realized that even if 'anyone' lived centuries ago, they were still a person.

"That's inconclusive," I shared, having been warned not to remind the children of their humanity. "It isn't like we can see a hole at the heart with centuries-old blood preserved inside, but my guess is the armor did its job and kept its owner safe." It was an educated guess based on a gut feeling and simply wanting it to be true.

ONCE THE KIDS LEFT, I went to catalogue the shipment for our next exhibition. Dr. Richards had to sign off on everything, but he let me check it all out first. This one was on anthropology and archeology, with a focus on how they could be used in modern society, such as solving mysteries and crimes. It felt like Dr. Richards' obvious attempt at keeping me at the museum after I graduated, but the possibility of that life disappeared years ago when I turned down the archeology program and chose business. Still, it was fascinating.

Normally, I would check off the item once I found it and move on, but today I took a little longer, knowing it would be my last shipment until September.

"Miss Carmichael, a word?" Dr. Richards surprised me into nearly dropping a vase worth more than my house.

"Of course," I assured him, placing the vase gently back in the crate.

Dr. Richards was close to eighty years old, with wispy white hair, a manicured beard, and the cutest horn-rimmed glasses. I knew the museum's board of directors wanted him to retire so he could be replaced by someone younger who was still publishing and making discoveries, but I liked him. He was the one who hired me, and who had a story for every piece in the vast collections, his face lighting up for each one. I would take excited over prestigious any day.

"That was a fascinating presentation," he told me. "I usually have to steer students back to their groups, but your passion has always been so refreshing."

"Thank you," I told him, flushed with pride, but he just smiled back.

"How was Professor Mallory's talk on the weekend?"

"Very interesting. Thank you." He'd given me his comp tickets, so I wasn't about to tell him I'd missed the live version and watched a bootlegged copy with my sister on Sunday night.

"I'm glad you enjoyed it. I've always found her wonderful to listen to," he shared. "How much longer do we have you for?"

"I'm on the schedule until Sunday, but we only leave the following Friday if you need an extra student wrangler."

"Have you considered a summer internship? We partner with the university, summer camps, and other organizations in a variety of fields to demonstrate all the ways history and archeology are still useful today. Other than for curating museums." He gave me a smile like I was in on a joke, so I smiled back.

"I'm studying Business Administration for a reason," I argued, more to remind myself than to be rude to him.

"I have to admit it surprised me when you chose that field." He waited for me to comment, but I didn't. "You should do something for yourself that makes you happy."

"I will. Once Sybill is better." I didn't mention my father's firm, which would also impede my happiness once I graduated.

"The internships are a really exciting, worthy opportunity, Miss Carmichael. Archeology shouldn't just be something you do as an after-school hobby before getting an office job." He sighed, almost sounding disappointed. "Professor Mallory is hosting a little get-together before she wraps up her Society Talks and leads a team in Europe. I would love for you to be there."

In addition to being the famed archeologist I wished I could be, Professor Mallory was the head of my university's Archeology Department. As in, she had final say on who got into the internships Dr. Richards mentioned.

"I appreciate that, but it would be a waste of a spot to invite me. I'm spending the summer in California."

"The invitation is yours, regardless. You can come just because you'll have fun, and you might learn something. We'll be at the Villa at eight pm. You can meet Professor Mallory one-on-one and make an educated decision afterwards."

"I really need to—"

"You have a true Gift, Miss Carmichael. It would be a shame if you didn't use it," he said before I could argue.

"Did you want me to lock up on my way out?" I offered,

packing up my things. I felt terrible for blowing him off, but I didn't want to get into it.

"No, I'll take care of it," he assured me.

"I'll see you tomorrow, Dr. Richards."

"Hopefully sooner, Miss Carmichael."

CHAPTER FIVE

"Sibby?" I called when I got home and found it eerily quiet. I was a few minutes late, but my little sister was usually in one of her online worlds by now. "Sibby?" I tried again, walking around the main level, hoping she wasn't in bed, when I saw her through the kitchen window.

"Is it already six?" she asked, alerted by the wind chimes when I opened the back door.

"I'm a little late. Have you been out here all day?"

"It was so sunny and beautiful, I couldn't help it," she explained, giving me a bright smile.

"When was the last time you ate?" I asked, kissing the top of her head to say hello. The fever still hadn't come back.

"I'm fine, Allie. Why are you late?"

"Dr. Richards wanted to talk to me, so I missed my usual train," I shared.

"What did Brontosaurus Rex want?" She followed me inside so we could get dinner started. Her hair stuck to the back of her neck from the exertion of that two-minute walk.

"You shouldn't call him that," I reproached, setting a knife and some vegetables on the table so she could sit down and chop them. She insisted on helping me cook, but standing was exhausting for her, and she refused to use a walker.

"You're the one who showed me the reviews," she reminded me. I'd asked her for help with the museum's website, and we'd combed through the Yelp and TripAdvisor reviews to find the best ones. Unfortunately, even the ones that raved about how fun and educational the museum was still referred to Dr. Richards as Brontosaurus Rex, a nickname from the museum's first review. Sybill had suggested they embrace it and put a page of pictures with him and some children he gave tours to over the years. Dr. Richards had been heartbroken that everyone thought of him as a fossil, even if he said she could do whatever she felt was best for the museum.

"He wants me to do a summer internship thing...but I told him I couldn't." I stole a piece of the pepper she was cutting. "It's just a summer program for archeology students where you're matched with archeologists in different fields and sort of intern with them to see what you want to do with your degree," I added when her eyebrows shot up at me.

"Are you able to do it if you've only taken electives?"

"Probably not. But he knows the person in charge of the program, Professor Mallory, so he wants me to meet her at a get-together tonight."

"That's amazing, Al. You love her. And you would be so good at it."

"You don't even know what *it* is."

"It doesn't matter. Digging, research, cataloguing...you're the only person I've ever encountered who sees more than a lump of clay and a bunch of rocks when they look at that junk."

"That's because you haven't encountered any archeologists."

"It's because you love that stuff."

"Can't you feel the history in the pieces?" She'd sat through every single one of my school presentations, even pretending to be interested while I had her touch every imaginary piece to practice for school groups at the museum. She was not a very good actress, but neither were the students.

"No, I definitely can't. It's a gift only you have, and you should use it." She used the same words as Dr. Richards.

"We have the new drug trial," I reminded her.

"No, *I* have a new drug trial. You're hanging out in a hospital so you can worry about me up close instead of from afar."

"I do more than worry about you," I argued.

"You deserve a bit of fun before settling down to a life of boring numbers and caretaking."

"Syb!"

I scowled, like every other time she was defeatist. She put her hands up in surrender, but I could also see she meant it.

"Maybe we both need to live a little," she tried. "You can play with old stuff, and I might get the chance to actually meet new people if I'm not constantly being shadowed by my overbearing older sister." She brought the back of her hand to her forehead to be extra dramatic, but she smiled to let me know she didn't hate having me around. "When does he want you there?" she asked, dumping the cucumber she'd sliced into the bowl of garden salad. She picked out the red cabbage chunks before chopping celery.

"I have nothing to wear," I argued, but she looked at me like that was an excuse and she didn't care.

I usually dressed practically in case something happened. Everything I bought was washing machine safe and easy to run around in, thanks to one too many mishaps while semi-carrying Sybill to a nurse's station, home from the park, to the ER, and so on. You only need to be caught wearing a dress that rides up once before you don't wear that kind of thing again. If you asked me, skorts were the greatest thing since sliced bread.

"Maybe a cute, earthy-toned short set to show how ready you are to dig and talk about fossils?" she teased.

"It's at the Villa, which is way fancier than anything in my closet."

"So, we need to make a really good impression," she understood. "Lucky for you, I am killing it with the flowy dresses. Most of them should fit you."

She got excited, rifling through her closet. We were the same height, but I probably weighed at least fifty pounds more than she did. Thankfully, she liked long, flowy dresses that she paired with Converse shoes. They completely hid her shape, so her face was the only way you could tell if she was withering away or doing better.

I had what I guess you would call an athletic build from years of jogging with my dad and playing tennis with my mom. Not to mention the yoga all four of us did whenever Sybill was feeling up to it. While it was supposed to strengthen her muscles and bring her peaceful meditation, we ended up giggling more than we meditated.

Sybill took out her rainbow-colored assortment of dress options, so I indulged her in a fashion show, modeling each dress to loud whoops before we settled on a burgundy one just tight enough to show that I had a shape, but not enough for you to realize I didn't have any curves. I knew it was the perfect combination of sophistication and *wow* when, instead of whistling at me when I turned around, her jaw dropped, and she fell silent.

"It's perfect," she told me, biting her bottom lip and looking at me like I was a sculpture and she was the artist, which terrified me. "What were you thinking for your hair? And makeup?"

"This." I shrugged, which was clearly the wrong answer. I ran my hand through my blond locks to give them some volume, but she looked at me with a tilted head and scrunched face as if to say, 'Is it, though?'

"I don't want one of your YouTube tutorials, Syb," I warned. Sometimes, when she needed a boost, my mom and I would plan makeover parties where Sybill loved using neon colors and way too much glitter. We would look like we walked off edgy runways, not like normal human beings.

"Give me twenty minutes. If you don't like it, I'll wipe it off and you can go like that," she decided, grabbing brushes and bottles before I had the chance to argue.

❧

IT TOOK HER HALF AN HOUR, but by the end, she made me look like a classic movie star. It was like she accented everything I already was and covered up the blemishes, so I only felt slightly out of place.

"Anyone who isn't blind will notice you in this dress. And with that brain of yours, you're the full package."

"It's leading them on," I argued.

"Give it a chance. And if you see something you find the least bit interesting, don't you dare turn it down so you can take care of me. Fight for it." She got this intense look in her eyes, like there would be hell to pay if I didn't.

"Thank you," I said instead of all the arguments swirling around in my head.

"Knock 'em dead," she told me with a smile before I headed out.

CHAPTER SIX

I power-walked to the station closest to my house and rode the train seven stops before transferring to the orange line. I was three stops away from the Villa's when they announced it was the end of the line and ushered everyone off the train.

"Due to an unforeseen incident, we are experiencing a temporary delay on the Orange line. Please standby," the automated system sounded.

"Great." I sighed, slumping my shoulders before going to stand by the wall. I caught a glimpse of myself in an empty ad space and felt overdressed and out of place. I should have told Syb not to bother doing my eyelashes with her torture device and gotten to the station on time. But it made her happy. And my eyes *did* pop.

There were only a handful of people on the platform with me. A middle-aged couple occupied the only seats, a group of teenagers stood in a circle with their noses glued to their cell phones, and a young guy with unruly black hair talked on the phone. He paced while he did so, walking past me a couple of times. He looked like a Calvin Klein model in his Levi's and dark grey t-shirt, but it was his constant smile that hooked me.

"I need to do this, Delia." He sounded reassuring, but his hand was at his temple, massaging it to relieve the tension. "I'm still at the station. I've been here almost half an hour and the trains keep turning around, but I'll let you know once I'm there."

At least foregoing the torture device wouldn't have made a difference.

I knew I shouldn't be eavesdropping, but there was something about his energy that drew me in. He was the only person in the station who didn't look miserable. He looked over to me while the other person was talking, and I don't know if he caught me staring or if he simply had a habit of smiling at strangers, but he smiled back at me with such warmth that I felt a flutter in my stomach before I turned away and focused on the notice board to my left. Apparently, the track would be cleared within the hour.

I checked my watch and let out a sigh. It felt like the universe was mocking me. I cursed myself for not bringing a bigger purse that could hold a book. Not to mention my phone was dying, so I couldn't text to pass the time or read from one of my apps. There was nothing to do but wait.

Fifteen minutes later, I was still standing there with the system announcing more delays. At this rate, I would probably get there faster if I had just ridden my bike. The minutes of my watch had never moved so fast, but nothing was happening.

Hopefully, tonight's get-together would be so crowded that no one would notice I was late. Or maybe I should have stayed home and worked on my summer reading. But I couldn't let Dr. Richards down. He seemed to believe in me, and even if I didn't see what he saw in me, I really wanted it to be there.

I decided I would wait five more minutes, then I would give up and go home.

"Today is not the day for public transit."

I almost jumped when the guy with the phone came to stand beside me.

"What?" I asked, more because I wasn't sure why he was talking to me than because I didn't hear him.

"They're saying it'll probably take hours to get it running again," he shared.

"Another announcement?" I asked.

"On the website," he agreed, showing me his phone.

"Great." I sighed, considering my options.

"I'm Tristan." He introduced himself with such an earnest smile that I couldn't help but respond.

"Alison."

"Where are you headed?"

"The Villa," I told him after a slight hesitation. "You?"

"The Owens Plantation." He looked over to see if I knew what that was. "At this point it would be faster if we walked."

"Then go for it," I told him, still not sure why he suddenly started up a conversation. "I'd rather take my chances with the bus than trek up and down muddy nature trails in the dark."

"Or we could take Beverly," he suggested.

"Who's Beverly?" I asked.

"It's a road that doesn't get much use anymore, but you can take it straight from here to the back of the Villa, bypassing the big hill and the marshes."

"Why have I never heard of it?" I was skeptical.

"Part of it flooded maybe a century ago, but they've asphalted it since. The tides have been low lately."

"That doesn't sound dangerous at all." I shook my head at him. "History or urban planning?" I tried to guess his major, but it was a subtle way to find out if he was also a student.

"Why not both?" he countered. The answer should have made me roll my eyes, but he had an easy smile that made me want to smile back. And trust him. "I stayed here a few years ago with someone who loved telling me all about how it used to be. I'm more of a modernist when it comes to art, but I'm easy to please either way. What about you?"

"Business Administration," I answered what I hoped he was asking. "But I love any piece that tells a story."

"What about the pieces that make you feel things?" he asked.

"Aren't they the same?"

"Touché." He smiled. "I'm going to walk so I can make it home before next week. I could accompany you if that isn't too—"

"Stalkerish? Creepy?" I finished for him, but at the same time, I wouldn't mind spending more time getting to know him. Unless he killed me.

"I promise I'm neither. Not that you have any reason to trust me, but here's my ID. You can call your family and tell them I'm the one taking you home before we go. If that makes you feel any better," he said, fishing around in his pocket before showing me a license picture of him with braces. *Tristan Elijah Davis.* He'd changed a lot since it was taken. Not that he was bulky now, but he looked incredibly scrawny in the picture. His smile, however, was the same. I tried to make out his age, but he had his thumb on the date. I would assume he was about twenty, like me, but I was terrible at guessing things like that. I would be much better at using his clothes and accessories to figure out what period he was from, but he wasn't an artifact.

"You're just a really Good Samaritan?" I asked, doubting it but also convinced that his eyes couldn't lie. The way they lit up was mesmerizing because the color of them was so dark. Like brown, only...darker.

"I have my mom's voice in the back of my head warning me I shouldn't leave you here alone, basically stranded," he shot back at me. The teenagers had given up and gone in the opposite direction, while the couple was on their feet, looking to do the same once the next train arrived.

"With a savior complex."

"I might also be terrified of the dark," he teased.

"Are you saying Beverly isn't a well-lit, safe road to take with strangers in the middle of the night?"

"This is good, I wouldn't want it to be easy." He shrugged like he would wait there with me all night.

"It's always more rewarding if you have to convince your victims to follow you into the woods than when they just come willingly."

"You're a lot darker than your pretty dress and angelic appearance would suggest."

"Angelic?" I asked.

"I guess the red should have tipped me off."

"I thought you were walking?"

"I was," he agreed, holding eye contact in a way that should have been creepy coming from a stranger, but it gave me butter-flies more than anything. "Then I remembered I don't really need to rush back to the empty house I'm sitting."

"How long are you in town for?" I asked, surprised that it made me sad to know he wasn't staying.

"A couple of weeks," he shared. "Are you staying at the Villa?"

"No, I have a faculty mixer thing there at eight." I didn't mention that I wasn't a part of the faculty and shouldn't really be going at all.

"Aren't you going to be late?"

"Probably." I sighed, smiling at his obvious attempt to convince me to go with him.

"The truth is, I've spent a really long time feeling...lonely, though never actually being alone. So, full disclosure, I am hoping to make an excellent first impression, so you'll give me the chance to make a second one."

His honesty was intimidating, but also refreshing.

"Well, when you ask like that..."

"Come on, what have you got to lose?" He headed for the

door as they announced that the replacement buses would be there within the hour. I bit my lip and debated it for half a second before following him out.

"Just follow Bishop until the fork where it turns left onto Beverly, right?" Tristan asked whoever he called. All I could tell was that it was a she. "Yeah, the little slope, I remember. Thanks Delia." He hung up and turned to me. "We're good to go."

"You brought me out here alone at night under false pretenses?" I asked, trying not to bring up how that was his second call to this Delia person. It would make me the creepy and stalkerish one for noticing.

"It was a while ago, and I wasn't completely paying attention at the time. I didn't want to have misrepresented myself, but she confirmed it all."

"She being your…" I trailed off for his answer, slightly hating myself for asking, but I wanted to know.

"Delia." He smiled, then continued when he realized that wasn't really an answer. "She's like a very maternal older sister. I came here…not without a goodbye, but definitely without a plan of what I would do once I got here, and she's worried about me. I'm usually the reliable, old-faithful type."

"Now you tell me," I teased.

"Have you ever felt like you needed a change, to go off on your own so you could…find yourself? It sounds cheesy, but I've been part of a family for so long that I know my role, but I don't know who I am."

"Philosophy." I made another guess at his field of study to lighten the mood.

"You think I'm crazy now." He shook his head at himself.

"No, I…I get it. I came here tonight for this internship program that sounds amazing, but it would mean being on my own without all the pressure and responsibilities of…" I stopped myself, ashamed I would go that far.

"Of what?" he asked.

"Where is home to you?" I changed the subject.

"I was a military brat." He went along with it. "My dad retired when I was twelve though, so we've been on the East Coast for the past few years."

"Where is your favorite place you've lived?"

"South Carolina," he answered without hesitation.

"We went there when I was little. I remember having so much fun just running through the waves all day."

"You should go back," he suggested.

"That wouldn't work."

"You're all booked until the end of time?" he pried.

"I went with my family and…" I sighed before deciding to just tell him. "My sister has been really sick, practically her whole life. We went there for a breakthrough trial that didn't work, but my parents were great at making the trips fun for us. She has another experimental treatment at a facility in California this summer, which is why I can't do the summer program. It wouldn't feel right to have fun while she is suffering alone."

I was afraid he would become weird and quiet as people often did, or tell me I was crazy and overbearing. Part of me hoped he would tell me I was right, that I shouldn't do the program here instead of being there for my sister in California. But a part of me also wanted him to want me to stay. Which was ridiculous.

"How did she convince you to come tonight?" He accurately analyzed our relationship, and why I came when I had no intentions of doing an internship.

"She said I have a gift and need to live a little," I admitted. "And she may have implied that my constant hovering is the reason she doesn't have more friends."

"Sounds like you have an awesome little sister." He smiled, but there was a sadness to it.

"She's my world, in the best way possible. I can't imagine not going with her because those experimental things are usually hell. I always find a way to sneak in past visiting hours and read with her, but…I can't remember the last time I was this excited about school. And part of me thinks it might be nice to sleep without waking up a dozen times to make sure she's still breathing. And I know that makes me a terrible person, but—"

"It doesn't."

"That's sweet, but—"

"The thing I hated the most about being sick was what it did to my parents. They never once complained about it, at least not to me, but even an eight-year-old can tell."

"I'm sorry, I had no idea." I tried to figure out what he meant by 'sick', but it would be rude to ask.

"Cancer," he answered anyway. "Started out in my stomach, then popped up a few years later in my blood, which sucked. I was in remission for almost a year before it got to my knee, then kind of spread to my bones."

"That's—"

"I know."

"How did you…" I wanted to ask how he got better but realized he might not be. Maybe I didn't want to know.

"They were about to take my leg as a last-ditch effort to save me, but—" A darkness filled his eyes, as if he was reliving it.

"The chemo worked?" I offered.

"Um, yeah. Yeah, that's what happened." He snapped out of it.

I seemed to lose him when we talked about his past, so I tried to convince him I wasn't as heartless as I felt.

"I really don't mind. Taking care of my sister. I love her and she brings way more to my life than she takes...but this program could be my last chance," I tried to explain, but I still felt terrible. Sybill had been relatively stable for years, but there were always risks with new trials. I would never forgive myself if I chose the program over her.

"Because you're graduating?" he asked.

"Not for a couple of years, but I'll be graduating with a degree that will help me work at my dad's accounting firm while the program is in archeology. My boss was talking like this program was my destiny or something, which is a lot of pressure and makes me think he's seeing things..."

"But you feel it, too," he finished for me.

"Now *I* sound crazy."

"You're a good person, Alison."

"Why?" I had expected him to tell me I wasn't crazy, because it was the polite thing to do, but his response was out of left field.

"You know exactly what you want to do, but you're waiting for the world to tell you it's okay because you're terrified of letting people down. It's noble, but you need to do what makes you happy. What sets your soul on fire. Otherwise, you'll spend your life hating yourself for resenting your sister and she'll hate herself for making you miss out."

I was offended and wanted to argue with everything he said until I remembered he'd been Sibby and could have a unique perspective I was too busy being the big sister to see. "Talking from experience?" I asked.

"Delia also says that we all have a purpose; most of us are just wasting time until we figure it out. It can be hard to step up and own it, but depriving the world of your Gifts is selfish and kills your soul."

"She sounds sweet," I said sarcastically.

"The circumstances were a little different, but the point is that you can't hide from it once you figure out what it is."

"I'll keep that in mind."

"And here we are," he pointed out, guiding me around a tiny fence. The second his hand touched my arm, it was like I could feel sparks of electricity coursing through my veins. More like static than a shock, but my skin tingled where his fingers had been.

I could have sworn he felt it as well, but he went back to smiling like nothing happened almost immediately.

"In record time, too." I was impressed. I could already see the lights from the patio with a couple drinking wine and enjoying the sunset.

"I'm nothing if not a man of my word," he agreed.

"Well, thank you. Really, I appreciate it."

"Anytime," he assured me, continuing on Beverly, presumably to The Owens Plantation. I knew it was somewhere around The Villa, but the Owens Estate had too many stories of being haunted and cursed to ever make me want to go near it.

I hesitated before saying, "You can have a second."

"Second what?"

"Impression." I fished through my clutch for a scrap of paper and wrote down my number. I was not used to any of this, but I wanted to see him again.

"Are you free this week?"

"I could be."

"Dinner?" he offered.

"Okay," I agreed before heading to the door, very aware that I had taken on his trait; I couldn't stop smiling.

CHAPTER EIGHT

I followed the signs once a gloved doorman let me in. Orchestra music floated down the hall and the faint murmur of conversation grew louder until I entered a ballroom. I was shocked to find the six-piece orchestra was for us. So much for a little get-together.

Dr. Richards stood in the corner with a group of academics talking on couches while Beethoven played in the background.

"Ah, there you are!" He got up and came to greet me.

"I'm so sorry. There was a delay with the train, so I walked," I apologized.

"Don't worry about it. We finally convinced Professor Mallory to play." His smile was one of pure joy.

"What game?" I asked. I assumed she would be testing the students who wanted to be a part of her summer programs. It was smart of her to look at more than resumes, but I wondered if she was testing their knowledge or figuring out who would be the most entertaining on location. I didn't know all the program options, but I knew that digs were often on remote locations for months in close quarters.

Dr. Richards smiled in a way that made it clear he was

simply too polite to laugh at me before nodding to the orchestra. "We hired a five-piece orchestra for ambiance during the cocktails, but she can't resist when Beethoven comes on. This kind of performance is priceless."

"The cellist," I realized. It was obvious to see which one she was, but I hadn't recognized her when I came in. Professor Mallory was in her late thirties, with rust-colored hair that she famously kept in a perfect and elegant bun, whether she was teaching at school or digging up Egyptian tombs. I'd seen her from afar on campus as well as for her Talk, but she looked completely different with a cello. She always gave off the impression of being strict and scary, but there was a melancholy to her when she played with her eyes closed, one with the music.

"Some people never find their calling, yet she has two," he said, clearly in awe of her.

"That's why she's so interested in the development of musical instruments." Her talk had gone into detail about the Neanderthal flute, but I thought it was just one of the many discoveries she made throughout her career, not one of her greatest passions. "Where are the others?" They set the room up with rows of chairs facing a podium, but it seemed all the attendees, about thirty of them, sat on those couches in the corner.

"Now that you're here, that's everyone. Tonight is an invitation-only, informal kind of thing."

"So nice of you to finally join us. I'm Philomena Mallory." She came over and introduced herself to me after the song ended and we all gave her a standing ovation.

"Alison Carmichael. Thank you for waiting for me." I remembered an article Sibby had read to me about women always apologizing for their existence, and how we should say 'Thank you' instead of 'I'm Sorry'. I'd thought it was silly at the time, but I got the feeling Professor Mallory wouldn't care about my apology, so I might as well try something.

"Miss Carmichael is the one I was telling you about earlier, who recognized the armor."

"Most students would think it was a dish."

"Most dishes don't have blood stains and arrow indentations." I shrugged. I was used to Dr. Richards saying I had talent, but she went from walking past me to engaging.

"That's a fair point," she said, giving me a second look. I reached to tuck my hair behind my ear, something I did when I felt like I was being judged. It only got worse when her eyes flickered to my hand, showing me she noticed. "I hope you wouldn't be late for our programs if you were accepted."

"No, ma'am," I said, more because she made me nervous than because I had any intention of applying.

"Come sit beside me. I'll fill you in on what you missed."

I QUICKLY UNDERSTOOD WHAT DR. Richards had referred to as an opportunity to meet Professor Mallory and find out about the different programs was more of an opportunity for her to evaluate the applicants before making her final decision. The most coveted program was a month-long dig in Italy, orchestrated by Professor Mallory, and she hand-picked her people. She had five spots to fill and thirty eager candidates, which was what tonight was all about. I received death stares from a few of the other students when she made someone give me their seat, but the couple on the middle couch that I'd spotted outside smiled at me with the confidence of people who knew they'd already won.

"This is Logan, my TA," Professor Mallory introduced the guy across from us, who passed me a single sheet of paper. I'd expected details on the program, but I found a map of their

Italian excavation site, along with handwritten notes. "I thought it would be fun to see where everyone would start if they were leading the team. As a 'get to know you' game."

Professor Mallory looked genuinely excited, but it was easy to see who'd already spoken, who was still figuring out their answer, and who wanted a second chance. She liked games, and although I hadn't experienced much of this in my electives or cared enough in my program, I used to thrive on this kind of thing in high school.

"I was just telling Logan you're so right about the church. It would be smarter to start the dig here and work my way across like this, so I don't miss anything. My team would be experienced by the time we got to the mummies," the girl to my left shared, moving her hand around the map and nervously awaiting Professor Mallory's response. Her fingernails were nonexistent, the skin at the tips raw from nervous biting.

"Jane, you marvel me with whatever task is given to you. Your research is impeccable and your eye for details and imperfections is flawless… but I'm afraid you're not meant to take the initiative."

I was as shocked as the rest of them at the Professor's bluntness.

"I told Jane I would never start by searching through the church's ruins for mummified corpses," she explained to me. "Her new plan would involve weeks of digging without the expectation of any finds. It would be a stroke of luck to stumble upon something of value in the stables."

"You start with the master's house, not the Lord's." The guy beside Logan was more cocky than confident as he gave his answer to Jane rather than the Professor. He grated on my nerves.

Dr. Richards watched the scene with interest, giving me an encouraging nod when he caught my gaze.

"I would still start with the church," I spoke up, surprising myself as well as the others. Even my competitive side liked to study the problem from all angles before making a decision. I had very little idea where I was going with this. "The mummified corpses of historical priests would get you news coverage and investments from the church, but a lot of these cities fell to Viking invasions, where anything of value was vandalized or taken."

"That makes no sense. Why start there if you think there's nothing?" the guy asked me.

"When they saw it coming, a lot of priests hid the gold and other treasured items under the floorboards, which were usually stone, not wood, so the goods weren't revealed in fires; they were preserved. Your note in the margin mentions this church burned down, but the stone walls show you the outline. I would find the altar and start there. Anything we found would secure funding for future digging, so I could let the advanced team work on historic finds, while the newly experienced team would feel more confident and be capable of recreating the process in the 'master's house,' as you call it."

"I'm guessing you're in the History department?" Professor Mallory asked, having probably been told that archeology was just an elective for me.

"I'm in Business Administration, but I've read an embarrassing amount of historical fiction novels with my sister," I admitted, knowing it would bring me down a notch in her esteem. But it was also the truth. Anything I hadn't learned in class was guessed from the tales of Bjorn and Maria Isabella or whatever other fictional couple I read to Sybill about. It used to be children's books like Harry Potter when we were younger, but when we grew up and she still needed to go to bed and rest her eyes, I'd read her the romantic adventures of made-up heroes until she fell asleep.

"Kenny, what are your thoughts?" Professor Mallory called on another student, resuming the suggestions. Some of them were safe or given with absolutely no clue of what should be done, while others amazed me with their obscure-yet-brilliant ideas.

It wasn't until everyone said their piece that Professor Mallory went out for a cigarette, and Logan shared her plans for the dig. Those going with her this summer would be prepared, while those who answered wrong could learn something.

"Professor Mallory likes out of the box thinking. Every team needs a Jane, who can get you the information you need and do everything you ask to the letter, but the Professor encourages us to pursue other interests and develop skills so we can bring more to the table than what she can teach us." Logan came to find me when everyone dispersed. The others weren't warming up to me now that I seemed to have Professor Mallory's approval.

"What's your expertise?" I asked him. He wore beige dockers with a light burgundy sweater, drinking an amber liquid while everyone else had wine. I didn't need to see the crown logo on his watch to know he came from money, but he seemed genuinely interested in me. Academically, at least.

"Jewels," he admitted. "My father owned a jewelry store, but he was also a gemologist. He taught me how to deal with customers as well as everything he knew about the gems in his shop. Whenever there's an interesting find, I can give an educated guess as to what we're dealing with, and then bring it to contacts who can authenticate it, restore it, or even sell it, depending on the situation."

"Your father must be sad you didn't follow in his footsteps," I guessed. My comment was about me more than about him, as just being here felt like a betrayal. I hadn't told my dad I didn't want to join the 'family business' once I graduated, probably because I planned on doing it anyway to make him happy. Most of the time.

"He was, at first, but I worked with him for over a decade

before I left. And when I called him to one of our digs, he got to see firsthand what I was doing. Then he was glad I'd found something that makes me as happy as stones made him."

"I'm glad it worked out for you." I gave him a smile, wondering how young he was when his father put him to work. He had to be younger than thirty.

"I have a feeling it will for you, too." He gave me a weird look, as if he knew something I didn't, before someone else called him over.

This left me alone to watch the orchestra. I absolutely hated it when my dad put classical music on the radio, but seeing it in person had this weird, magical beauty to it. I could have stayed there all night, getting lost in the musical notes that went straight to my heart, but that wasn't why I came.

There was a bar in the corner, so I decided to get a drink before exploring the options.

"A lime and soda, please," I asked the woman behind the bar.

"Single or a double?" She grabbed a bottle of vodka.

"Neither," I stopped her. "But I wouldn't say no to one of those mint leaves." I was halfway to a Virgin Mojito.

"It's open bar. Tips and alcohol are included," she pointed out, either not realizing or not caring that most of us were underage.

"I like to stay sharp."

"You'll need it." She gave me a smile, then handed over my drink.

WHEN PROFESSOR MALLORY came back to the room, everyone had broken into small groups with different conversations going on. She went to talk with the couple she'd clearly already chosen for the Italy trip, then to Dr. Richards, all the while keeping an eye on the rest of us. I couldn't help but feel like she was a cheetah watching her prey, which made me just as uneasy as it made me excited.

I went through the program brochures that were laid out over three tables, wondering if the other students had already looked at them all or if they were going for the Italian dig without even considering the other options.

My family did okay, but we were lower middle class. If, by some miracle, they selected me for the internship in Italy and I told my parents about it, they would find a way for me to be able to go, just like they did for every other after-school program or class trip. But I couldn't justify spending thousands of dollars to go somewhere other than helping with Sibby's treatments in California.

"Have we convinced you to come to the dark side?" Professor Mallory found me as I explored a display on putting your degree to use in museums. She had a glass of red wine and a knowing smile.

"The dark side?"

"Are you sticking to a Fortune 500 company for your internship or trying one of ours?"

"I wasn't planning on doing any internships this summer," I argued. "My family is spending a few months in California, so I shouldn't even be here tonight."

"Why did you come?"

"Just in case. To see what was out there. And it's not every day a non-archeology student gets invited to try an archeology internship," I shared.

"It doesn't happen," she agreed. "Dr. Richards went out on a limb for you because he believes in you and thinks you would be a great asset to our programs. I thought he was exaggerating, that you reminded him of a granddaughter or some other senti-mental nonsense, but seeing you in action tonight...he's right. You have a gift for this stuff. And your mind is very interesting."

"Because I read books?" I blushed.

"Because you're not afraid to share an idea from things you read in time travel romance novels. You consider the human element, which most people forget. In our line of work, when every dig brings up bones, you can't dwell on it, or you'll go mad. But some students don't even acknowledge that the bones were people once, and I find that terribly sad."

"One of my favorite parts of archeology is that we're not studying how a population lived at a certain time; we're discovering how individual people went about their lives based on the objects they left behind."

"It's a shame you're not interested in any of our internships. I could use someone like you in Italy."

I studied her face, trying to figure out if she was serious, that I really could have one of the most coveted spots in her program based on our five-minutes of interaction.

"What exactly do they do in the Cold Case internship?" I asked, surprising her. And myself, to be honest. It was the one that originally caught my attention, but I was still convincing myself that I wasn't doing any of them.

"You don't want that one," she shot me down.

"Why?"

"Because no one does. Graciela has been trying to get an intern for years, but it's hard and depressing work." I wasn't discouraged, so she went on. "You would think it's low pressure, but she usually works on the cold cases that have people actively pushing her to work on them, which means that every time you can't find answers, you're disappointing a very real person whose heart is breaking in front of you."

"How long did you do it for?"

"I've tried all the programs before approving them for internships. It takes a lot of paperwork for placements to count for course credit, and I didn't want people just using us for free labor. It's incredibly rewarding when the pieces come together, but I prefer my bones and murder weapons to be hundreds of years old, so I never have to meet the people who lost them."

"That sounds like a good rule."

"Not if I was one of the parents needing answers." She shrugged, taking a long sip of her wine. "The internship is yours if you want it, Miss Carmichael. You just need to decide what you want," she told me before going back to the couches. I considered following her, but I was pretty sure I was dismissed.

CHAPTER NINE

My last table was the Cold Case one with the same tagline from the email I'd received. It was mostly made up of a bunch of random items in what appeared to be evidence bags. Some of them looked like buried murder weapons, while one of them held what Sibby would call 'more lumps of metal'.

I picked up the bag to see if there was a description, but all I found was a case number and 'EVIDENCE' written in black marker.

"It's not the actual evidence." Dr. Richards came over and explained. "Just to illustrate the point."

"Chain of custody and all that?" I asked, well-versed in police procedurals thanks to my dad.

"Among other things," he agreed. "Any idea what they are?"

"Very smooth rocks..." I tried to look at them for more details. "I'm not sure."

"You can take them out of the bag to get a better look," he offered.

"Right, they're not actually evidence."

"Just a piece of history," he agreed, smiling as he often did when he watched me discover a new artifact.

I took out one of the pieces and touched the smooth surface, but the fear hit me like a ton of bricks. I could practically hear the screams of women and children being burned alive.

"They were coins," I realized. I could sort of make out scratches on the side, probably of some Roman's face.

"Why yes, Miss Carmichael, they were. Did you notice the faint outline of Caesar over here?" he asked, using a magnifying glass to point it out to me.

"That must be it." I didn't have a logical explanation as to how I knew. From looking at them, they could have been absolutely anything before they melted into nothing.

"Or did you feel it?" he asked.

"Feel what?"

"Everything that happened to them?"

"To who?" My first thought was that he was having an episode or going senile, but then something in his look scared me. Not that it was scary, per se, but he looked at me like he *knew*.

"When you touch the items, both the ones here and throughout the museum, I believe you either see or feel what happened to them," he told me.

"To the objects? That doesn't make any sense," I argued. I might have described it similarly in my head while it was happening, but saying it out loud sounded wrong. Very wrong.

"Your work is extraordinary; it's why I let you do all the cataloguing, even though that should be done by someone with a degree in the field or at least an intern. But you're better than any of the students who've interned for me, even some of the so-called experts who've given Society Talks." He gave me a warm smile, but there was more. "I say this with all the respect in the world, but you don't have the knowledge or experience to come to most of the conclusions you've been reaching. You initially thought these were rocks because that is what they look like. Only when you touched them did you realize they were melted down coins. It wasn't because you studied the pieces with all the tools at your disposal; it was because touching them did something to you."

"Like what?" I asked cautiously. He didn't seem shocked or concerned by the fact that he believed objects were talking to me. I was living through it, and it still made absolutely no sense to me.

"I believe you're Gifted," he said, like I should know what it meant. I knew the word, but it was clear he meant it differently than simply being good at something.

Before I had the chance to ask, Dr. Richards guided me over to an alcove, then pointed his palm into the unlit part of it. I stared into the darkness to see what he was trying to show me within the light of his flashlight until I turned back and saw his hand. The light was coming directly from his palm. There was no flashlight.

"How are you doing that?" I asked, forgetting myself enough to reach out and touch his hand before the light disappeared. For the life of me, I couldn't figure out where it was coming from.

"I'm Gifted, too," he admitted.

"I don't know what that means."

"It means we have special abilities that can help us accomplish specific things."

"Like seeing in the dark?" I asked. It was a weird party trick, but I didn't see the connection between his bright hands and the feelings I got when I touched certain things.

"It comes in handy on digs, in tight spaces, when you're trapped, or lost—"

"I'm not Gifted," I argued. He had to be going crazy.

"You can call it what you want, but what did you see when

you touched the coins? How did you know the breastplate had arrows and swords in it rather than knives and forks?"

"Because it didn't look like—"

"Alison," he cut me off with my first name. I felt like we had gotten close over the years—I even considered him my surrogate grandfather—but he always called me Miss Carmichael.

"I have a vivid imagination, okay? I hear a story once and then I put myself in their shoes and I imagine what it was like. I must have realized the metal was partly melted or seen the Caesar outline, and that's how I figured out they were coins. The breastplate was research, Google, and my due diligence about the things we display at the museum, because it's a part of my job."

"Do you truly believe that?"

"It makes more sense than your fortune teller theory."

"It does. But that doesn't make it true. I believe I could hand you a dozen random objects from any collection without a description or any backstory and you could identify each one. Or at least give me intimate details of how it was used. Like the necklace," he brought up the object that started my obsession with his museum.

"I'm pretty sure I would go mad if everything I touched showed me its story," I argued, thinking I might already be. At least one, if not both of us, had lost their minds.

"I would choose the ones that would," he said with confidence, already looking around the room in case he had to prove it.

"Which ones are those?"

"From what I understand, the ones that held high emotions. Your face lit up at the bowl that was crafted over a decade to prove a man's love and devotion. But I saw the pain when you touched those coins, and the breastplate, or any other weapon that was used before being hung on a wall. If I had to guess, a painting that was commissioned for money would be like any other painting for you, but one painted by a lover would give you chills. I must confess, I've never seen a Gift quite like yours before, so I don't know the particularities. But I know I'm not mistaken about you having one. And the fact that you haven't gone off to find me psychiatric help tells me that on some level, you believe me."

"Maybe I'm just a very empathetic person."

"No, I've met Empaths, and they did not get visions from objects," he argued.

"There still has to be another explanation."

He gave me a moment, allowing me to come up with a better one, but I couldn't. "You should do the summer internship because all of this makes you happy. That's what I would tell anyone else with your drive and passion for antiquities. But knowing that you have this Gift and all the incredible things you could accomplish with it, I implore you not to let it go to waste."

"I'm sure someone else can dig just as well as I can."

"The team that goes with Professor Mallory is very prestigious, but I thought you would like the cold case placement better. They comb through the evidence, examining everything that was used in a crime to find clues and figure out who used what to kill who. I know the woman who runs it, and she would be more than happy to help you figure all this out. The program, but mostly your Gift. If I've discovered anything about our purpose, it's that we have one for a reason."

"I appreciate your enthusiasm, but you're clearly mistaken." I tried to break it to him as gently as I could before walking past him and leaving the party.

Once I was outside, I lifted the hem of my dress and ran as fast as I could away from Dr. Richards' crazy ideas, and from whatever happened when my hand touched those coins.

CHAPTER TEN

It was just past midnight when I got home. The house was dark other than the TV through our bedroom window. I moved carefully and quietly to not wake my father, who slept on the couch in the living room until my mom got home. It rendered my creeping pointless when I got into the bedroom and Sybill immediately asked, "How was it?" with absolutely no volume control.

"Shh!" I warned, pushing her over so I could get into the bed with her. She was watching the ending of Legally Blonde with a cucumber facemask and a bowl of popcorn.

"If his snoring doesn't wake him, nothing will," she pointed out, putting the volume lower so we could talk.

"The get-together was...kind of like I fell into a shark tank while covered in fish guts," I shared.

"That's a disgusting analogy." She grimaced. "I'm sorry I convinced you to go."

"Don't be. Professor Mallory kind of told me I could choose any program I wanted," I said, trying to decide how much I wanted to share about the rest. I settled on keeping Dr. Richards' ridiculous theories to myself. "And there was a delay at the station, but you can apparently get to the Villa without going through the woods. Tristan walked me there."

"And Tristan is…" she let it linger so I could fill in the blanks, but she also sat up in bed and turned to face me, armed with a Red Vine.

"He's very nice. And easy on the eyes," I added reluctantly, knowing it would be her next question. I rattled off everything I knew she wanted to hear, which was basically everything I knew about him.

"But," she pressed, knowing me better than that.

"But he's not from here and is very close to a woman named Delia. He says she's like an older sister, but I just met him and I'm already sensing all kinds of shared history, secrets, and baggage."

"It's nice to know the smart ones get jealous, too." She smiled at me, undeterred by my fears.

"I'm not jealous. It's called being cautious," I argued.

"I'm pretty sure it's called excuses to write the poor guy off," she called me on it.

"We're having dinner this week." I raised my eyebrows, knowing it would surprise her.

"Color me impressed, and I'm sorry." She looked at me like I was a completely different person than a minute ago.

"Maybe this is how I live a little; a couple of dates with a really nice boy."

"Could you make that sound more boring?" she reproached.

"I'm sure I could," I informed her. "I'm setting my expectations low."

"Don't set them too low," she warned. "You need to give him a chance to sweep you off your feet before you write him off."

"But what if I like him?"

"You're supposed to."

"Normally, yes. But I'm leaving next week, and he's not from here."

"What do you mean, you're leaving? Where is the summer internship?"

"Syb," I said pointedly, but she initiated a staring competition that I quickly lost. "I'm going to California with you."

"Not after Professor Mallory told you you're the best student she's ever seen and you can have any position you want," she argued.

"That is not at all what she said."

"But she did say the internship was yours if you wanted it."

"She did."

"And you want it."

"I'm not sure." I kept thinking of the weird conversation I'd had with Dr. Richards.

"Of course you do. You have to do this Allie, otherwise I will never forgive you. Wouldn't you be heartbroken if I spent the entire summer hating you?"

"Might give me some peace and quiet for a change," I teased.

"Allie," she snapped.

"I know."

"You need an adventure, which means you jump in, and then you figure it out. You can't stand on the ledge and analyze everything you might find at the bottom," she said, grabbing her tablet so she could look at my options. "Which one are you going to do? It's last minute for a trip to Italy, but that's obviously the best one. Or at least the one I would choose," she added when she saw my look.

"There's the internship with the Cold Case Unit where I would look at stuff from old crime scenes—"

"Like digging up dead bodies?" she asked.

"I'm pretty sure it's all in evidence bags or it wouldn't be a cold case," I argued, basing myself entirely off TV shows. "I think it's murder weapons and random objects they found on the scene that might be related...I'm not sure."

"Then why do you want to do it?" she asked.

"They had a bag that looked like scrap metal, but the archeologist working on it realized they were coins that were melted down after a huge fire that killed a lot of people. Forensic anthropology is a thing, so this is that without the bones."

"But wouldn't cold cases be a lot more recent than those coins? Would you want to be digging through stuff that could belong to someone you've met?"

"Not really. But if it's recent, it means that there's probably someone out there who is still waiting for the answers."

"And you want to give that to them."

"Or get rid of my obsession for once and for all," I teased, trying to get away from the seriousness of that conversation.

"Well, either way, I'm proud of you, big sis. Both for taking a chance and for not just wasting it on artifacts," she teased.

"I'm shocked by that one myself."

"Enjoy it while it lasts." I was pretty sure she meant it to be encouraging, but I felt the weight of it.

CHAPTER ELEVEN

I t was great that Sybill was so convinced I should stay here and do the summer program, but I still had my parents to talk it over with. I woke up early and made apple muffins with a caramel glaze that took away any of the apple's health benefits. I timed it perfectly, so that I was waiting in the kitchen when my dad came down for coffee and my mom walked in after her night shift.

"That smells delicious," my mom said, taking me in her arms.

"How was the party?" my dad asked once he'd taken a sip of his coffee.

"Um, interesting." I'd spent a lot of time in bed last night thinking about what I would say and whether I would ask them at all. I remembered none of it. "It was more of a get-together for Archeology students, so they can apply to summer programs in their field."

"Syb said Dr. Richards invited you?" Mom bit into a muffin and collapsed onto one of the stools at the island.

"He thinks I have a talent for it and wanted me to see what was out there."

I told them most of what happened at the party and how he

kept hinting that I should do the summer programs, leaving out any mention of being Gifted and what happens when I touch things.

"One of them is an internship with the police department going through cold cases and archiving the evidence with fresh eyes to help solve them. I know we do the family trip for Sybill every summer, so I know it makes no sense, but I thought that maybe I might stay here and do it." I finished what must have been the least persuasive request of all time.

Part of me hoped they would say no, that they needed me this summer and I was wasting my time with this hobby. Then I would be blameless when I turned Dr. Richards down, finished out my week, and never had to think about our conversation and 'Gifted' abilities ever again.

"What do you think?"

"I think it's fantastic," my dad said before noticing my mom's look. "I'll miss you more than words can say, obviously, but you take on so much and put all this pressure on yourself that I think it will be nice for you to do something you enjoy for a change."

"You're implying that looking at murder cases would be more fun than a trip to California with my family," I pointed out.

"You know what I mean." He looked to my mom for support.

"We don't need the three of us by her bedside waiting to see if she'll get better, worrying about every little detail. If Dr. Richards sees something in you, I think you should pursue it."

"It's just for the summer, right?" My dad took a sip of his coffee, as if he didn't really care about the answer. This was the perfect opportunity to tell him it was a chance to explore other avenues because I didn't want to work at his accounting firm.

"Of course. Carmichael and Daughter for the win." I smiled at the ridiculous name change he wanted to make once I graduated, but even if I got a pang in my chest for what I was giving up, his beaming smile was worth it.

"When do you start?" my mom asked, grabbing a muffin without looking at it, as if that would prevent us from realizing it was her third.

"I have to hand in some paperwork, but it should start on Monday if they take me."

"Of course, they will," Mom said with certainty.

"My daughter, the gifted one." Dad raised his eyebrows excitedly, but I froze at his choice of words.

"I'm sure I said talented and dedicated."

"Own it, Allie. You deserve it." Mom kissed my forehead before going up to bed while dad did the same before heading to work. I sighed once I was alone, then went to my room to print out the paperwork.

ONCE I FILLED IT OUT, I rode my bike to the museum, arriving just in time for my shift. I was usually someone who liked to rip the band aid off in one shot to get the bad stuff over with, but I put off Dr. Richards, avoiding him at work and even having lunch outside in case he tried to sit with me in the staff room.

I waited until four o'clock to knock on his office door.

"Miss Carmichael." He looked happy to see me, but also nervous.

"I came to give you my forms," I said after taking a deep breath. "And I'm sorry for running out last night."

"Don't worry about it. I left after midnight. Professor Mallory was still discussing her adventures with those who remained."

"I'm sorry I missed that."

"I'm sure you'll hear all about it in Italy. It's our version of war stories."

"I was actually hoping for the Cold Case internship."

He smiled, understanding this was because I believed him. "It will be tough." He inhaled sharply. "Especially for you." He furrowed his brow and sighed. Dr. Richards was the first one to mention anything unusual about me, but it was already hard before that.

"If you say I have a Gift, isn't it better to use it solving crimes rather than finding out what armor soldiers wore centuries ago in Italy?"

"I suppose you could just ask them," he said to himself.

If it wasn't for the light he'd had bursting from his hand last night, I would assume he truly was going mad in his old age, and I was a fool to pay any attention to the crazy ideas he had about me.

"What you said last night—"

"About your Gift." He nodded. "I'm terribly sorry. I meant to do it with a lot more tact and consideration of your feelings. It wasn't my place to push you to use it. I just thought it would be a shame if you buried it away, then settled for a job you…there I go again," he cut himself off.

"I don't really know what you meant or what you thought I would do, but if I can help them find peace, I'd like to do that. For the summer," I added, so he knew I was going back to my business classes.

"We would be incredibly lucky to have you." He smiled. "Graciela oversees the interns at the precinct. I think you'll get along great."

"You won't be there?" I asked.

"Looks can be deceiving. Graciela knows a lot more than I do. I'll let her know you're coming."

"Can you give these to Professor Mallory?" I handed him my application.

"Of course," he assured me.

~

I WAS UNLOCKING my bike when my phone rang.

"Hello?" I asked, not recognizing the number, but assuming it was the fastest response ever about the internship.

"Hello, Alison." It was neither Graciela, nor Professor Mallory. "This is Tristan. We met last night when I tried to lure you down dark alleys."

My cheeks warmed as I blushed, hoping he couldn't hear my smile through the phone. "If I remember correctly, you did more than try."

"You sound surprised," he called me on it.

"I wasn't sure you would call."

"I didn't give you my number, so I didn't really have a choice," he pointed out. "I wanted to make sure you got in safe."

"All good," I assured him. "Is that the only reason you're calling?" Heat rose to my cheeks again, which was weird. I wasn't used to being this nervous, especially not about a guy. Sybill was waiting for her knight in shining armor, but I usually turned down idiots I didn't have time for.

"That was my main goal," he agreed. "But I guess I would feel better if I could see it with my own eyes. Maybe over dinner," he suggested.

"You're very thorough, Mr. Davis."

"I try my best." He laughed, then cleared his throat.

"Well, if your well-being is at stake, I guess we better have dinner."

"I wouldn't want you to put yourself out and do something you didn't want to." We were still teasing, but I was also positive he meant it.

"I would love to have dinner with you." I rolled my eyes that I had to drop the charade, but I meant it. And maybe Sybill was right; I could benefit from living a little without setting my hopes so terribly low.

"How do you feel about tomorrow?" he asked.

"I finish work at four," I shared. "It's a museum just off-campus enough to be more of a tourist attraction than an academic one."

"Could I meet you on campus at 4:15 then? Or would you need to go home first?"

"Campus is perfect." I would feel more glamorous if I went home and let Sibby work her magic on my face and my hair and maybe lend me another dress…but that wasn't exactly me. I was a no-fuss, race you to that rock, dressed for anything girl that I thought was pretty outstanding, but would probably be a disappointment if you expected the girl I looked like last night.

"I'll meet you by the statue with the one-armed pirate."

"Lord Dashwell?" I asked. He was the only one-armed statue I could think of, but he was the university's second president. Famous for discovering a rare plant in the woods around campus, not being a pirate.

"I'll see you tomorrow."

I could hear his smile, not the constant one he wore, but a big one that might be accompanied by a blush. It only made mine bigger. "I'll see you tomorrow."

CHAPTER TWELVE

Even though I was only going to be working at the museum for a couple of days with the new exhibition, it was still mandatory that I attend the orientation. Instead of doing inventory, I spent my morning listening to a visiting academic give us 'interesting' tidbits about the pieces. By the time we were allowed to leave, Sybill was waiting on the bench for me.

"I thought I was meeting you by the fountain," I pointed out when I saw her. She had to get blood work and other tests every couple of months, so my dad dropped her off on his way to work, she got poked and prodded, then hung out with me until my dad's lunch break, which he spent driving her home before going back to the office.

"I was worried you were being held hostage," she explained, getting up so we could walk over to the café and get milkshakes.

"Were you mentally preparing yourself to barge in and rescue me?" I asked.

"I asked a man who came out what was going on and he told me it was a lost cause, so I was mourning you."

"I'm touched."

"You should be. My first instinct was to have a pre-emptive milkshake while I waited for you."

"Maybe then you wouldn't steal half of mine," I pointed out while paying for our order.

"Not half. I just need some vanilla to cut into the chocolate, but vanilla on its own tastes like chalk."

"You mean it's delicious."

"Agree to disagree. Where's the pirate?"

"Over there." I nodded, handing her the milkshake.

"He doesn't look intimidating at all. But he does have a parrot," she pointed out.

"So he does."

"I'm liking this Tristan guy more and more," she shared.

"He's definitely interesting."

"You sure you don't want me to just do a bit of..." She pretended to type at an invisible computer.

"No, I do not want you to cyber-stalk him or hack into the DMV," I warned.

"Then what about—"

"No contouring!" I swatted her hand away from my face where I knew she was going to point out what she wanted to fix.

"You know it's more about giving me something to do than there being anything wrong with the way you look without makeup."

"I do, but thank you for saying it."

"You're meant for so much more, Allie. I don't know what it is yet, but I can feel it. Have you tried talking to Dad?" she suggested.

"And say what? 'I know you've spent your entire life building up this business and dreaming of your kids taking over, but I have no interest in it?'"

"Might make it easier when my turn comes."

"You're unbelievable." I shook my head at her.

"But I'm cute, so you still love me."

"Always."

"Want me to tell them you're working late when you don't come home tonight?" she offered.

"I'm telling Tristan I need to be home by seven. I told Dad I would look over the renovation plans."

"You're so clueless sometimes." She sighed, shaking her head at me again. "If you're home, you can look them over all you want, but please try not to be. Tomorrow is another day."

MY AFTERNOON at the museum flew by with a group of kids from science camp. The teacher had clearly done the tour beforehand to prepare, as I hadn't ever seen a group have more fun learning. She split the class in two and had them compete on their knowledge after each room, finishing with a speed round. It was insane.

I was worried they would go over with all the questions the kids asked me at the end, but they were incredibly punctual and left at the exact time they were supposed to, leaving nothing behind, which was rare. Dr. Richards let me out a few minutes early, since there wouldn't be any more visitors until after dinner.

I debated if I should go to the ladies' room to make myself more presentable, but I saw Tristan walking across the campus and my mind went blank. I had spent most of my time with him in the dark, other than the few minutes under the harsh, artificial lights of the underground, but he was gorgeous in the sunlight.

"Tristan," I greeted. He'd smiled at the sight of me.

"Are you ducking out early?" he asked with a suspicious grin.

"My group was very efficient."

"Lucky for me. Do you have anything else planned for tonight?" he asked, checking his watch.

I looked at him and bit my bottom lip. My dad was counting on me, and I wanted to do some research on the precinct and cold case statistics for the area. But Tristan was only in town for a couple of weeks. And I liked him. "No, tonight I'm yours."

I heard how it sounded once the words were out of my mouth, but it was too late to take them back. Thankfully, his smile stayed in place as he looked at me. He bit his bottom lip too, but didn't seem to debate anything as his eyes traveled to my lips.

"Are you hungry?" he asked me.

"I could eat," I said, noncommittally.

"That's perfect, because I know a place that serves food."

He hesitated for a nanosecond before he showed me the way instead of taking my hand to lead me.

"You never told me what you studied," I stated as we passed the engineering building.

"That's because I never went to college," he admitted.

"Really?" I was surprised. Not that it mattered, or that there was anything wrong with it, but he talked about things and knew way more than I would expect from someone who didn't go past high school.

"After the cancer and my...miraculous recovery..." He sounded bitter, but shook it off quickly. "It didn't make sense for me to spend years in classrooms when I wanted to be out there living."

"Remove foot from mouth," I said guiltily.

"No, I...I've regretted it sometimes. I even took a few courses here and there, but when the kids I grew up with were going to university, it seemed really pointless."

"I guess it kind of is. I love my archeology classes, but I doubt even a quarter of us will do anything with it."

"Aren't you going to dig for buried treasure?"

"I don't think they have much of that here," I argued.

"What got you interested in archeology?" he asked. "Not that it isn't…"

"No, it sounds boring," I acknowledged. "And I die thinking about how careless I was with it now, but I didn't understand why it was wrong at the time…" I paused, then realized that I was giving the wrong impression. "When I was maybe twelve years old, my class went to the museum for a special exhibit on Tudor England. I don't know if they were cleaning the glass or if they just trusted everyone to obey the signs and not touch anything, but there was this pearl necklace with a ruby hanging down like a teardrop. I swear it was calling to me." My teacher thought I was making an excuse, but I couldn't explain how connected I felt to the necklace in that moment.

"The card beneath it had this story about a princess who died during a plague, so the king had a necklace made in her honor that her sister wore to keep her close. I didn't know if it was because my sister was always sick, but I had to reach out to it. When I put my fingers on the pearls, it was like I felt that little girl's pain, losing her sister, and…" I couldn't find the words to explain it, but I had felt her grief as if it were my own. Dr. Richards was the one who found me and rewarded my curiosity rather than punishing my disobedience. He warned me about damaging the pieces and why they ask people not to touch, but he also gave me a summer job when I turned sixteen.

"Yeah, I see why that's appealing." Tristan said it with a straight face, then smiled to show me he was being sarcastic.

"That might be an awful example, or I might just be morbid, but I loved the idea of uncovering the past and sharing these stories. I've always been really interested in history, and archeology makes it all come alive." I looked over and tried to read his expression. "You think I'm crazy."

"No, I like how passionate you are about this. I don't think there's anything that excites me that much."

"There has to be something," I argued.

"I used to really like basketball." He shrugged.

"Playing or watching?" I asked instead of why he was no longer into it, which was what I was curious about.

"That's a loaded question." He let out a breath before looking at me in a way that made the answer painfully obvious.

"That was stupid of me. I didn't think." Someone who'd battled cancer from the age of eight probably wouldn't have been playing basketball in any real capacity.

"No, it's fine. I loved both up until about the third resurgence. Once it was in my bones and they wanted to take my leg, there was no going back. I could no longer play on the days it felt better because it never felt better."

"Not even now?" I asked, bolder than I should be. It was clearly a sore subject I shouldn't make him relive, but his face never reflected the sadness and pain of his words. I saw it in his eyes and knew the cheerful attitude was entirely for my benefit, but he had either worked past his issues, was a psychopath, or perhaps a master at compartmentalizing.

"I find it's like when you break an arm. You get so used to not using it and modifying your routine that once it heals, you'll still favor the other side, and adapt yourself so you don't put too much pressure on it. Even though the arm is completely back to normal, you're not."

"You should definitely go into philosophy." I gave him a tentative smile and got a sad but grateful one in return. I considered it a victory when I saw the twinkle in his dark eyes.

"Oh, I can spew it and wax poetic for ages, but I would be terrible at remembering what anyone else said," he argued, leading us down a quiet alley.

"Is this a second attempt at kidnapping me now you've researched how much livers go for on the black market?"

"I would never kidnap you unless you came willingly."

"I don't think that's considered kidnapping."

"Then it's settled. I can't kidnap you because you want to come with me."

He was teasing, but it got me to smile as he opened the door to a little Greek place. The inside had maybe four tables ranging from two to eight seats, all of them mismatched. They covered the walls in pictures of a family that I guessed were the owners. It followed them from a couple's wedding day to beach days in what could only be Greece—gorgeous backdrops and sceneries of it—before their story continued here in America.

"Opened in 1918," Tristan shared, "with the best tzatziki I've ever had in my life. You do like Greek food, right?"

"I don't like olives and have never understood the pink mousse thing, but otherwise, yes, I love Greek food," I assured him.

"Perfect." He smiled before ringing the bell.

The man who came to greet us looked miserable until he saw Tristan and his face lit up.

"How come you don't tell me you're in town?" the man asked, coming out from behind the counter.

"I didn't know how long I was staying. It's just me," Tristan warned. I raised an eyebrow at him, but no one explained who else we should be expecting.

"No matter. You brought a pretty girl." He took Tristan in his arms for a hug, then did the same to me. He looked like he would smell like fried onions, garlic, and grease, but I was surprised by the freshness, like mint and cucumber.

"This is Alison," Tristan introduced me. "And this is Mr. Aetos. He's an old friend of Delia's." The two of them exchanged a look, as if that wasn't quite how Mr. Aetos would describe it, before he decided it didn't matter.

"Find a seat, I'll bring you food."

~

"Do you come here often?" I asked Tristan once we were alone.

"Maybe a handful of times with Delia, but if I come to town without her, she asks me to check in on him."

"That's sweet of you."

"Oh no, it's very selfish. You'll agree once you taste the food," he assured me.

It took less than fifteen minutes before our table was covered with every Greek food I'd ever heard of. Salad, potatoes, gyros, tzatziki, bread baked with cheese and spinach, as well as that weird pink mousse thing.

"What did you decide about the internship?" Tristan asked before taking a chunk out of his pita. He was right; the tzatziki was out of this world, and the tomatoes tasted like they were fresh from a garden out back.

"I handed in my application yesterday, and got the acceptance email this afternoon," I admitted, biting my bottom lip.

"Is that your terrified yet excited face or your 'I can't believe I just did that, is it too late to take it back' face?"

"Is that the vibe I'm giving off?" I couldn't help but laugh at his suggestions. For someone who just met me, he read me pretty well.

He considered it before deciding, "A combination."

"It just isn't very me." I shrugged before realizing that wasn't entirely true.

"Or maybe it is, and you'll find what sets your soul on fire."

"I think that's aiming a little high, but hopefully I'll learn something and figure stuff out."

"I don't think it is," he argued. "You deserve to have your soul go up in flames."

I was about to defend my pessimism and low expectations, but he'd purposely phrased the last part so wrong that I burst out laughing.

"In a good way, of course," he amended with a knowing smile.

"So, you're not suggesting I go straight to hell?"

"You can take some detours." *God, that smile.* "I think hell is being powerless."

"That's one kind," I agreed. I knew he was probably talking about his cancer and not my career choice. It sure felt like hell when Syb was having one of her bad days and all I could do was watch.

"Aren't we just rays of sunshine?" Every time he revealed something deep about himself, he masked it behind a smile or with a joke. I wanted to let him know it was okay, that he could be as vulnerable as he wanted with me, but Mr. Aetos came out with a tray of baklava.

"Oh, I don't think I have any more room," I told him apologetically.

"You'll find it," Tristan assured me.

"Or you'll take home," Mr. Aetos added.

WE TOOK the dessert in a to-go box, and after a lengthy conversation with Mr. Aetos in the kitchen, Tristan brought me home. It would have been a ten-minute subway ride, but I was grateful when he suggested we walk instead. It wasn't quite dark yet, but I felt the sparks when Tristan took my hand. I tried to hide the smile, but that just made my cheeks go red, and Tristan wasn't hiding his. He looked perfectly content holding my hand and telling me all the trivia he could remember from when Delia had first brought him to Boston. He didn't mention her by name, which I appreciated, but I knew she was the friend he kept referring to. Although the more I listened, he talked about her like a motherly presence in his life. Add in the fact that Mr. Aetos was an old friend of hers, and I hoped she might be my grandmother's age.

I stopped us on the street before we got to the house. I enjoyed having it just be the two of us and crickets.

"I had a really nice time getting to know you tonight."

"Likewise." I swallowed, nervous because I knew this was where he would kiss me. Not that I had never been kissed, but not any that counted.

"Goodnight, Allie." He kissed the top of my hand and stepped back, letting me walk up to the house alone.

I willed myself not to look back because I didn't want him to see my confusion and disappointment. When I did, he was still in the middle of the street, watching to make sure I got in safely. He obviously cared, but why didn't he kiss me?

CHAPTER THIRTEEN

I showed up at the precinct on Monday for my first day of work and immediately encountered an incredibly large officer who looked at me like he was trying to decide if I was a criminal or needed help. I took off my dad's bright yellow raincoat and saw him let out a breath.

"The new secretary?" he asked, making me rethink the outfit. I wore the fanciest skort I owned, my Dr. Martens with the slightest heel, and a blue blouse.

"New intern, actually. I'm supposed to find Graciela Goncalves in B-473?" I checked my paper to make sure. After confirming that I really did want to intern in the Law Enforcement Outreach program, Professor Mallory sent me a single lined email with a woman's name, a room, and a time. No 'please bring the following items', 'business casual', or any insight into what the program entailed. Then again, according to Dr. Richards, the main point was for me to master my 'Gift'.

"Oh." He sized me up with suspicion. "Take the elevator down to the basement, turn right, and it'll be at the end of the hallway. The light is wonky, but there are no axe murderers. We keep them on the second floor."

It took me forever to realize that he was joking.

"Thank you," I told him with a polite smile before I followed his instructions.

I WAS glad he warned me about the light. When I was halfway down the long hallway, the fluorescent lights above me flickered in a way that made me feel like I was in a horror film.

I mostly believed him about the lack of axe murderers down here, but I still made it a point to cautiously look around every corner and doorway before darting past, just in case someone jumped out at me.

I sped to the end of the hallway, where I finally found room B-473. 'Department of Archeology' was written on a piece of loose-leaf paper taped to the other side of the glass. If they didn't want to be found, they were doing an excellent job.

I knocked first in case this was Mrs. Goncalves' office, then let myself in.

The right side of the room consisted entirely of shelves filled with boxes, probably the evidence from cold cases. There was a huge white board in front of me, but all it had was a long list of numbers in different colors, some with check marks, some crossed off, and others intact. The left side of the room had two long metal tables. One of them had a hairbrush, a key chain, and a wooden box on it, while the other had a sealed box.

I thought I was alone, but there was an alcove behind me to the right. A girl with huge headphones on her ears sat at a desk. She was probably in her late twenties, chewing the straw of her smoothie down to nothing. I could faintly hear La Bamba as her Converse shoes tapped along to the beat.

"Mrs. Goncalves?" I asked. Based on what Dr. Richards said about her, I'd assumed she was much older. Like, roughly his age. "Mrs. Graciela Goncalves!" I tried it a bit louder.

She looked up and smiled when she saw me. "You must be

Miss Carmichael," she said, taking off the headphones and motioning for me to sit in the chair across from her.

"Alison," I let her know she didn't have to be so formal.

"Grace," she did the same. "Graciela is an eighty-year-old grandmother."

"So, the internship…"

"Of course, you need the introduction. We basically re-examine cold cases, not just when they're reopened, but I methodically go through every single one like they did when DNA testing first came out. I've been posting for interns for years, but you're our first victim."

"That sounds promising," I stated. "When you say *our…*"

"Technically, Detective Cortez oversees this department, so I meet up with him occasionally to go over anything we find. I find," she corrected herself. "I like that you were more concerned about another colleague than me calling you a victim."

"Or I wanted to make sure you didn't see anyone standing behind me."

"Because of the flickering lights?" She nodded in under-standing.

"And I want to be prepared if my boss is crazy." *Before* they decide I have superpowers.

"Smart," she approved. I was really liking this girl. "As far as the internship goes, your job will be to help me catalogue every-thing from an archeological point of view. Try to see what other people have missed. It's about ten percent looking at things and ninety percent writing about what you see, with other boring paperwork mixed in."

"I appreciate your honesty."

"But Isaiah also implied you might be here for another reason."

It took me a minute to understand she meant Dr. Richards. It was odd to hear her call him by his first name, like a friend.

Growing up, my parents' rule was that adults were either Mr. and Mrs. So-and-so or they were Aunt and Uncle So-and-so. "He said you had a lot of things you could teach me. And that looks can be deceiving."

"That they can," she agreed. "If what he says is true, then your job is the same, but there's an extra percent of the time that you'll spend figuring out what will go in the paperwork to explain whatever we found out in a way that will hold up in court. To be honest, that will probably be the hardest part of this whole thing."

"If what he says is true," I repeated, not sure how useful I would actually be.

"If Isaiah is anything, it's thorough. And he's always right. Annoyingly so most of the time, but I wouldn't be half as good as I am if it wasn't for him."

"What exactly do you do?" I asked in a way that could be about the precinct, but I was mostly wondering if she also had weird flashlight hands.

"I figure out what's inside the boxes," she answered.

"Of course."

She looked at me, sizing me up. So far, we'd both hinted at it, but neither of us had come out and said anything about Dr. Richards' crazy theories. We clearly didn't trust each other yet, and I hadn't handled it so well when Dr. Richards brought it up.

"Come on, I'll give you the tour," she decided, hopping down from her office chair. She was almost half a foot shorter than me, but the messy bun on top of her head probably made us even. "Cold cases have their own evidence locker at the other end of the basement, and there's a whole warehouse that you'll never have to go to. We have about a dozen boxes in here at a time. Then, once we're done with them all, we get another twelve. I've been working backwards, but they'll occasionally send us stuff from a cold case they're reopening or if a current case has something we can help with."

"Which one is this?" I asked of the box on the other table. I assumed it was what she wanted me to work on while she did the hairbrush and stuff.

"This is from 1947," she shared, putting on a pair of gloves before removing the lid. "They took it out of the warehouse to compare the blood to an inmate who was executed over a decade ago."

"Was it a match?"

"I like to form my own opinions before getting the answers. Bias clouds your judgment, which can be annoying when you have to build your theories from scratch, but it's really awesome when we think outside the box and solve a case."

Her face lit up as she said it, but it worried me that solving cases was a rare occurrence.

"See, I can tell that this vase is porcelain, made with kaolin and bone ash, probably from the late 1920s. It held lilacs in it before it got smashed, and that dark stuff is blood. A positive," she shared. While she held the piece in her gloved hands, she purposely put her inner forearm on top of it before telling me what it was made of.

"Was that in the report? Or the inventory?" I asked, not seeing any instructions as to the contents.

"The case files tell us the crimes and all that morbid stuff. I like to open the boxes and look inside, making sure I have all the items on the list, and kind of get a feel for them before I read the case file. It doesn't always make a difference, but sometimes you get so used to seeing something one way, that you forget you can see it another."

"You've already read this case file?"

"No. I have no idea what happened other than Elizabeth Boyle ended up dead. They're testing the blood against someone named John Lemmings."

"Then how would you know about the blood type and the flowers?" I asked.

"You asked what I do." She shrugged.

"Like a microscope?" I asked.

"Sort of? It depends on the thing, but it's kind of like I can break it down more and more until I find what I'm looking for. When I eat a piece of dark chocolate, I know it's seventy percent, but I don't want to know how many spider legs and fly wings got through the inspection. For this, I was looking for anything that could help, so I kept going."

"Could you have figured out whose blood it is on your own?"

"I'm not a computer," she argued. "I know the composites of porcelain because I see it a lot. I've learned to tell the difference between the different blood types, but I am always going through textbooks and Google to figure out what things are."

The way she said it and the way she looked at me sent a shiver down my spine that I quickly shook off.

"I try not to use it on people." She read my expression. "Isaiah won't shake my hand without gloves on. Others avoid touching me entirely, so I get it if you're not comfortable with that either."

"You need to touch it, not like an x-ray?" I verified.

"No, but that would be cool." She smiled. "But only if I could control it. Imagine just staring at skeletons everywhere you went?" It was her turn to shiver.

"Is it hard?" I asked.

"It can be. At first, it came sporadically, like if I touched something and really wanted to know what it comprised. But it can become a rabbit hole that never ends. I made the mistake of 'predicting' a brain tumor and unofficially headed a cult for a few days before I ran away."

I looked at her, trying to figure out if she was serious, but she didn't seem like she made jokes. She said things in a joking manner, but I got the feeling it was always the truth.

"The point is that I did figure it out, and now I can shake your hand without seeing the cancer in your lungs, and I can eat a twinkie without knowing all the horrible things they put inside it."

"Does Dr. Richards know that?" I asked.

"He does. But he also knows that I would use it if I thought something was wrong with him, and we don't want to go through that again."

I found her fascinating, and could have kept asking her questions all day, but she looked at me expectantly and I remembered that I was mostly here because Dr. Richards thought the way pieces spoke to me was a Gift.

"What do you see?" Grace asked me.

"A smashed vase. Dried blood."

"We're not allowed to handle the evidence with our bare hands for obvious reasons, but it shouldn't be too hard to use your Gift from your wrist or your forearm. Unless you don't want to use it."

"I think you guys might be mistaken. I read a lot, which gives me a very vivid imagination, and I probably just make things up when I try to imagine what happened."

"If that's what you think, why did you come?"

"Apparently, depriving the world of your Gift is selfish and kills your soul." I remembered Tristan's words. I'd texted him a few times after the date, but he either replied with a one-word answer or not at all. It was weird until I figured he probably had a girlfriend back home and didn't want to lead me on. Hence foregoing the kiss. Unless I completely misread things and blew it somehow.

"Spoken like a true Gifted." Grace shook her head with a sigh, then held the piece of porcelain in front of me. "There's an easy way to find out."

I wasn't sure I wanted to find out, but if I could help put bad guys away and figure this out ... wasn't it always better to know than to be in the dark?

I took a deep breath and let it out, then brought my wrist to the smooth side of the shard of porcelain. I did it cautiously, like I expected an explosion, but nothing happened.

"I guess that's our answer." It was silly to think I was capable of anything more than imagining things.

"How does it normally happen?" she asked.

"I just…it's like everyone else. I look at something, I touch it, try to imagine what it was for, how it was used, and then I see it." I shrugged. She didn't need to know that sometimes the pieces called to me, and I saw the stories unfolding before my hand barely grazed their surface.

"Do you think it's because you don't want to see a murder?" she suggested.

"I don't think anybody wants to see a murder, but that hasn't stopped me before."

"Can you try to see the flowers that used to be in it? Or where the vase used to be?"

"I'm not a computer either," I argued. "When it works, I don't see the years the plate hung on the wall, watching life happen."

"What do you see?"

"The man who spent hours painstakingly adding jewels so he could give the woman he loved something he felt worthy of her. How touched she was when he gave it to her, and she held it to her chest. I couldn't tell you where they were or what their house looked like. I just get snippets."

"You might not see the day it smashed, but you could see the day someone painted the flowers on the side or whoever gave it to her."

"Right," I agreed.

"We'll work on that," she decided. "But first, you need to want to see what this piece has to show you and do what you would have done with your fingers, but with your wrist.

Explore it, be curious, and try to want to know about the vase more than you want to prove Isaiah wrong," she encouraged.

I wanted to argue, but she was right. My life would be a lot easier if Dr. Richards was wrong. Clearly, some people had unusual Gifts, but that didn't mean that I was one of them.

I took another deep breath, and a closer look at the small chunk of porcelain she was holding in her purple-gloved hand. She purposely chose a piece that you could see the blood on, but I was careful to avoid that spot as I rubbed my wrist along the smooth, cold side of it.

Like every other time, it was the emotion that hit me before the images. My heart beat faster with boundless joy before two pinky fingers brushed on the surface of the vase as two people held it. There was the overwhelming smell of a flower, possibly lilacs like Grace had said, but also apple pie wafting in from the distance. A door opened and while my heart still beat fast, there was also fear, the connection with the other finger now broken.

There was a loud shout, but I couldn't make out the words before the vase crashed to the floor into a dozen pieces. I thought the snippet would end there, but all I could see was a girl with long, honey colored hair reaching across the shards, cutting her arms in the process, trying to hold his hand with her last dying breath.

I snapped out of it with a sharp intake of breath, then took a moment to regain my composure. Now that I'd felt a death, I was very certain that the soldier had not died wearing the breastplate because I wouldn't have touched it again. It was sort of like the coins. Only whoever held them must have dropped them before the flames got to them, whereas this woman sped up her death by slicing into her own skin to reach her lover.

"What did you see?" Grace asked, grabbing a Lindt chocolate ball from a bowl I hadn't noticed. She then pushed the bowl closer to me. "Chocolate makes most things better," she explained.

"I saw her die," I shared. "Or dying at least."

"Was she hit over the head with it?"

"Not the vase," I said with certainty. "I think she dropped it, then fell to the floor and cut herself on the broken pieces."

"And the person who did it?" she pressed.

"I don't think any of the blood is from the killer," I warned. "It was just flashes, but she was holding the vase with someone she trusted and loved. Someone else came in and scared her, causing them both to drop the vase. I think the new person hit her on the head and once she was on the ground, she used the last of her strength to reach for the man she was with at the start. She was bleeding from a gash on her head, and the sharp pieces of the vase only made it worse."

"Do you know what he looked like?" Grace asked me, opening the file and going through the pages of the report.

"I didn't see him, only her. Or maybe a finger. I mostly felt what she felt for him. They were in love," I said. I must have been feeling both of their emotions while they were holding the vase together.

"And how accurate are your...flashes?" she asked after reading a couple of pages and looking at what looked like crime scene photos and mugshots. Something I said didn't fit.

"You think I'm wrong?"

"I think you could have just provided motive, but only if you're jumping to the most obvious conclusions."

"What do you mean?"

"All you saw of the other person was a finger?"

"Yes."

She considered it a moment before saying, "Then how do you know it was a man?"

"What's in the file?" I asked, trying to pick through the flashes to see if there was any sign of who she was with other than the pinky.

"They found Elizabeth with her best friend, Margaret, who survived with severe brain damage and no recollection of the events. The convict they're testing it against had worked for Margaret's parents, so it was a far-fetched theory to put the case to rest. They never suspected Elizabeth's husband, who found them, because every single person they interviewed gushed about how much he loved his wife and would never hurt her..."

"But if he came home and found her with someone else..." my chest got tight at the realization that the actual killer had gone free.

"The notes continue like they reopened the case every few years to see if anything new came up. They checked fingerprints and DNA when the technology became available, but nothing ever came of it. Each time, the detective in charge visited Mr. Boyle, and he mentions how sad it is that the widower visited Margaret every week to share his grief with someone who understood."

"Rather his guilt," I argued.

"They were looking for a jealous lover. They just didn't realize..."

"I see what you mean about not wanting to be biased when you look at things."

"It's a lesson learned the hard way," she said, starting a report, although I wasn't sure how she was going to explain our new theory as to what happened.

"What happens when you solve them?" I asked.

"I'm not sure it'll make much of a difference in this case, but if I can find a plausible explanation, they'll officially reopen the case and work it. They have specific forensics people for court, so I rarely do anything after the initial report, but Detective Cortez lets me know the outcomes of the trials. Or at least the ones we win."

"That must be really rewarding."

"They won't all be like this," she warned. "Most cases are unsolved because the killer was really good and they're unsolvable with what we have."

"You said it would mostly be paperwork on random household items," I assured her.

"But sometimes you get to make a difference." She smiled, and I could see why she did this. "Either way, welcome to the club."

CHAPTER FOURTEEN

Grace was right about the day-to-day of my new job. So far, other than the case with the vase, it had been three days of occasional flashes that amounted to nothing.

"I don't think you're reading the objects so much as experiencing the life people poured into them. Unless someone was holding the flashlight when they died, why would you see anything?" Grace sighed. She'd warned me it would be like this, but I think she'd been trying to downplay how useful she thought I would be. Even if she tried her best to hide it, I was letting her down.

"Dr. Richards said something similar," I agreed.

"He warned me. I've just never been good at listening to cautions, which is probably why I ended up here. But I don't see a reason to change that now."

"When I concentrate really hard on finding the emotion, I can feel a child who is terrified of the dark and clutching the flashlight for dear life, but no one is getting hit over the head with it," I shared, wishing I could be more useful.

"Well, it says the flashlight was new, so maybe…"

"The kid worried they found a monster and bashed an old

man on the head with it?" I did not like where that thought was going. "I think that would be a more traumatizing event than being afraid of the dark," I argued.

"I highly doubt a kid could have pulled this scene off." She shuddered, and although she hadn't let me see the crime scene photographs, I could imagine how terrible they were from the state of the flashlight. The hardest part of my job with this particular object was finding a spot that didn't have too much blood caked on it to risk touching it. Apparently, the flashlight had been left by the victim's head while they bled out for days until they were found. This was the most depressing summer job I could have found.

"Then what are you thinking?" I asked. I could tell when the wheels were spinning in her mind because she usually stopped speaking, stared blankly at something in the distance, and tapped her finger down on the table in rhythmic succession.

"The victim didn't have children or grandchildren, and this flashlight has been locked up in evidence since the late eighties," she pointed out. "If there was ever a child who clutched it in fear, the child would have to be linked to the killer. And if he wasn't overwhelmed with regret or hatred or any strong emotion the whole time he was doing…what he did with that thing…then I hope it wasn't his child."

"Or hers," I corrected. Ever since I assumed Elizabeth Boyle's lover was a man, I was trying very hard to have an open mind about all our cases.

"I'll let the detective know to look for a suspect with a kid in their mid-twenties to late thirties," Grace decided.

"How will you explain it?" I asked. Her Gift allowed her to suggest they investigate certain things where they should be able to find the same compounds she did if they took the time to break the object down. The precinct had microscopes and mass spectrometers and everything you could possibly need to analyze something. My Gift, however, highlighted a specific moment in time that, for the most part, didn't leave any kind of trace.

"Not in a way that can hold up in court, but I can find a way to get Malcolm to look into it."

"Is he…Gifted?" I asked, using the proper terminology. I was going to ask if he was like us, but even if I had proven it to myself time and time again that I could see something in the objects no one else could, I still didn't see myself as Gifted. At least not in the sense that Grace implied, where it was a vast community of people with incredible Gifts and purposes. I still felt like I had neither.

"His mother was, so he gets that sometimes we know things we can't explain. If I tell him we think the killer had a kid, he'll look into the old case file, find anyone who fits the profile, and build a case against them."

"You make it sound so simple." As did all the TV shows. But I was seeing that there were way more unsolved crimes and cold cases than most procedural TV shows implied.

"Getting someone to follow a lead I believe in is easy, building a case and actually getting a conviction is damn near impossible, especially for cold cases."

"Why do we do this then?" I was curious about her motivations, but I had no intentions of stopping.

"Getting killers off the street, giving families closure, solving crimes…" she listed off reasons someone should do it.

"But what's your why?" I pressed.

"Someday we can finish early, hit a happy hour, and I'll tell you all about it," she decided before taking out the next object from the box. She smiled when she said it, but I could see there was a darkness she wasn't ready to share yet, so I let her keep it.

CHAPTER FIFTEEN

I walked into B-473 and found Grace talking to a man my father's age, dressed in an old brown suit. I assumed he was a detective, but despite the smiles and teasing banter they had going on, I could tell he was here on official business. Something awful, judging by the way he looked at me apologetically.

"This is Alison," Grace told him, motioning for me to come closer.

"I've heard nice things, which is a tremendous compliment with this one," he told me.

"He lies. I'm nice to everyone," she argued.

"There's a reason your office is in the basement as far as we can get you from other human beings. I'm Detective Cortez," he introduced himself with a smile that twinkled all the way to his eyes. I got the feeling he thought she was amazing, but I wasn't getting a romantic vibe. There was a bit of a familiarity that could make them related, but they had different last names, and I got the impression she was the one in charge, even if he was clearly our boss. I could maybe see a bit of my dynamic with Sybill, but I didn't think they were siblings either.

"Nice to meet you," I said, nervous for some reason. Probably because he was an officer of the law, and whatever we were doing down here wasn't legal.

"I came down to see if you two would like to see some newer evidence we're stumped on."

"A recent case?" Grace asked. I guess they didn't get to the point of his visit while they were catching up.

"Two days ago. We found some evidence they've analyzed every which way they know how, but we don't even have a name yet."

"Not a single suspect?" I asked. I felt like cold cases could go unsolved a lot easier than recent ones, where everyone has GPS and a camera on their phone, there's CCTV on every corner, and they have the tools to analyze everything you leave behind in international databases. But that could also be another lie from TV shows.

"No suspect and no victim."

"You couldn't ID them?" Grace pressed, swallowing hard. Facial recognition, fingerprints, dental records…how messed up did someone have to be for none of them to work?

"We don't have *them*," he admitted. "We literally only have two objects. No idea who the victim is or even what they've done to her."

"But the blood must…"

"None of that either."

"Then how do you know anything happened?" I asked, wondering what the two objects were.

"A kid saw a man half-carrying a struggling woman into the woods while on a Boy Scouts Camping Trip. He tried to tell an adult, but the man put his finger to his lips, so the kid kept his mouth shut until he got home to his mom on Sunday. The kid insists there was a trail of blood, and that the woman was covered in it, but by the time we went to look—"

"The rain washed it all away," I guessed. The weather had been miserable since my first day here, until today.

"Do you think he buried her in the woods, or is there a chance she got away?" Grace was hopeful.

"I've sent guys to search every inch of those woods, but without a body and on the delayed word of a seven-year-old … it'll take a while. We haven't found anything other than what we have upstairs so it's possible she got away, but no hospitals have her, and according to the kid's description, she lost too much blood to just put a Band-Aid on it and move on."

"What do you want us to do?" Grace asked.

"We're going to give your new intern a tour, so she can see how we handle current cases, not just cold ones. If you can do your things, the tiniest of leads or even a hunch would be greatly appreciated."

"There are cameras upstairs," Grace warned. I'd thought they had the kind of arrangement where he didn't ask questions and she didn't give him the details, but I was getting the feeling that she'd even told him about me, which wasn't cool.

"They won't be a problem," he said with confidence.

"Why not wait for it to get to us?"

"Because they haven't opened a case yet. There's not enough evidence, but I believe that kid. And until I see a body, I'm going to assume she might still be out there. I always prefer solving an attempted murder than the alternative."

"What do you think?" Grace asked me.

"You really think there's a chance she's out there?"

"A tiny one. But I have been called an optimist," he warned.

"Any chance is worth fighting for." I shrugged.

"Follow me." He replaced his smile with a solemn, no nonsense detective look. The transition was impressive.

I took deep breaths as we walked, not sure if I was silly for being nervous or if I should be terrified of walking right into a trap. Really, what could they prove, though? They could arrest me for tampering with evidence if we got caught, but being delusional wasn't a crime.

Unfortunately, a mental institution instead of a prison wasn't as comforting as I wanted it to be.

DETECTIVE CORTEZ KNEW everyone and said hello to at least a dozen people as the three of us made our way through the lobby and up a set of stairs to the bullpen, private offices, and labs. He lied seamlessly about how he was just giving me a tour to anyone who asked, so he would point out different rooms and stations to sell the story.

Finally, we got to a brightly lit white room with huge machines and tables. There were also those wall freezers from morgues, but I didn't think there were bodies in them. More from wishful thinking than any actual indication. Then again, maybe I liked it better if the bodies were up here rather than down in the basement with us.

"Does she want to see how the machines work?" A girl in a lab coat asked after Detective Cortez explained what he was doing.

"Nah, I'm just giving a quick tour, so she knows where everything is."

"I was about to grab a coffee from next door. Do you want anything?" I got the distinct impression that she was interested in our detective. Or was a very nervous person.

"I'm good, but I forgot my lunch this morning, so if you're still going to Betty's…"

"I'll meet you there," she assured him before leaving the three of us alone in the room.

"The evidence is over here." Detective Cortez brought us to the other end of the room, where the long white tables were, acting like that whole interaction hadn't happened. Which wouldn't be weird, only Grace looked at him expectantly.

"Suzie Withers?" she asked, eyebrows raised.

"Dr. Withers. And it has been four years," he defended himself.

"I know. You're the one who's been insisting you don't have the time or the interest to get back out there."

"I don't," he agreed.

"But..." she pressed.

"But I need to eat, and Betty's has fantastic grilled cheese sandwiches," he said in a tone that would have made me drop it. Especially with the look he shot in my direction, like he did not want to have this conversation in front of me.

I turned away when he looked, as if I hadn't been following their every word. I took a closer look once he explained the evidence, wondering if maybe I was wrong, and they had been together once. Was Grace the one he was with four years ago, or was he turning Grace down in favor of Suzie Withers?

"We obviously can't have fingerprints on these because it would jeopardize the case when we open it and we would all lose our jobs, but they were wiped clean anyway," Detective Cortez shared, bringing me back to the crime we were trying to solve.

The table had two objects: your average kitchen knife and a necklace.

"I'm thinking the knife was the weapon, so that would probably be the one to start with," Detective Cortez suggested.

Grace went first, rattling off chemical compounds and explaining what they meant.

"Basically, it's a knife." The detective was clearly disappointed.

"That someone recently wiped clean," she agreed.

"With an over-the-counter bleach everyone has in their laundry room." He sighed, having clearly hoped she could find something his team—including Suzie—had missed.

He looked at me expectantly, so Grace said, "You're up, kid." Then added, "If you want to, of course."

"She deserves whatever help we can give her," I assured them, nervously tucking my hair behind my ear. I'd obviously used my Gift multiple times in front of dozens of people. Every oral presentation for my archeology class or with kids at the museum where I was front and center, rubbing old artifacts to calm myself down and find answers when I had none. Still, it was entirely different to do it now when it was some kind of divine Gift rather than just a wild imagination and some self-soothing.

I picked up the knife and hoped I would see someone lovingly cooking up a big meal for their family, pouring their heart and soul into it, but I knew it was more likely I would see a woman being stabbed. Unless you were a psychopath or in absolute shock, murdering someone should be the most traumatizing thing that happened to you.

Instead, when I gently touched my wrist to the handle, it felt like I was thrown into the wall and impaled.

"Are you okay?" The detective was behind me in an instant, ready to catch me if I collapsed.

"What happened?" Grace had seen me touch things before. Other than cringing or bringing my hands to where I felt the pain inside, I rarely had a physical reaction to the flashes. And never so guttural.

"I'm fine," I assured them, trying to shake it off, but that wasn't entirely true. I stared at the knife like I expected it to zap me, but I couldn't explain what had happened. It was like I felt the knife go into my stomach, but there was also something so horrifying that my mind blocked it out with such force that it almost knocked me off my feet.

"Did you see her attacker? Could you see a name or anything?" Detective Cortez asked. I got the impression he thought I was more like a psychic with visions than just someone with feelings, and bits and pieces of visuals.

"I don't think most of it was coming from the knife. I think it was my brain rejecting whatever horror the flash would have shown me." I shared my assumptions.

"You think she was butchered?" he asked, gritting his teeth in an anger he was trying not to show us.

"To be honest, I don't know. I think she was stabbed, which you already knew, but maybe the killer had a mental break-down. Or I could be broken," I suggested, thinking the Gift itself might be my broken part.

"It was a long shot, don't worry about it," Cortez tried to make me feel better.

"I'll check the other one," Grace suggested, going to the necklace.

"This could have belonged to anyone who wandered off the path because no one ever looks there unless a tree falls, or an animal is injured. We were just taking a stab in the dark," he explained.

"The amber is actually glass and polyethylene, but the chain is solid gold," she shared.

"And what's inside? I think Suzie plans on breaking it to find out more, but so far, they've just been using machines to get a better look."

"Paint, not DNA."

Her answer caused the detective to sigh, once more defeated.

I stepped forward, ready for my turn.

"You can head back downstairs, and I'll meet you," Grace assured me.

"You don't want me to try?"

"We don't want you to hurt yourself," Detective Cortez argued. "It's not like you guys come with a manual to tell us what's pushing it too far and what happens when something is so terrible you don't want to see it."

"I doubt it would knock me dead. I'll probably just get winded again if it's too much," I said with a confidence I was no longer sure I felt.

They exchanged a glance before Grace shrugged, so Detective Cortez said, "Okay," proving to me that while he was our boss, Grace was the one in charge.

I really wanted to help them find this woman, especially if she was still alive somewhere, terrified and either alone or with a monster. But at the same time, I didn't want to feel anything like that again.

I brushed the back of my wrist against the stone, apprehensive about what was going to happen, but I felt a rush of elation. I concentrated like Grace taught me, trying to see the moment the feelings were felt. At first, all I could feel was warmth and sunshine, but then the scene began to form.

"It's beautiful!" I could hear the amazement in her voice, feel her joy.

"It reminded me of you. You deserve something pretty."

I could see the blurry outline of a man. Or rather, a boy. He was five or six years younger than me, but I could clearly make out his red hair. Thankfully for him, it was more of a strawberry blonde than an actual Ronald McDonald red.

"I'll never take it off," she promised, clutching the stone in her hand. I knew it wasn't realistic, but I believed she had every intention of doing just that.

"An amber for my Amber." He looked deep into her eyes, but I knew how much he loved her from the rush of it I felt when he pressed his palm over the necklace, letting his fingers rest on her clavicle.

I don't know if these flashes had the power to show me what people felt at their cores, or just surface emotions, but I was drunk on what they felt for each other, and completely understood how teenage love led to things like Romeo & Juliet. It was intoxicating, and I couldn't think straight.

"Amber," I shared when the moment ended.

"It's not real," Grace told me. "It's a fancy enough knockoff, but there's no resin and no chance that anything could be preserved inside it."

"I think her name is Amber," I explained myself better. It was a weird nickname otherwise.

"Like an outside the box version of those necklaces with names on them?" Detective Cortez asked, not really buying it, but also wanting to. Solving a potential murder would be infinitely easier if you knew the victim's name. Any lead, no matter how crazy, was better than the nothing they had before.

"He said an amber for my Amber."

"I didn't know you could hear conversations." Grace was impressed.

"I don't, usually. It's always muffled, so I can distinguish yelling, whispers, and screams, but never the words they're saying."

"What do you think is different about this one?" the detective asked, taking all this weirdness a lot better than I would have.

"I don't know. Maybe because it's more recent? Or they both had strong emotions toward it? I usually only feel the person who is touching it, whose emotions with it are strongest, so there would be a buffer between me and anyone else. If I had to guess, it was her most prized possession when he gave it to her, and unless he's dead, he is one hundred percent tearing up the world to find her right now."

"Can you tell how old they are?" he tried.

"Early teens, but I don't know how long ago it was. I can usually identify time periods because I'm dealing with medieval technologies and can look up when certain things were invented."

"But no iPhone to figure out which generation we're in," he understood.

"None that I could see."

"We should have the reports by this afternoon." A man's

voice made me jump as he came in and went straight to the big white box I assumed was a powerful microscope.

"I'm not here to pressure you, I was just giving Miss Carmichael a tour of the other floors." Detective Cortez didn't miss a beat. He lied as seamlessly as if he were telling the truth. In a way he was, but he was also hiding things, which I never would have known from his self-assured smile.

"I don't know how you survive in the basement." The man shook his head at us like he found the prospect similar to torture.

"You get used to it. Anything else you wanted to show her, or can we get back to work?" Grace asked, as if the whole ordeal was a waste of her time.

"Nope, we're good here, but if there's anything else, or she has questions, you know where to find me."

DETECTIVE CORTEZ WENT BACK to what I assumed was his office, while Grace and I took two sets of stairs instead of the elevator to get down to the basement. There was a weird smell of bleach in the staircase, which gave me shivers and the impression that something sinister had happened in there, but it also brought us past the flickering lights, right across from B-473.

"Are you sure you're okay?" Grace asked me once we were inside, placing her bowl of chocolates in front of me.

"I'm fine," I insisted, but I still took one. "Can I ask you something not exactly work-related?"

"I think we're past work-related," she said, showing me her palm to remind me we knew each other's secrets.

"Were you and Detective Cortez...his first name is Malcolm, right?"

"Oh, sweetie, if that's how you ask a question...." She shook her head at me.

"I'm sorry, it's none of my business, I was just..."

"You were curious." She shrugged to let me know it was okay, but she made no effort to give me an answer. "What are you doing tomorrow night?" she asked with a sigh.

"Absolutely nothing."

"Meet me at Enrique's at eight. We can get to know each other."

"I don't really drink," I warned. Enrique's was a bar and a cop hangout, so there was very little chance I would get in without being twenty-one.

"They won't mind if you're with me," she assured me before going over to the box she'd been working on yesterday.

I did the same, but looked up when her cell phone buzzed. She got this proud smile when she read it. "Amber Dennis," she told me.

"Who is that?" I asked.

"You were right. Our missing Jane Doe." She showed me a picture of a blonde teenager wearing the necklace we'd both played with upstairs. "The case is officially open."

"I hope it helps them find her," I said, still feeling how happy that boy and the necklace made her, but also reeling from what happened with the knife.

CHAPTER SIXTEEN

The sun was beaming when I finished, so I tried to let it melt the chill in my bones. I'd seen, or rather felt, horrors from some of the weapons and instruments from class, the museum, and the cold case boxes, but none of them lingered on me for this long after I stopped touching them. It was like I could feel the knife in my gut, and something tearing at my heart. I couldn't explain the pushback either. Was that what Amber had felt when she was stabbed or did the inanimate object have feelings it was trying to keep me away from?

"Are you okay?" Sybill walked up to me from Dad's car.

"What are you doing here?" I asked, taking her in for a hug.

"Dad needed very particular jogging shorts, so I told him he could shop while we had ice cream, because I don't like that weird maple one they have at the clinic, and mom was excited for Yogurtland. I texted you," she added when I still looked confused.

"How dare she compare frozen yogurt to ice cream," I teased, trying to shake it off so she wouldn't worry. My sister knew me better than that, but she just gave me a meaningful look before letting it drop, probably afraid this was about my guilt for not going with them. "I'm guessing gelato is also blasphemous?" I verified.

"They're all fine as their own entity; they're just not ice cream."

"Very true," I agreed, leading her to the ice cream shop I passed every day on my ride over, wanting to stop, but I was usually too late to eat it before work. Even if Grace seemed to always have a smoothie or leftovers with her, I had no interest in bringing any food down to the basement. Even coffee was pushing it, although I knew it didn't really taste like death when I drank it down there.

"Anything exciting happen today?" she asked. I'd told her about solving that first cold case, leaving a lot of details out and making up others, but we hadn't talked much about my work since.

"I was brought in on a more recent case," I admitted.

"Is that like a promotion or are they trying to break you?" I couldn't help but laugh when I saw her face, which perfectly reflected my feelings. I was all for working on cases that had the potential to save someone rather than just bringing their killers to justice, but removing the curtain of academia made every-thing way more emotional and weird. It was always hard because they were people, but lives were on the line this time.

Sybill ordered two soft serves, paying extra so we could have sugar cones and sprinkles.

"Fancy," I commented.

"It's a special occasion." She shrugged.

"You know, you say the word and I'm there. Today, tomor-row, whenever."

"I know," she assured me. "But I won't. I mean, unless I'm dying within the next twenty-four hours. Then I might let you know."

She was teasing, and I could see the twinkle in her eye, but I could also see the bags under them. I knew we shouldn't have stayed up to finish the book yesterday. She used the fact that we would have to wait months to find out what happened if we didn't, but she looked so much worse for the wear that I knew my smile was not reaching my eyes today.

"You're really not as funny as you think you are," I warned.

"I'm way funnier." Her attitude was completely unfazed. I envied her that part.

She made a deal with my parents, where she agreed to be poked and prodded every summer without complaint in exchange for being allowed to go to school with the other kids her age. She took a lot more sick days than her classmates, but her grades were amazing.

I was probably about to reiterate how willing I was to ditch everything and join her in California, where I felt I was supposed to be, when I noticed Tristan across the busy fountain and lost my words. I hadn't heard from him since Monday when I told him how my first day went—minus a few details— and he told me how happy he was for me. Then radio silence.

"Are you having a stroke?" Sybill asked, mostly joking, but we'd also memorized the signs. I could hear the fear in her voice whenever I got sick or felt tired, like maybe I caught whatever she had. If she was feeling particularly well, she would try to take care of me, but I could tell that as much as it scared her, a tiny selfish part of her would welcome having a companion going through things with her.

"I'm fine," I repeated what I'd been saying since I first touched the knife, although I wasn't sure if the addition of butterflies in my stomach made me feel more or less fine.

"You've either seen a ghost or...it's him," she read off my expression.

"Tristan," I agreed.

"Are we calling him over or hiding in the bushes? Because if we're hiding, you'll have to go on your own and I'll report back once it's clear." She'd told me multiple times to give up on him and find someone better, but also gave me possible explanations for his silence, most of them unprompted.

Before she even finished her proposition, Tristan spotted me from across the crowd. His smile grew bigger and more authentic when his eyes met mine. It was like his entire face lit up. I didn't mean to, but my smile must have matched his because he hesitated half a second before walking over.

"Alison." He stopped a few feet from our table.

"This is my sister, Sybill. Syb, this is my friend, Tristan."

Sybill rolled her eyes at me for introducing him like she didn't know absolutely every single detail about our relationship, or rather lack of one.

"It's a pleasure to meet you, Sybill. I was debating if I should have ice cream when I saw you." His eyes offered me an apology, but he otherwise acted like there was nothing weird with not responding to days worth of texts.

"You should," Syb told him. "If the question involves ice cream, the answer should always be yes."

"I like how you think," he told her.

"You should get yourself a cone and come join us."

He looked over at me to gauge whether he was welcome, then smiled at her. "I'll be right back."

"You did not do him justice," Syb stated once he was out of earshot.

"I think I described him pretty accurately."

"I don't think you said absolutely perfect."

"It was implied." I rolled my eyes. "And he isn't."

"Well, now I get to find out what's going on. To be honest, the worst part of leaving was that I wouldn't get to meet him. Now I can ask him all the fun questions you're too shy to."

"I'm not shy, they're inappropriate," I reminded her. I wasn't worried. I knew she wouldn't embarrass me on purpose or call him out, but she wouldn't be opposed to guiding the conversation towards things she was curious about. Like why he didn't kiss me.

"Chocolate and nuts?" she commented on his selection.

"Peanut butter and chocolate is my favorite combination in the world," he explained. "Strike one?" he asked off her look.

"What's your all-time favorite TV show?" she asked, implying his answer would determine if he had a strike or not.

"Seinfeld," he said without hesitation.

"We watched that with our dad." She looked at him, surprised by his choice, but she approved.

"Scrubs felt a little too on the nose."

"Movie?" Syb asked.

"Terminator 2."

"Allie." She turned her head toward me after a few more questions, but kept her eyes on Tristan.

"Yes, Syb, how's your interrogation going?"

"I like him," she decided.

"Thank God," he said, winking at her. "But I think it's Allie's opinion that makes or breaks this."

"She likes you, too," Sybill said without hesitation.

"Well, that's a relief." He pretended to wipe the sweat from his brow.

"She's a little more boring than I am, but it's usually just because she takes a while to catch on," Syb shared.

"Is that so?" He looked at me, cocking his head in a way that made me blush.

"I guess I'm easy to wear down." I shrugged, garnering a giggle behind his smile.

"Lucky for you," Sybill said under her breath, but still loud enough for everyone to hear.

If looks could kill, the look I wanted to give my sister would have murdered her on the spot. Tristan didn't take his eyes off me as he said, "I'm not trying to wear her down. I would much rather sweep her off her feet."

His eyes told me he meant it, which raised some questions on my end, but he was saying it out loud to make me blush more than anything.

The conversation went on like this with Tristan trying to make me blush and impress my sister, while Sybill asked him every question she could think of. I mostly watched, except for when Tristan asked me questions or Syb went too far. It was entertaining as hell, and I knew I was smiling more than I should.

"This was surprisingly a lot of fun, but I have a meeting to get to," Tristan said, rising from the table. We'd finished our ice creams at least twenty minutes ago.

"Surprisingly?" Sybill called him on it.

"I don't think I've ever been so thoroughly interrogated, but I enjoyed it," he rephrased for her.

"Well, if ever you moved here—not necessarily for my sister —you would be invited to our Game Nights."

"Very tempting," he told her. "Every Friday?"

"Usually," she agreed. "We're leaving at an ungodly hour tomorrow morning, so we're doing an abridged version tonight instead."

"Oh, that's tomorrow?" he asked.

"Yep. Poor Allie will be all by her lonesome for the first time in…ever?"

"Peace at last!" I teased, throwing my hands up in the air.

"If ever you get tired of all the peace and quiet, you know where to find me."

"I might take you up on that," I warned, wondering if he would be more responsive to texts now.

"I look forward to it." He smiled and his eyes went down to my lips, making my cheeks flush for the millionth time today. "Sybill, an absolute pleasure," he told her before going off.

"I take back everything about the internship. You're staying for him," she decided once he was gone.

"We've literally been on one date," I reminded her.

"And he's completely into you. He's either been busy or just isn't good at texting. I know I'm charming, but he was a trooper and a half."

"I'll take it under advisement."

AFTER DINNER THAT NIGHT, we played a game of Scrabble, where my dad wiped the floor with us. Every time, Sybill and I assumed we would have the advantage because we read so much and know all the complicated words, but he killed us with the simple ones. He loved adding an 's' or an 'ed' to score triple points.

"Are you sure you have everything?" I asked Sybill, folding the last of the laundry she needed.

"It's California, not a third world country," she pointed out.

"I know, but—"

"But you're worried I'll be missing you."

"I know you're missing me; I'm trying to make sure I'm the only thing you'll be without."

"I've got a mountain of books and my laptop. That's pretty much all I'll need."

"And you've got this," I decided, reaching for the clasp at the back of my neck.

"Al…" she made a weak attempt at arguing.

"This doesn't mean you can skip out on the crappy stuff. If Dr. Bell says anything about you not cooperating, I'm coming to get it back."

"It's more of a reward than a bribe," she pointed out.

"Do you not want it?"

"Of course, I want it. I'm just saying that I'm not an idiot."

"I know."

"Thank you." She pressed the necklace to her heart. It had

belonged to our grandmother, who left it to me before she died when I was four. I wore it every single day until one of the trials wreaked havoc on my little sister. She wouldn't eat, didn't want any of her toys…there was nothing any of us could do but hold her and watch as she suffered. I was cuddling her one night in the hospital when she fell asleep clutching the necklace. When she woke up, I let her wear it until she felt better which obviously never happened. Still, she gave it back to me at Christmas, so it became a tradition that I would give it to her every summer, and she would give it back every winter.

"Have fun this summer. Save the world. I expect really interesting stories every single time I call."

"How often will that be?" I asked.

"I'll be extremely busy socializing and puking my guts out, but I should manage a call every week or so."

"Or so?" I asked, raising an eyebrow.

"Fine, I'll take a scintillating, well-developed story every Friday, and an entertaining tidbit every other time I call, which might be daily. But you better not pick up when you're with Tristan unless it's because he misses my sparkling personality."

"I'll miss it."

"Even with all those calls I just threatened you with?"

"Even with all those calls," I assured her.

She came and slept in my double bed, which we usually only did in hospitals and hotel rooms these days. At the hospital, I was there for her, but tonight, I knew she was humoring me. I spent most of the night listening to her labored breathing, watching her chest go up and down and praying they would be able to help her this time.

CHAPTER SEVENTEEN

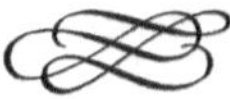

I woke up way earlier than I wanted to so that I could say goodbye to my family and see them off. I had never been away from them for more than a few days, and while I had no doubts that my parents could manage Sybill and she could handle her own pills, I couldn't help but think of all the hardships they would face without me, and how lonely Syb would be. The guilt was eating at me.

"But most importantly," my dad said, making me realize I'd completely been ignoring him for the past few minutes, "enjoy yourself. Have fun. Go on an adventure. Do things you wouldn't do."

"Like get a tattoo?" I asked. I knew he meant it with all the sincerity in the world, but it was weird to have your parents tell you to let loose and live a little.

"If that's what would make you happy then yes, get a tattoo. Preferably not a tramp stamp, but..."

"If it makes me happy," I finished for him, smiling as I felt the tickle in my nose that told me I was about to cry. I stared straight at the rising sun in the distance to stop it.

"He's making a point, but if you're serious, don't get it on your face. And make sure they disinfect everything. I have horror stories of—"

"I'm not going to get a tattoo," I assured my mom. "I'm going to go to work, look at dead people's things, hopefully help some people, then you'll come home, and everything will go back to normal." I tried to make the last part sound happy and exciting.

"That sounds promising."

"Just make sure you have fun between the dead stuff," my dad encouraged.

"I love you guys."

I got big hugs that lasted longer than they normally did because I would have to hold on to them longer. Syb was already asleep across the back seat with a mountain of pillows and blankets, but we'd said our goodbyes last night.

I watched them driving away and considered going back to bed, but the chances I would fall back to sleep were slim. Instead, I got ready and went to work way earlier than I should have. I planned to go to a coffee shop and wait for a more reasonable hour, but there was something I had to do inside the precinct, and the fewer people, the better.

I took a deep breath before going up the stairs in the lobby. I hoped that a combination of looking like I knew where I was going, pretending I belonged, and then acting lost and apologetic if caught, would allow me another chance to see something with the necklace.

Amber's face was all over the news last night. They'd found evidence of a struggle at her apartment, and one of her kitchen knives was missing. No one had seen her in over a week.

I rounded the corner to the lab and found myself inches away from Detective Cortez.

"Alison," he said, surprised.

"Detective Cortez." I smiled, taking a split second to decide if I wanted to get away from him or get his help. "I was wondering if I could see the necklace again. Or at least read the report?" If Grace trusted him with both our secrets, I had to be able to trust him with my mission.

"Do you think you missed something?" he asked, already bringing me to the room, using his key card to give us access.

"Not exactly. I was just…that gold chain was intact, right?"

"It was…" He waited for my reasoning.

"It was a short necklace. If it wasn't ripped off in the struggle, that means—"

"She wasn't wearing it." He understood what I was getting at. "Are you hoping you'll get another flash, or do you just want to look at it?"

"How long do we have?"

"Five minutes if we don't want to have to come up with an excuse as to why we're in here," he said after checking his watch.

"I'll take it." I knew it wasn't really an answer, but I didn't know what I was hoping to find. I just knew something felt off.

"Watch the door while I find it," he asked of me.

There were no windows, so I was mostly watching the door handle and the little keypad beside it, hoping there would be a noise to let me know if someone used it.

"Alison…"

"What's wrong?" I asked, taking my eyes off the door to see why he sounded so defeated. "They said they were going to crush it," I remembered, seeing the little baggy of what used to be her necklace. "Is the chain still there?"

"Here." He handed me another bag, but he didn't look optimistic.

I took a glove from the box on the wall and opened the bag to take out the golden chain. I didn't want to risk getting any of my hairs on it, so I let the chain brush gently against my palm.

The pain I felt in my chest and in my gut weren't physical, but I wanted to double over from the weight of them.

"Amber, please." I could hear his heart breaking, but I felt hers as she fumbled with the clasp at the back of her neck. She was emotional, and it's always hard to take a necklace like that off yourself, but she wasn't trying to go faster either.

"Don't touch me," she warned as he made to come close and help her.

"This isn't what I wanted."

"You should have thought of that."

She got the necklace off and it felt like a weight had been lifted, but not in the way the expression usually means. It was like she'd been wrapped up in one of those weighted blankets and suddenly found herself without it, exposed to the elements and the cold, lost and heartbroken. She wanted nothing more than to put the necklace back on, but instead, she let the chain linger in her fist for a few more seconds, then dropped it into his hand.

"The necklace is yours," he argued.

"Keep it. Or it'll end up in a landfill instead of with the next idiot who falls for you."

She walked away then because she knew that if she didn't, she would never be able to go. But he was the one holding on to the golden chain now, and it felt like my heart was ripped out of my chest.

"WE NEED TO GO." Detective Cortez suddenly had gloves on as he grabbed the chain from me and put everything back where he found it. "Suzie's on her way up with coffees," he explained, putting his hand behind my elbow to guide me into the hallway. All I wanted was to curl into the fetal position and cry.

"That's lucky," I said, referring to the fact that the lab technician happened to have a crush on him.

"I...maybe," he said. This wasn't the time to be discussing his love life. I was just curious to figure it all out.

. . .

HE BROUGHT me to a small office with 'Detective Malcolm Cortez' written on the frosted glass window. He took his seat behind the desk and motioned for me to sit across from him.

He started talking about different programs at the precinct just as Suzie knocked.

"Oh, I didn't realize you had company," she said when she saw me. I knew it was a cover, but I still felt bad when I saw the shock and subsequent hurt on her face.

"Just telling Miss Carmichael how everything works," he assured her, implying this was nothing out of the ordinary, but he had to know that everyone who saw me here with him at six in the morning would get the wrong idea.

"I was at the coffee shop, so I brought you one. Next time I can get three." She gave me a bright smile, and I got the impression she really was that kind of sweet girl who would get everyone coffee just to be nice, but I could also see that it stung.

"No, I'll be back in the basement as soon as he's done my orientation." I tried to be reassuring, but if she believed me that nothing was going on, she would question why there wasn't a more appropriate time to be doing this.

"You two have a great day," she said before leaving.

"I FEEL TERRIBLE," I said once it was just the two of us.

"I'll tell her it was a favor for…for Grace." Her name sounded weird on his lips. I wondered if there was a nickname he called her that he had to stop himself from using. "What did you see?"

"They broke up. He was the one who had the necklace at the end of it."

"The boyfriend did it?" He looked confused.

"What's wrong?" I asked.

"There's a serial killer we haven't caught yet who abducts

couples. Amber's boyfriend, whose name is Hunter, has also been missing, so they're looking for someone who matches the serial killer's profile."

"You don't agree?" I asked.

"Not if Amber and Hunter broke up." He looked at me, gauging how much he should trust me, the same questions I'd had about him earlier, but he came to the same conclusion. "I had my doubts when none of the other crime scenes had murder weapons left behind. Or personal effects. The knife is similar to what he would have used on his other victims, but he doesn't leave things behind."

"I know they broke up, but I don't think he would have killed her. I can still feel my heart breaking from when she handed him the necklace. There was no anger or wanting revenge, it was just pain."

"I'll keep an open mind," he assured me.

"I'm glad I don't have your job." I sighed, wrapping my arms around myself.

"I'm glad I don't have yours." He shivered as a shadow crossed his face. I knew it wasn't fear, but he made it feel ominous and dark.

"I better get down to work," I decided, even though I was still over an hour early.

"Of course. I'll let you know if I hear anything."

I WAS GOING to use the extra time to get ahead on the day's work, but I figured it couldn't hurt to Google Amber Dennis and see what the world was saying about her. Most of the sites used the same picture of her college graduation, where she is smiling with the cap, gown, and diploma. Others used one of her with a little girl, her sister according to the caption, but she wore the amber necklace in both. They all used the same words to describe her; kind, caring, brilliant, a spark of life. She sounded like a cheerleader who volunteered with orphans on weekends, but so did everyone when they went missing. Or died.

I tried to take that thought back, and nearly missed the one site that not only used a different, more recent picture of Amber, they also included her boyfriend, Hunter.

Only he didn't look anything like the guy with red hair from my flashes. Hunter was tall and blonde, making me think of my old Ken doll. The picture they chose looked like it was from an engagement shoot, as Amber had a very expensive-looking diamond ring on her finger. Hunter wore a suit and looked like a fancy lawyer. Someone important.

I got into a deep dive of the articles, trying to see if any of them mentioned an ex-boyfriend, or how long ago she and Hunter met, but all I could gather was that the engagement party was a month ago.

"Am I late?" Grace asked when she came in, putting her coat on a hook and juggling her breakfast to look at her watch. I noticed that both she and Malcolm wore the same kind of analog watch with a leather band, but this wasn't the time to get into that either.

"I'm early. Very early. I had Mal…Detective Cortez show me the necklace again."

She raised an eyebrow at my slip but didn't comment on it. "Did you see something different?"

"The chain gave me a new flash," I shared, pulling up the different articles on my phone.

"This is the couple you saw?" she asked me once I pulled up the engagement photo.

"No, that's the girl, but not the guy. At some point between these pictures and that one, she had a heart wrenching breakup and gave back the necklace."

"If she gave it back, how did it get into evidence?" she asked.

"That's exactly what I was wondering."

Grace called Malcolm and told him Hunter wasn't the boyfriend from the memories, but the necklace in the woods made the ex-boyfriend from my flashes the prime suspect.

❧

"ARE you sure you want to do this?" Grace asked me that afternoon once Detective Cortez let us back into the crime lab. The knife was on the table, waiting for me.

"You heard Detective Cortez. They've handed the case off to the federal agents, who are all convinced this is a serial killer. The few people who listened to him now believe her ex-boyfriend saw the engagement announcement and went after them. I know I don't know him, and I literally only felt a few seconds of him, but I can't imagine him ever hurting her." We'd found the guy from my flashes on Amber's Facebook, an ex-boyfriend named Matthew Crawford. He joined the military when he turned eighteen and just got back from his second tour in Afghanistan.

"Even after she hurt him and moved on with Mr. Perfect?"

"I don't know what happened, but if you'd felt what they were feeling…"

"You're a bit of a hopeless romantic, aren't you?" she asked me.

"I don't think it's hopeless." I proved her point more than mine.

"Good luck," she said before going out to distract the lab techs.

I PLACED the knife carefully on the counter, then took off my purple glove. I was apprehensive, knowing I was either going to get emotional pain, physical pain, or both. I took a deep breath,

110

closed my eyes, and let the back of my hand brush against the handle.

I expected the pain in my gut, but hoped I wouldn't be knocked back again.

Was my fear blocking me, or did the knife not want to share its secrets?

I took another deep breath and thought of Amber. I remembered how happy she'd been when Matthew gave her the necklace. How heartbroken they'd both been when she gave it back. Then I thought of her alone in the woods somewhere or in a cell-like basement, praying for someone to find her while the cops were busy looking in the wrong place. I clenched my hand into a fist and braced myself for the blow before pressing the back of my hand onto the handle, nothing uncertain about it.

This time, nothing tried to knock me off my feet. There were so many voices screaming inside my head as rage mixed with sorrow, but the feeling of the knife slicing into my gut made me sink to my knees. I tried to focus on one of them, to single someone out, but then I felt fear and desperation. I didn't know them enough to know who felt what yet, but I started to recognize what emotions and sounds went together. This wasn't the first time that multiple battles had overwhelmed me at the same time. It was a given whenever I touched swords or things that were worn by many people with high emotions, but I wouldn't have expected a kitchen knife to have such a sordid history.

I tried to focus and single out Amber, since I could so vividly recall her pain from previous flashes. I expected it, but it still stung when the pain in my stomach grew more pronounced. I assumed actually getting stabbed hurt more, but I felt like I was going to pass out from my experience of it. More than her pain, I could feel her fear.

Maybe they were right, and this was a case of a jealous ex-boyfriend trying to steal his ex's happiness. One of those, 'if I can't have her, no one else will'. I was crushed and dreading it as I tried to focus on Matthew, remembering his pain from the breakup so I could lock onto him. He only held the handle briefly before he pulled the knife out and I lost him, but his regret and guilt were overwhelming. I could feel his urgency, praying that she would be okay, that he wouldn't lose her.

I focused on Hunter, the one I didn't know with the fancy suit, on the anger and the betrayal that were screaming at me. He wore his emotions on his sleeve, or in this case, on the handle of his knife, but there were so many of them. A jumble of rage and pride, pain and hatred. I got whiplash from how quickly he bounced from one to the next as he held the knife in his hands, pacing. I knew what was coming, but it still shocked me when he plunged the blade into Amber's stomach with one hand, pulling her closer with the other. He also felt remorse, but it was buried deep underneath his anger.

I took my hand off the knife and took a few steadying breaths, waiting for the pain to go away, but I only had a couple of minutes until the time Detective Cortez warned us he would be back with Suzie. I put the evidence into its bag, the box back on the shelf, and left the room, hoping I didn't look as bad as I felt.

I WAITED until I was in the basement to lift my shirt and look at the spot where I felt the blade go in. My skin was untouched, but it felt like I should be able to see a knife stuck inside, with blood pouring out of me.

"You took your time," Grace warned, coming in barely a minute after me.

"I couldn't make sense of it." I quickly dropped my shirt and smoothed it down over my non-existent wound.

"Did you get what you needed?"

"Hunter stabbed Amber. I think he stabbed her and dragged her across the forest floor until I don't know what happened, but Matthew pulled the knife out and tried to bandage her up."

"And you're basing this on…"

"A jumble of flashes."

"I'll tell Malcolm."

"I don't know why nobody's found them yet. Matthew was terrified; I'm sure he was going to bring her to a hospital."

"Is Hunter dead?" she asked, reminding me that he was missing too.

"They can't be playing cat and mouse out there with hundreds of people looking for them." As soon as the world had realized Hunter was missing, his father, who owned a law firm, put out a reward for anything that helped bring his son home safe. There were more volunteers than the search party knew what to do with.

"The search parties started today, but the rangers said that part of the mountain had been off-limits for months because of bear sightings. Only trained rangers and officers were allowed, so it could take days, maybe even weeks, to search it all."

"If they're just hiding out there to get away from him…" My stomach was in agony, and even if I knew they were most likely dead, my chest grew tight at the thought of them alone in the woods.

"Grab your coat," Grace decided.

"Where are we going?" I asked, already following her.

"You need a distraction, and I need a drink."

CHAPTER EIGHTEEN

Enrique's was crowded for this early in the afternoon. It was just like the cop bars from my dad's shows, but Grace walked past the bar to a very narrow staircase in the back. I expected it to bring us to a second level like the first, but there was just a hallway with offices, and a heavy black door at the end.

She pushed it open to reveal a gorgeous rooftop terrace, surrounded by light green plants and beautiful flowers of every color.

"Garden of good and evil?"

"I garden when I'm stressed." She shrugged, fixing one of the hanging plants before taking a seat at one of the two tables. They looked more like backyard furniture than bar staples; low tables with couches.

"You did this?"

"Enrique pays people to do it now," she corrected.

"And Enrique is..."

As if to answer my question, a man came over to us with a couple of what looked like mojitos in handled mason jars.

"Enrique is incredibly talented at figuring out exactly what you want to drink. Or eat," Grace said with a flirtatious smile, biting down on her bottom lip. He was attractive and kept in shape, but he was at least a decade older than my dad.

"I have nachos and cheese sticks that Johnny will bring up soon." He gave her a look like he wanted nothing more than to kiss her, but held back for my benefit.

"What do I do to deserve you?" she asked him.

"I ask myself that same question every day." He sighed and smiled at her before leaving us alone on the roof.

"We met in Spain, and he swept me off my feet like it was nobody's business. I tried to fight it, for his sake and Malcolm's, but why be miserable when all you need to be happy is staring right at you?" I could see she still wrestled with that decision, but she'd also looked at Enrique with that look my mom gave my dad whenever he asked her to dance. Usually in the living room to no music, but she loved it. And him.

"Four years ago," I guessed. Then swallowed back the sick as I considered how much younger she would have been back then, while he would still have been in his early fifties. I took a sip of the mojito, hoping it could dull whatever was going on in my stomach. The stabby feeling didn't help either.

"A little longer than that." She watched for my reaction.

"Detective Cortez seems like a nice, standup guy. And Suzie has it really bad for him," I said like I was just making conversation, but she knew I was saying I didn't approve, and she should let Malcolm know it was okay for him to move on, so he could be happy too.

"How long ago did it happen?" she asked.

"Did what happen?"

I waited for more details, but she stopped and chatted with the waiter who brought us the food Enrique had promised. The cheese sticks were golden brown and oozing, while the nachos were piled high with cheese, meat, and vegetables. The waiter looked more Grace's age, and they seemed to know each other well.

"When did you become Gifted?" she elaborated once he was gone.

I had no idea what it had to do with anything, but I answered anyway. "I don't know. The first time I felt the pull was maybe nine years ago."

"But you know when you died, don't you?" she pressed, looking at me strangely, but I was looking at her the same way.

"When I died?" I was shocked by the question, but then I wondered how the hell she knew. "You mean when I drowned?"

"That sounds terrifying." She shivered and wrapped her arms around herself as I did the same.

"I don't remember much of it. I just remember Sybill was wearing this red bathing suit, and I wanted it instead of the yellow one they bought me. Everyone was fussing over my baby cousin, and I was trying to figure out whether I could fit in Syb's bathing suit, and what I could trade her for it, when I saw her fall off the dock. I screamed her name and ran after her without thinking. She was crying, so terrified, and I remember I kept bobbing under, but I wasn't afraid. I just kept thinking that as long as I could keep her head above water, we would be okay. The current was strong, so I couldn't get her back onto the dock, but there was a boat anchored nearby, so I got her to grab onto the ladder before my leg got caught on something. I tried to stay above water, but the more I moved my foot, the tighter it got, and with the waves... I saw her big eyes go wide, then I went under, and everything was black." I shivered, even with the sun beating down on us. I knew it would make the chill worse, but I took another sip of my mojito to calm my nerves. I guess I remembered a lot more than I want to. "This is a terrible distraction," I warned.

"We're here to get to know each other," she reminded me.

I nodded and took another sip, but I had never asked

someone about the time they almost died as a get-to-know-you question.

"What happened when you woke up?" she asked delicately.

"My chest hurt so bad. I cried because I opened my eyes and all I saw was my dad pounding on my chest while my mom begged me to breathe. I didn't put it together and realize he was doing compressions until I spat out the water and remembered what happened."

I expected more sympathy from Grace, something about how hard that must have been, but she looked confused.

"I know that's not exactly how CPR works, but that's what it felt like," I amended.

"You didn't die."

"I'm not currently dead, but I was. Just under two minutes, so my dad won't let me use brain damage as an excuse when I make a stupid decision or get bad grades." I'd tried it once, but the look on my parents' faces ensured that I never mentioned it again. That day at the beach before Sybill fell into the water was one of the last times I could remember us all being care-free and perfectly happy. After that day, we spent weeks, or maybe months, making sure I was okay without my parents ever leaving my side. I would wake up in the middle of the night and find one of them standing over me and Syb. She took to sleeping in the bed with me, maybe as a thank you, or an apology for making me go into the water in the first place, or maybe my parents put her there so they only had one bed to watch over. It was when they finally loosened up and treated me like a normal child again that we realized something was wrong with Sybill. All the symptoms of cancer but without a tumor or any sign of cancer. That was how her pediatrician had described it. Another said it was a constant and severe case of mono, which I'd teased her about because I knew mono was also called the kissing disease. I don't know at what point we realized it wasn't something we were going to fix, rather something we would live with for the rest of our lives. I always wondered if she got it in the lake because I wasn't fast enough or if my parents were so focused on me that they missed the sickness taking hold of her until it was too late.

"How old were you?" Grace asked.

"Almost seven. Labor Day weekend," I shared, which was not what she wanted to hear, even though she seemed to be expecting it.

"I'm beginning to think this will sound like a really weird question for you, but have you ever been dead? Or blacked out for longer than a couple of minutes?"

"I had my tonsils removed, so they put me under for the surgery," I shared, but I could tell that wasn't what she meant.

"But you're Gifted," she said like it didn't make sense.

"That's what you tell me," I agreed.

"You're still in your First Life."

"You only have one life to live." I shrugged.

Grace's confusion and the way she looked at me made me very nervous.

"This explains some, but it raises so many more questions."

"All I'm getting is questions," I said, but I wouldn't know where to start. "What's going on?"

"I brought you out to tell you how I became Gifted and ended up here, so you would understand better about Malcolm and Enrique, without the possibility of someone overhearing or walking in on us."

"That's what I thought we were going to do," I agreed. I was more interested in her love life because the Gifted stuff made me uneasy.

"I thought it would be easier if I knew where you were coming from, how long you'd been Gifted, what you've had to deal with, whether anyone answered your questions before…"

"But I answered wrong?"

"I don't know," she admitted. "In my experience, every Gifted person dies, and that's how they acquire their Gift."

"I'm like this because I drowned?"

"No, I'm like this because I had an abusive husband I didn't get away from fast enough. I'm not sure what you are."

"What I am?" I asked. I was fine and perfectly normal until they decided I was Gifted. This was on them, not on me.

"No, I'm sorry, I don't mean that. I just mean that I died when I was twenty-six years old, and no one was there to bring me back to life and save me. I woke up a couple of days later in the trunk of a car in an impound lot, scheduled to be compacted into junk. I was scared, confused, and so lost, until I found Isaiah."

"That's terrible," I said, trying to find better words to describe her horror. "How did you survive?"

"I didn't, Alison, that's what I'm trying to tell you. I died. As in completely dead, not coming back through any medical miracles, but then I did. The stab wounds were gone, the bruising…I was exactly like I had been before he found me."

"That's impossible," I argued.

"So is your Gift," she pointed out.

"You think Dr. Richards died, too?"

"He was in the Great War."

"Which one?" I knew World War I was the only war referred to by that name, but maybe Grace didn't.

"The one from 1914 to 1918."

"If he fought in the First World War, he would be at least…he would be over a hundred years old," I argued, but she just shrugged.

"He was lucky to figure out what he was made for."

"You're making this up," I accused her, but I couldn't think of an angle. Unless she wanted to see how many crazy things I would believe just because I had what they called a Gift. Maybe it was all hallucinations.

"I thought the hard part would be explaining Enrique."

"Is he dead, too?"

"No, he's just a normal fifty-eight-year-old man who deserves a nice, fifty-something year old woman, but still wants me."

"Most men want a younger woman," I said without thinking, my mind on all the other things she'd said.

"I'm not younger than him."

"You're not much older than me."

"Malcolm is my son," she admitted.

I looked at her, thinking this was the most ridiculous joke she was trying to pass by me, but she was dead serious.

"He has to be—"

"Forty-five years old," she finished for me. "I had him hidden away with a friend the night his father found me. When I woke up, I went to get my son, then I tried to start over as if nothing had happened, but I wasn't getting any older. We moved around whenever people commented on it, until I met Enrique. By then Malcolm was pretending to be my little brother, but I wasn't ready to trust anyone else with my secrets. Enrique was the guy I should have married and lived happily ever after with."

"When you said his mother was like us…"

"His mother is me," she agreed. "I didn't think it would all be new to you. I knew my relationship with Malcolm would be easy to understand once you found out who he is, so I was going to ply you with alcohol to tell me all about your impressions of him and Suzie, because I so want him to be happy. And then I was going to tell you how hard it is to be with Enrique in secret, to have to stay away for long periods of time then hear people talking about how he has a type whenever I come back… but you don't have any of that."

"My head is spinning, and the mojito isn't helping," I shared.

"I thought you only looked underage. I shouldn't have given you alcohol," she realized, but made no attempt to take the drink away from me. "I was a mess for months after it happened to me. Nothing made sense. I thought I was crazy, but then I met Isaiah, who was digging in the little Mexican town we were staying in."

"Did he know what you were from looking at you?" I asked.

"No, he…he would come into the little cantina I worked at, flirting with the woman who owned it. For months. One day he comes in and tells us he's going home, thanks us for putting a smile on his face, then springs into action when a group of cartel members come in, fully armed, asking for my boss' daughter. He jumped in front of us like he had no fear, did something with his hand that sent the sun in their eyes, and managed to knock two of them out before the cops arrived."

"Dr. Richards?" I asked, not buying it. I knew old people had pasts and were young once, but none of that sounded even remotely like his current personality.

"You met him after he spent decades being reminded just how mortal he was."

"You saw him come back?"

"You don't come back after you accomplish whatever it is you're here for," she explained. "He'd been shot, and I didn't know he was Gifted, so I tried to stop the bleeding, but he kept telling me it was fine, not to worry about it. Before he passed out, he said he would just wake up good as new. I'd never met anyone else like me, so I waited for him at the hospital. Thank God the doctors were able to save him."

"Because the thing he had to do was save you guys?"

"Margarita, my boss' daughter. We think. He didn't know he was in his Last Life until years later when he realized he was growing older again. Margarita became a doctor and developed treatments for diseases, and better ways to perform surgeries. Every time I Google her, she's done something new that's incredible and revolutionary. She couldn't do that if he hadn't taken that bullet for her."

CHAPTER NINETEEN

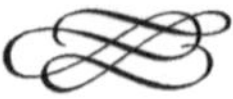

I spent the weekend at home Googling 'Gifted' and reading the book Grace lent me once she understood just how clueless I was. My brain was exhausted, so I tried to do some mindless reading. Unfortunately, the historical romances made me wonder if the author was Gifted, and that was how they painted such an accurate picture of England in the sixteenth century. Maybe Anne Boleyn really did have these conversations, and this book was written by a lady's maid who overheard them. Or Anne Boleyn herself, for that matter.

I couldn't decide if I was more convinced that none of it was real, or excited about all the incredible things I could discover through meeting more Gifted. I would assume there weren't that many, but at the same time, Grace and Dr. Richards found each other, I found them...either we were drawn to each other or there were more Gifted than the books and online forums imagined.

I had mostly researched people who were Gifted without dying. While someone coming back to life after being dead for a few days—exactly like Jesus—was the part I was having trouble digesting, Grace had been more intrigued by me. When I asked if there was anyone she could ask, she told me that I could trust her to keep my secret, but she felt very strongly that this was the type of thing you didn't go around advertising.

"Like having weird magical powers?" I'd asked, thinking she was being ridiculous, and I was being funny.

"Much worse," she'd replied, without even the hint of a smile.

~

AFTER TWO DAYS, the best I could come up with was a single paragraph in one of the eBooks I downloaded. It was the kind of book I would have loved when I was little and wanted to be a Charmed sister. *The Gifted* happened to be in their table of Contents, along with spells, potions, and magical creatures.

"On very rare occasions, the Gift is exhibited in a Gifted's First Life. Like witches, they remain human, but have a supernatural ability. Studies have been attempted, but no conclusions were made."

So I was like a witch, bringing my childhood dream to life, only it was nothing like I'd imagined. The book made it seem scientific rather than mystical, which gave me shivers every time I thought about it. What did they mean by studies being attempted? None of it was FDA approved, so my guess was they cut into those 'First Lifers' and couldn't figure out what made them special. Or maybe the subjects died and became Full-Gifted, thus solving the problem. Either way, it made me think Grace was right about not telling anyone about it. Which included my family.

At first, I was relieved that they were just texting, because it meant that I didn't have to lie to them and pretend to be okay, but by Sunday night, I gave in and facetimed them.

"Hey, Pumpkin." My dad picked up on the first ring. "How was your weekend?"

I analyzed his voice before responding, since the trials were hit or miss. He sounded exhausted, but not worried or drained. "Quiet. I had research to do for work."

I was saved from having to explain when my mom joined in, telling me how much she missed me already.

"How are you guys?"

"Oh, you know, day one is always tests, poking, prodding, and lists of dos and don'ts—"

"But I got my first dose and didn't burst into flames, so I'm calling it a win." Sybill cut Mom off, sounding worse than my dad, but still optimistic.

"How are you feeling? Did Damian give you his pudding?" I tried to put my worries aside and be enthusiastic for her. Damian had a blood disorder and often ended up in the same trials, or at least centers as Sybill, and they bonded over their love of everything computers. They led campaigns together to build cities and kill bad guys all year long, and she's been in love with him for as long as I can remember.

"You make it sound so trivial, but the way those pills taste, it's a profession of love. In the highest order."

"I don't doubt it, Syb. I'm very happy for you."

"We should get some food in her, but call us when you get in tomorrow," my mom requested.

"Next time we do a video call, I'll make sure he's sitting behind me. He started growing a beard, and it makes him a thousand times sexier." Syb was stuck on Damian.

"I look forward to it." I rolled my eyes at her, but I was just going through the motions.

ANOTHER TEXT from Tristan popped up when I put my phone on the charger, hoping I was feeling better. He'd texted a few times since the ice creams, which was a welcome change, but I told him I was under the weather and staying home all weekend. He'd even called once, so I had to make those fake coughing noises, which was embarrassing. Luckily, I had the Gifted websites in front of me, reminding me why getting involved with anyone right now was a bad idea.

CHAPTER TWENTY

"I got you one of those fancy coffees with the whipped cream and the caramel." Grace wasn't even remotely surprised to find me already working when she came in early on Monday morning.

"You did?" I asked, seeing her green smoothie.

"You deserve a treat. And you look as exhausted as I thought you would," she explained.

"That's very sweet," I said sarcastically about the comment on my looks, but meant it for the coffee.

"It is overly sweet, but if you top it off with the sludge from down here, it might be drinkable." She nodded to the ancient coffee pot she continuously complained about, but often drank.

"I'll keep that in mind."

"Any progress?" she asked.

I was staring into space and thinking when she walked in, but I had my work in front of me with occasional moments of productivity.

"Those need to be checked and signed off on. Then I can bring them back to the evidence room for you," I offered.

"Like a real assistant," she teased before getting to work.

. . .

I was painfully aware of how much longer it took us to do things than if we were normal people. Sure, it came in handy when we found discrepancies or foul play, but most of the time, I had to sift through flashes of mundane lives, in addition to the actual work we were supposed to be doing. Very rarely did Grace need to know the chemical compounds inside snow globes and knockoff purses.

Around ten, I took her advice and refilled my sweet caramel coffee with what was left from the pot she brewed at eight. It was surprisingly okay, unless that was the exhaustion talking.

I took a walk at lunch, even though Grace invited me to a bistro with her and Malcolm. Now that I knew who he was, he was more obvious about how much he cared about her when he came to the basement, but I didn't think I would ever get used to him calling her Mamá.

When I got to the ice cream shop, it hit me how much I missed Sybill. We were one of those weird, awkwardly close families who could use the time apart, but I didn't want it. Everything would be so much easier if I had skipped the get-together and gone to California with them. Although it was nice to wake up and not immediately go quiet to make sure I could hear my sister breathing. I did not miss her illness.

I found myself thinking that even Tristan would be more than welcome. Not that I could tell him about any of this without him running in the opposite direction. It was what I wanted to do, not that it would be much use if I did. When you're the problem, running away doesn't help.

. . .

WHEN I GOT BACK to the basement, Grace was poring over a golden block the size of a watermelon.

"Another recent case?" I asked, not looking forward to it. The more I thought about my body's reaction to the knife, the more I thought maybe time heals wounds for objects, too. The longer it had been since the traumatic or emotional events, the less they affected me.

"Isaiah stopped by with it," she corrected. "He was sad he missed you, but he had to get back to the museum. I'm not sure what help I can be, but it is pretty. And interesting."

"Looks like it belongs in a tomb. Protected by mummies." Whenever he had experts look at our pieces, I assumed they went to other museums or academic institutions, not police precincts.

"It does, doesn't it?"

"Any luck so far?"

"The outside is solid gold and gemstones, with things like dirt and whatnot from centuries...probably thousands of years of exposure," she shared.

"And the inside?"

"I'm not sure."

"Is it empty?"

"No, if it was empty, there would be air or gas or something. This is like...a mental lock that's stopping me from seeing farther than...what you can see," she finished.

"Is it for the museum?" I knew the fall schedule would be all about Queen Victoria and the industrial revolution, with an emphasis on the working class. I didn't need Logan's gemologist skills to know this piece was way older than that, and worth more than I could ever afford.

"A friend's private collection," she shared, turning it over and sliding her hands along it, as if trying to find a secret opening.

"I'm guessing it's the kind of thing you don't just break open to see what's inside."

"I mean, the gold makes it worth more than my salary no matter what state it's in, and any one of those jewels could buy me a mansion in Brookline without a mortgage. But he brought it to me because I shouldn't need to break it to see inside."

"And he just left it with you?" I asked, realizing it was worth way more than I had initially assumed. Dr. Richards was good with letting me handle any piece I wanted, which I now realized he had an ulterior motive for, but even moving something to a different room within the museum required paperwork and permission.

"I'm a very trustworthy person," she reminded me.

"Are you going to use the machines upstairs?"

"The mass spectrometer?" she asked. "I'm sure his friend already used every scientific clue you can think of. I'm the last resort of thinking outside the box. Not that it's helping."

"What if it's just gold all the way through, and there's nothing inside?" I suggested.

"That would be a terrible joke to play on someone. But it's still weird that I can't feel the center, whether it's hollow or not." She resorted to shaking it, like someone trying to figure out their Christmas present by any means necessary. "Do you want to try?"

"Shaking it for answers?" I asked.

"Touching it. Maybe they felt really proud and accomplished as they were sealing it."

"If you think it will help." I played nonchalant, but I was intrigued. Not just because I had never been this close to something so expensive before, even in exhibitions, but I couldn't figure out what it was. It didn't have a base to be put on display or any obvious use, other than protecting whatever may or may not be inside.

I knew it wasn't evidence, but I still wasn't going to put my fingerprints all over it. I placed the back of my fingers on the gold.

There wasn't any pain, unlike the lingering pinch in my abdomen from the knife, but it felt like someone shoved me in the chest so I would lose contact with the object.

"It's blocking you, too?" Grace asked, to which I nodded.

I tried again with the entire back of my hand, running it along different parts of the object, concentrating harder, focusing on specific elements or emotions I was looking for, but it felt like the object was getting angry with me, pushing back harder every single time.

"It's weird because this must be a defense mechanism to keep whatever's inside of it safe. But every time it kicks me out, I'm even more curious to find out what's inside."

"Welcome to the club," Grace assured me before sighing. "Better get back to work."

I agreed, but I kept my eyes on that golden box, wondering what mysteries it contained.

CHAPTER TWENTY-ONE

We were a bit behind on Grace's usual rate for going through cases, not to mention we should be going a lot faster now Grace had an assistant who knew what was going on. So, when Tristan asked if I was interested in going out for dinner, I told him I had to work.

"You don't have to stay," Grace told me for the dozenth time since five o'clock came and went without me leaving.

"We're behind and that thing is staring at me," I teased, though we both knew it was the truth. Every time we finished with one of the evidence baggies, we filed it back into its place and stopped to see if the object was any more forgiving. It wasn't like the necklace from the museum when I was twelve, whose pain called out to me, but there was something about it that compelled me to try and understand it.

"I was debating putting a sheet over it, but I thought that might be a bit much."

"I'd be a lot less curious if it wouldn't push us out."

"It's like a neon sign saying, 'I'm hiding something super valuable, please don't try to come in.'"

"Maybe it wants to be found out, and this isn't a defense

mechanism so much as how it makes sure we don't give up," I suggested.

"That's a valid point."

She was going to say more, but something behind me stopped her. I turned around, expecting Malcolm, but found Tristan.

"You said you had to work late, and you weren't feeling great this weekend, so I made you some soup." He explained what he was doing in the basement of the precinct. "I tried to leave it at the front desk for you, but the girl made it seem like unless I brought it down myself, you weren't going to get it."

"People may or may not think the basement is haunted." Grace shrugged, reminding me she was there.

"This is Grace Goncalves, my boss," I introduced her. "This is my friend Tristan."

"Who shows up with soup." She sounded impressed.

"I had a lot of time on my hands," he dismissed it.

"You should go enjoy the soup upstairs in the atrium. I have to check this box before we can open a new one anyway."

"I wouldn't want to impose. If you're busy..."

"A girl's gotta eat," Grace assured him, practically shooing me away.

"I'll be back soon," I promised her, hoping he didn't see the wink she gave me.

"I'M SORRY; I didn't mean to get you in trouble or pull you away from your work. I just thought you might need some warm, hearty comfort food." Tristan looked nervous, and I realized I'd been pretty standoffish with him. I responded to every text, but there was so much going on in my brain that I hadn't wanted to complicate things with the butterflies he gave me. Part of me figured it was fine, considering his hot and cold routine with me. "And I wanted to apologize for disappearing."

"No, don't worry about it. This is sweet of you. Kind of perfect, actually." I smiled, only feeling *extremely* guilty for lying to him.

"Are you sure you're okay with this?"

"I could use a break. And it smells really good."

"It's a family recipe." He looked both proud and nervous.

"You *made* me soup," I realized.

"I did," he agreed. "I'm by no means a chef, so I won't be offended if it's disgusting and you have to throw it out."

"I wouldn't dream of it," I assured him, taking one of the seats in the open area on the main level of the precinct. The basement was like a dilapidated old building, but the upper levels were designed by architects, possibly with the goal of ensuring the officers didn't burn out. It was very peaceful.

"When you kept turning me down, I was worried I'd lost you. Or that I didn't pass Sybill's test." He smiled teasingly, handing me a thermos filled with chicken noodle soup, only instead of noodles, it had gnocchi.

"Are you kidding? She'd be the first in line if...she likes you. A lot." I stopped myself mid-sentence and swallowed, trying to remove my foot from my mouth. What was I going to say? If we break up?

"She's funny. And she adores you. Not really what I expected," he shared, taking out another thermos for himself. I wondered if he'd hoped this would happen or if he brought extra for Grace.

"Because I made it sound like she was sickly and on her death bed?" I asked.

"Kind of."

"She hates that. She has good days and bad days, and she likes to remember the good ones, but I always picture her from the bad days. There's more of them and..."

"And they leave an impression," he finished for me. "That's

kind of depressing though." He gave me a sad smile, probably thinking about how his parents and sisters saw him.

"We did family therapy for a while when she first got sick, and she literally said, 'It's like Allie sucks all the light and happiness out of the room'. She apologized, and the shrink gave a bunch of explanations for what Sybill really meant to say, but I guess I've kind of always been the dark shadow that doesn't trust the good stuff." I didn't know why I shared it unless I truly was trying to scare him off.

"And ignoring you for the better part of a week proved your point." He looked up at me with a guilty smile, as if he knew he'd done wrong but was hoping to be forgiven.

"You didn't owe me anything. I found it confusing more than anything." I downplayed how much it hurt at the time.

"I like you," he admitted. "A lot. And when I'm with you, I want nothing more than to spend more time with you. But then I remember that you live here, and I'm going home soon and…I would not be good in a relationship right now. I have a lot of issues I need to work through, and things to figure out. But when I saw you with your sister, I couldn't have stopped myself if I'd tried."

"If it makes you feel any better, I'm also going through stuff and not really looking for anything long-term." Even as I said the words, I knew I didn't mean them. My brain did, but my heart was looking for a solution. "Although I did think I could last two weeks before boring you into avoiding me."

"I knew that was why you were so aloof. It's payback," he teased with a smile that didn't meet his eyes.

"Or you're just so positive that I didn't want to drag you down." I should have made a joke and called us even, keeping it light. A part of it was me not wanting to be the reason he stopped smiling. Because if transit delays and cancer didn't crush him, what kind of monster would I be if I did?

"Impossible," he assured me. "I mean, you can try, but I've

been trained for these very occasions. I'm excellent at making people laugh when they want to cry."

"Is that a very marketable skill?" I asked, realizing I didn't know what he did for a living.

"People don't usually pay that much, but I get a lot out of it," he teased.

"Sybill's really good at it, too."

"It's a special club with years of training." He was trying to get me to smile, and it worked.

"This is really delicious," I shared. "I'm wondering if maybe you bought it and put it in a thermos."

"I see that subject change and raise you an 'I made those gnocchi from scratch with my bare hands.'"

"You didn't."

"I did. Thought I might need to grovel and bribe you."

"Would you teach me?"

"Reveal all my secrets so you don't need me anymore?" he asked.

"Even if I know how, it would still be easier to have you make them for me," I teased back. "And you do live…not where I live, remember?"

"That's a fair point. But I was thinking about it, and I do travel. Could even do it often."

"For work?" I asked.

"Or for dark clouds who need some sun."

"Don't you have a job?"

"Independently wealthy." I couldn't tell if he was still teasing.

"And you wait until now to tell me?"

"I had to make sure you actually liked me first."

"I do," I admitted.

His smile not only reached his eyes; it made them sparkle.

"My friends are getting back tomorrow and won't need me to house sit, so I'll probably head home." My face must have dropped because he quickly added, "Can I take you out on

Thursday? I don't know where yet, but I want a second chance to sweep you off your feet without the mistakes I made last time."

"I would love that."

I could tell he wanted to kiss me, both from his smile and the way his eyes lingered on my lips, but we were in a police station, so he settled for reaching across the table to hold my hand.

A shock passed through me when his fingers touched mine, but I didn't pull back.

CHAPTER TWENTY-TWO

Tristan offered to walk me back to the basement, but the woman who worked the desk at night didn't look like she wanted to let him in when the place was empty. I left him at the main lobby and took the stairs that bypassed the ghostly lights.

I checked my phone as I walked across the hall and saw I had a text message from Grace.

"Enrique and Malcolm convinced me to call it a night. Tomorrow is another day. I locked up, but your keycard will let you get back in for your stuff. Take care."

My first impulse was to run upstairs to see if Tristan had left yet and ask him to stay if he hadn't. I couldn't really do that, but the idea put a smile on my face as I gathered my coat and my purse from B-473.

I was about to turn off the lights and leave when I remembered the paperwork I'd left out when Tristan showed up. Chances were Grace would be in before me in the morning, and I didn't want to leave the place a mess.

I put all my reports and notes into a file folder, then went to put it in the inbox on Grace's desk, but got a paper cut in the process. I usually got them all the time in the winter when my skin was dry and cracked easily, but the mountains of paperwork were wreaking havoc on my skin this summer.

I noticed a drop of blood forming, so I put my finger in my mouth, deciding against looking for a Band-Aid, when I suddenly felt something in the room pulling at me. It was exactly how I felt all those years ago in the museum, before I touched the necklace, propelled by forces I didn't even try to control.

When I couldn't see what caused the feeling, I debated leaving and trying again in the morning, when Grace would be there to okay me rifling through her things on a supernatural hunch, but I didn't know whether the feeling would come back or if it was a now or never kind of deal.

The guilt ate me alive as I went through her desk drawers, but at the same time, I was compelled, like a part of me would be missing until I found whatever it was. Finally, I uncovered a black box hidden behind a bookshelf. I knew what it was the moment I opened it, even though the object was wrapped in a red cloth. I knew I should be more cautious, that this was the thing we'd spent a good chunk of our day trying to crack with absolutely no success. I knew I shouldn't trust anything that called out to me, but then again, the necklace hadn't done me any wrong. Other than to show me the pain I would experience if my fears came true and I lost Sybill.

I unwrapped the red cloth to reveal the golden object incrusted with jewels. It probably would have been safer for Grace to take it home with her, but then again, you were supposed to trust cops. A police precinct would be harder to break into than wherever she lived. I wondered if that was with Enrique, or if she had to have her own place to keep up appearances. I knew I was stalling, but while the object called to me now, it had very unceremoniously been pushing me out all day, getting stronger and more painful with each shove. I wasn't worried that the shove would hurt; I was terrified of what I would see once it let me inside.

I WAS careful not to leave fingerprints, but I'm not even sure if the back of my finger was touching the golden exterior before I was pulled into a flash.

If I had any illusions about a happy, peaceful memory lurking inside the mystery box, I was immediately freed of them when I found myself in a suffocatingly warm room with the faint smell of honey. A woman was lying on a metal table, chained and terrified. I could feel her heart pounding in her chest, so fast and hard that it was painful, but on the outside, she was the image of calm, cool, and collected.

The golden object was on her bare stomach, held in place by a system of tubes that were carrying blood from a needle in her arm to a crevice on the top of the golden object. It was very elaborate with the blood pouring out normally from her arm, ending up in a rustic beaker, suctioned into more tubing, into another beaker, before going into the golden object's center, drip by drip.

"You come from a line of Monsters among Men. Helping us put an end to it can be your redemption," a man's voice taunted.

"My redemption?" she asked, as if she was mocking him. Maybe he didn't hear the quiver in her voice, but I could feel it. "I'm not the one kidnapping little girls and torturing them because I'm jealous I wasn't born special."

"You're not special, you're despicable. Cursed." He glared at her, then nodded off to where I couldn't see. Someone took an antique blow torch to the golden object, so it heated up, but the gold wasn't melting. It burnt red, burrowing deeper into her stomach, eating away at her skin. I couldn't believe she was still conscious.

.   .   .

I CAME BACK to the basement, my heart beating even faster than hers had been. It took longer than I was comfortable with until I believed that I was safe, not burning from the inside. I took a few steadying breaths before wrapping the golden artifact in the red cloth and putting it back behind the bookshelf. I wanted to run straight to Grace to tell her what happened. I could text her or see if she was at Enrique's…but that would involve telling her that I snooped around to find something that had nothing to do with me, or our job here.

CHAPTER TWENTY-THREE

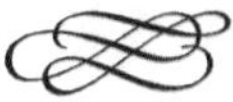

"You're making a habit of coming in incredibly early." Malcolm stopped me as I walked into the precinct.

"Couldn't sleep, so I figured I might as well work." It was true, I was having a lot of trouble sleeping lately. I was getting to a point where I would wake up and not even have to remind myself that Sybill wasn't there to check on, which just made me feel guilty. But more than anything, that cursed gold thing had given me nightmares, and I couldn't shake the guilt of not telling Grace about it. Hence coming in over an hour early for work.

"I'm not sure if we have the budget for a full-time employee to assist my mom, but if we do, the position is yours the second you graduate."

"I won't have any of the qualifications," I argued.

"To be honest, an archeology degree would make you more qualified than Grace is on paper. It's not like we expect a police officer."

"How qualified would I be with a degree in Business Administration and a couple of archeology electives?"

"Seriously?" he asked.

"Seriously." I'd never had to justify my major this much. "What brings you in so early?"

"Late," he corrected. "We found Hunter in one of the hunting cabins last night. Alone. I've been trying to get a confession, but he's sticking to his story that Matthew came to their apartment, knocked him over the head, and abducted them." It was a statement, but he looked to me at the end like he wanted me to confirm that Hunter wasn't an innocent victim, even if they had no evidence to go on. I knew they always confessed on TV so viewers would be satisfied and have all the answers, but I couldn't imagine real life criminals were that stupid.

"I don't know how they got to the woods, but Hunter definitely stabbed her." I prayed that he believed me. "What's his excuse for hiding instead of calling the cops when he got away?"

"He says he's been wandering the woods looking for Amber because he didn't want to leave without her." I scoffed at the blatant lie. "My guess is he wanted to wait until he knew they were dead before getting people to look for her."

I flinched at the thought. I knew it was silly, that I didn't actually know either of them, but after feeling their feelings so vividly, I really wanted them to be okay. It felt personal. I also wanted them to get over whatever broke them up so they could live happily ever after.

"Any luck on that front?" I asked. I should have spent my weekend volunteering with the search party, not wallowing in my research depression.

"None yet, but I'll keep you posted," he assured me.

"And get some rest," I encouraged.

GRACE WAS ALREADY WORKING when I got to the basement. I recognized the gold object on the table, with a red smoothie, the one she calls her brain juice, beside her.

"No luck?" I asked.

"I may or may not have gotten here over half an hour ago and have been staring at it ever since. I'm bringing it back to Isaiah tonight and I want to give him something more than 'I see nothing.' Not like there's nothing inside, but whatever it is, I can't see it."

"What about blood?" I asked.

"There's a drop of it here, where the setting got loose and is sharper than a knife, but it's from the last century. I'll still tell him about it, but I'm sure he knows, and I don't know what use it will be." She shrugged, bringing her hand through her hair. "How was last night? Your dinner?"

It took me a moment to remember she knew about Tristan, but not what I got up to after he left me.

"It was nice, thank you for letting us go off."

"Ah, young love," she teased. "You were sick this weekend?"

"I was trying to process the whole, 'everyone else like me had to die to be like me and is now immortal' thing."

"I'm sorry, I would have kept my mouth shut if I knew you didn't know."

"Then I would never know," I argued. "It's just taking some getting used to."

"Of course. Any progress?" she asked.

I knew she was talking about me and the Gifted reveal, but I saw an opening and I took it.

"A bit with that thing," I admitted.

"With this?" she asked, confused.

"When I came in to grab my stuff last night, it was calling to me."

"Like the necklace?"

I nodded. "I was going to call you, but I wasn't sure what it was, and it felt crazy saying something was calling to me, but..."

"It told you where I hid it," she understood. "And you saw something."

"A flash. Two people. And weird science stuff?"

"In a lab?" she asked, calmer than I expected. Like a part of her expected this to happen.

"More like a mad scientist's torture room from the industrial revolution." I tried to guess at a time period, but I hadn't seen much of the actual room.

"So, it contains a secret formula?"

"He couldn't get it open, but I'm pretty sure it contains her blood. Or her blood can somehow open it...he was doing something with her blood."

"The young woman's?"

"He said she came from a line of Monsters among men. He wanted her help to put an end to them."

"Do you think he meant Gifted?"

"He did call them Cursed, which is another name for us, right?"

"Was she Gifted?"

"I didn't see any powers. But the way she didn't give in with that much fear and pain...that took superpowers," I said with confidence.

"I'm thinking she must have been Gifted, but it isn't something you pass on. People can take our lives, but I don't think they can take our Gifts."

"How do they determine whether someone becomes Gifted?"

"I met a guy once who called it an insurance policy for people who needed to contribute something to the world. Sometimes good, sometimes bad, but the contributions were always necessary."

"But you don't figure out what that is until..."

"If you accomplish it before dying, you never find out. Otherwise, you figure it out when you suddenly start growing old, like Isaiah. Or when you don't come back."

"Why can't there be bright lights, and a 'congratulations, you did it' banner?" I asked. God help me, but I believed all her stories about the Gifted. Even if it sounded ridiculous and made up.

"Some people do know what they're here for, and I have heard of bright lights that appear and give you the choice to grow old or move on."

"Do the Gifts have something to do with your purpose? Was it dark when Dr. Richards saved your boss' daughter?" I asked, thinking of the triviality of our Gifts.

"He was able to temporarily blind the men with it, and he learned to use it to his advantage in a million ways I never would have thought of. Just like my Gift could have been a parlor trick until I put it toward science and solving crimes. I think our Gifts have something to do with who we are, and our purpose is usually linked to our values. They do play a part together, but not necessarily so. My use may come from something like identifying an unknown substance that goes on to cure cancer, or I can be walking home from work and be the only person who yells "look out!" before someone would have been run over by a train."

"Is there a collection of this information somewhere or is it all 'this happened to a friend of a friend of mine'? Because that book had some interesting facts, but I wouldn't know where to start if I wanted to find out who that woman was."

"I think there are collections of stories and Chronicles in personal libraries, but I haven't seen anything like that. I don't think you're supposed to find her, but if I wanted to figure it out, I would go to the oldest Gifted I know, and ask them about the oldest Gifted they know, until I got to the right time period."

"Who is the oldest Gifted you know?" I tried.

"Minnie," she said after thinking about it for a while. I waited, so she added, "I thought Isaiah was joking when he dragged us to her bicentennial, but she was taught to play piano by a friend of her father's, who went on to compose Fur Elise. I can't remember if that's Bach or Mozart or..."

"Beethoven." I looked at her with disbelief.

"Yeah, the dog one."

"I feel like I would have a million questions to ask her."

"Last I saw her she was really busy and stressed about some new partnership research thing she's doing, but when the bags under her eyes disappear, I'm sure she'll resurface."

"Seriously?"

"Isaiah knows her better than I do. He usually shrugs and uses a platitude like 'it was what it was,' but Minnie will talk for hours about her childhood and historical figures she's met…she loves history."

"I do, too."

"I think this is the first time I've seen you actually be excited by the Gifted."

"I guess I'm an academic at heart."

"So, you'll enjoy writing a fun essay on every detail from that memory?" she tried.

"I'll add it to the other reports I'll spend my day writing," I assured her.

WHEN I GOT HOME, I realized that I'd forgotten to call my parents when I got home last night and felt terrible, until I realized they hadn't called me either. Or texted.

My sister's phone went straight to voicemail, so I tried my mom.

"Is Syb okay?" I asked as soon as she picked up, not even bothering with hello.

"She went to get ice cream with Damian."

Of all the terrible scenarios running through my head, not even once did I consider that the silence was because she was too busy with a boy. "I thought she hated that maple one?"

"Oh, she does. They went to the ice cream shop on the other side."

"She was cleared for that?" I usually made the trek on my own, hoping that a milkshake would make her feel better after a bad day, but she rarely kept it down.

"I'll let her tell you," she assured me before my sister came on the screen, looking rosy-cheeked and out of breath, but not in the way I was used to.

"I think he's the one." She beamed.

"Damian?" She had been going on about him for years, it was true, but it was in a schoolgirl crush kind of way. But then again, I'd just met Tristan and sometimes my brain would wander before I could stop myself.

"No, Herbert. That's what I'm calling this latest trial. Ever since it started, it's like...I haven't felt this healthy and alive since...I don't think I ever have. I tried to read the paperwork to see what they're putting in me, but I don't understand any of the words. All I know is that I feel great. I can't wait until the six weeks are up so we can go home, and I can take care of you for a change. Or actually, I don't want you to be sick. I want us to go bike riding. Or hiking. Rock climbing maybe."

"Rock climbing?"

"We can work our way up to that one. I just feel like the world is full of possibilities, and I can't wait for us to experience all of them."

"I'm so happy," I told her, aware that I was tearing up. For once, it was happy tears.

"Me too. And Damian is definitely living up to expectations."

"A complete gentleman, I hope?"

"Unfortunately. How's Tristan?"

"A complete gentleman," I assured her.

"Unfortunately?"

"I'm still in the room," Mom called.

"No side effects?" I asked Sybill to change the subject, but I also couldn't believe this miracle drug was fixing her without giving so much as an upset stomach or a headache.

"Not yet. And Dr. Bell says my tests are all good, no damage to anything." The closest we'd gotten to making her feel better for an extended period was a powerful drug that was like chemo, only it made her dangerously toxic. We had to wear gowns and masks to go near her, but even that wasn't recommended. She'd been miserable, and it was doing something to her kidneys, so the trial ended before the six weeks were up.

"That's amazing."

"I never thought I would be happy to stay up at night waiting for my daughter to come home," my dad contributed.

"You're allowed to stay at the hotel?" I asked.

"I told you, Al, I feel normal. And a bunch of the families are staying here, so the doctors and nurses come by all the time, on top of the daily appointments."

"Did you make it to Disney?"

"Dad's bringing us tomorrow. Damian and me. We considered season passes, but Mom reminded me that it's still a two-hour drive, and I'm not that dedicated. Although I have decided that you're either spending a weekend here before the summer is over or you're coming with me next summer, because I'm not ready for Damian to see what a nerd I am."

"If he's worth anything, he'll love you anyway. But I can't wait to go with you."

"Keep kicking ass so you can get some time off."

"I'll try my best."

My dad came on and we all talked about random things until they had to go to dinner. I felt like my heart was bursting from the happiness and relief of Sybill looking so happy and healthy, almost enough to make me forget about the Gifted stuff, missing persons, and ancient artifacts.

CHAPTER TWENTY-FOUR

"Where is Prince Charming taking you tonight?" Grace asked me while I helped Malcolm unload a trolley covered with a fresh batch of file boxes filled with evidence from more cold cases. Grace had to sign for them and be responsible, but her son insisted that while she might look younger than him, she was a woman in her sixties who shouldn't be lifting heavy boxes.

"He hasn't told me," I shared. "Does that mean you have old and brittle bones with arthritis, or are your insides young, too?" I had a million questions now that he'd brought it up.

"Is he kidnapping you?" Malcolm asked.

Grace focused on, "My insides?"

"He's surprising me. I'm not a fan of surprises, so I am very nervous and trying not to think about it," I warned Malcolm. "And I'm sorry, I regretted my choice of words the second I said them, but you haven't answered."

"I'm an eternal twenty-six-year-old." She smiled, lauding it over me, but her smile faded when she looked at her son.

"She's immortal, but she still goes for yearly checkups," Malcolm confided.

"I'm not immortal, mijo. And even if you come back, you still go through the pain and suffering of dying."

"Did it just happen the once?" Was it just one abusive ex-husband her Gift saved her from, or had fate intervened multiple times to keep her on course?

"Does he know you don't like surprises?"

I was going to tell Malcolm to drop it, but I saw my question made Grace uncomfortable, so I answered him instead. "I don't not like them, I just haven't had a lot of good surprises, so I'm apprehensive. He's picking me up here, so it's the same as if we met up and wandered around to find something to do, only he already figured it out," I told him the perfectly sound logic I reminded myself of whenever I got nervous. It wasn't surprises so much as not knowing what to expect, or what was going to happen. I prepared for absolutely every outcome, which was why I was such a good student.

"Did he warn you to wear something specific?" Grace joined in.

"He said whatever I feel comfortable in would be perfect."

"So, dinner and a movie, but trying to sound mysterious?" she suggested.

"I don't think so."

"And he knows you're home alone?" Malcolm pressed.

"I am a twenty-year-old university student," I reminded him. "Do you want me to invite him here so you can ask what his intentions are?"

"I'm sorry, that was overstepping." He shook his head and brought his hand to his temple.

"I'm sure my dad would appreciate it. Tristan knows I'm on my own, but I've made it abundantly clear that I talk to my parents every night before I go to sleep."

"You told him you do that, or you actually do that?"

"Sometimes we text instead, but it's like a habit, you know? I'm home, I'm safe, I love you, goodnight."

I felt self-conscious about my overly close family that I was keeping at arm's length while I worked through what I could tell them about this weird Gifted stuff, but Grace was looking at her son like he had some explaining to do.

"Mamá," he started.

"Mijo."

"I'm forty-five years old," he reminded her.

"You're still my baby," she pointed out. "Always."

"I better get back to work. Good luck on your date," Malcolm told me, kissing his mother on the cheek before going upstairs. Hunter's father was no longer garnering the same number of volunteers now that Hunter was safe, but Malcolm was pouring through his files for any clue as to where Amber and Matthew were, or what happened.

"Once," Grace told me when she was sure her son was gone, pulling me from my thoughts.

"Once what?" I asked.

"I died once more after the first time. Technically I'm in my third life."

"I shouldn't have asked. I'm curious and you're so open, but I forget that it's your life, it's traumatic, and it hurts."

"There are so few people I can tell." She sighed, preparing herself. "About seven years ago, my granddaughter was in terrible shape, wasting away, but a heart transplant could make everything better. I don't know if you've ever prayed for someone to die, but it does something to you." She paused and swallowed before continuing. "I went to see if I could be a match, hypothetically. I think they were used to family members willing to trade their life for a child's, but I didn't have the life ahead of me they thought I had, and I didn't have the heart of the grandparents who usually volunteer. I found a shady character who did the tests and told me my heart was strong and seemed to be a match, so I…I made it happen."

"You saved her," I understood. I assumed my Gift meant that I would also come back to life when I eventually died, if I hadn't accomplished something memorable. My brain immediately went to Sybill, and I knew without a doubt that I would give her my liver, my kidney…if she was dying, I would very seriously consider giving her my heart.

"I gave her a year," she corrected me. "A good one, where she got to run and play and be a kid, but I had to stay away and miss it. I would do it again. I would have died and given her a new heart every year if it would have helped, but it didn't. Not long after she died, my daughter-in-law went back to her family in Colorado, so my son moved here and hasn't gotten out much."

"Four years ago?" I asked.

"You got there eventually." She gave me a sad smile. "And his daughter would have been a few years younger than you by now, which is why he sometimes fails to turn off the protective father gene. When you lose a child, you're still a parent; you just don't have anyone to take care of anymore."

"I'm so sorry," I told her.

"Me too," she agreed, rubbing her thumb against a ring I'd never noticed on her right index finger. "Have you ever gotten more than one memory from an object?"

"I got three disturbing memories from the knife," I reminded her. And different parts of the necklace showed me different moments.

"I mean, from the same person. You see the strongest emotion, but this ring has seen me through unbridled joy, as well as devastating loss. Maybe the necklace upstairs did, too."

"The one they smashed into pieces?"

"It took me years to figure out everything I could do with my Gift. Maybe decades. Why not try it?"

"After you." I couldn't help but smile, thinking she was crazy, but also hoping she was right.

THE TECHS WERE on a field assignment, so Malcolm had no problem getting us into the lab. He looked doubtful this would work, but clearly knew better than to question his mother. I put on a pair of purple gloves and carefully opened the bag.

"How should I proceed?"

"Try it like you've never touched it before and see what happens," she suggested. I put my knuckles in, careful not to touch anything with my fingers, and saw when Matthew first gave the necklace to Amber. It was a failure, but I felt so warm and fuzzy that I also considered it a victory.

Grace rubbed her ring some more, then tapped her thumb against her middle finger, thinking. "Do you think you could focus on the emotions you got from Amber on the knife? If that's what you used to single them out from the jumble of emotions..."

She would have kept going, but I nodded. I didn't want to go from pure, young love to pain and fear, but they were running out of time.

I took a deep breath and remembered the ache in my chest, the pain in my stomach, everything I got from Amber on the knife, which inevitably brought me to Matt, since he was the one who pulled it out of her. I pressed my knuckles into the plastic, imagining myself sucking all the memories out of it.

To be honest, I expected it not to work, and to just replay that same memory over and over again, since I usually got the same thing every time I touched the pieces in the museum.

Instead, a wave of pain and regret washed over me, and I recognized Matthew's emotions. I thought it might be from after Amber gave the necklace back to him, but then I saw her. She wasn't clear, but she was sitting in front of a mirror, doing her makeup while he walked up to her. She had to know he was there, but she made no effort to move, or acknowledge him. When she did speak, the memory wasn't letting me hear it, so I pushed harder.

"I'm pretty sure no one invited you."

"I'm not staying." He paused. Now that he was close enough, I could see the faint markings of a black eye that she was trying to cover up. "And you shouldn't either."

"It's my party," she argued.

"He's hurting you." I could hear the pain in his voice as badly as I could feel it. I knew that I had warm tears pouring down my cheek, but he was somehow managing to hold his in, the necklace clutched in his right hand.

"You don't know what you're talking about."

"I can confront you and let you tell me you walked into a doorknob. I can even pretend to believe you if that's what's best for you. But this is me talking, Amber. The guy who will love you until the day I die and do anything to keep you safe."

"That's not your job anymore, Matt." Her voice shook at times, but she kept her head held high and her eyes steady on him through the mirror.

"It'll always be my job," he said simply, taking her hand and pressing the necklace into it. "When you remember that you are Amber Dennis, the most amazing woman I have ever met, who deserves all the best in the world, more than an asshole who hurts you, put this on. If I see you wearing it, no questions asked, I will find you and I will rescue you. You can go home if that's what you want. This isn't about that...but if you stay and he breaks you...I will kill him," he said in a way that implied he would be next. That even if they weren't together, he couldn't live in a world where he lost her. I believed him, but I also think he wanted to make sure she wouldn't let it happen.

I shivered when I let go of the necklace, so Grace handed me a chocolate from her pocket.

"I knew you'd get it," she assured me, but Malcolm rolled his eyes, knowing she'd had no such conviction.

"What did you see?" he asked.

I told them while eating the chocolate. By the end, Grace had her hand on her heart, and Malcolm's hands were in fists, ready to knock Hunter out. Instead, he went to the computer and pulled up all the social media images they had of Amber. "This one had the TBT hashtag, but I found she looked older than in the other ones with the necklace."

"She's changed her clothing style to long sleeves, her foundation goes down to the neckline, and I would bet that chunky bracelet is hiding a bruised wrist." Grace stared at the screen, but Malcolm and I both looked to her, knowing what she had been through to know the signs.

"I know we were hoping for something to find them, or more concrete so you could charge him, but can this help you build a domestic abuse case in the meantime?" I was grabbing at strings.

"This is very helpful," he assured me. "Thank you."

He went to his office while we put the evidence back. I wanted to find Amber and Matthew, hopefully alive, but I needed to nail Hunter so he couldn't do that to anyone else, with a case his father couldn't get dismissed.

"Do you have more chocolate?" I asked Grace.

"Are you sure?" she asked, emptying two more chocolates from her other pocket as I grabbed the bag containing the knife.

"It can't hurt," I said, shrugging my shoulders with nonchalance to hide my reluctance and fear.

I concentrated on Hunter, trying to remove my hatred for him and focus on his emotions.

I touched my knuckles to the blade, hoping for something that would get us a conviction, or lead us to Amber, but I was overcome with rage. When Hunter planted the knife deep inside Matthew's chest, all I felt from him was hatred and twisted satisfaction.

CHAPTER TWENTY-FIVE

At five o'clock, I stood outside the precinct and waited, unable to shake off Matthew's pain or Hunter's bad vibes. After the dozenth time I asked Grace if Malcolm had sent her an update, she decided my energy was killing her concentration and asked me to leave a few minutes early.

I smiled when Tristan walked over, right on time.

"For some reason, I didn't think you would be punctual," he shared once he was close, the right side of his mouth going up into a smile he tried to hide.

"Oh, I hate being late," I assured him. "I'm often there hours early for class, with a book, so I don't have to cut it close."

"I was the opposite. On good days I would roll out of bed and run like hell to try and make it on time." He smiled, but I saw a shadow when he thought of the bad days, where he must have gotten up hours early to be on time, but probably didn't make it. Or at least that's how it was with Sybill.

"I said I hate being late, but on those days when I'm not there hours early...I'm sometimes late. Luckily, people remember you waiting there hours ahead of schedule, so they tend to forget the couple of minutes that make you late. And I'm usually very apologetic."

"The whole, 'I'm never late' thing?" he asked.

"It's why honest people are so much better at lying." I shrugged before realizing what that implied.

"Are you counting yourself as an honest person?" he asked, but I knew it was a trap.

"Where are we going tonight?" I changed the subject.

"We are on a very tight schedule, which will all be revealed in time, but the first stop is right over here." He played along.

"And is that the burlap sack you'll use to kidnap me?"

"This is a surprise. All their other bags were see-through," he explained.

"The potato vendor's bags?" I teased.

"Do you trust me?" he asked.

"I think so." I looked at him with uncertainty, but when his eyes met mine, I was surprised by just how much I did trust him.

"Good." He took my hand to bring me through a side alley. I felt the sparks when his hand touched mine. Whether by coincidence or because he felt them too, he looked back at me and smiled before making his way through rows of street vendors.

"Is it like this every Thursday?" The vendors stretched on for as far as my eyes could see. The first few stands were exactly as I'd expected, merchant farmers selling fruits and vegetables. Then we got into the derivatives like honey, artisanal cheeses, and organic hand creams from essential oils with homemade packaging. The next area was like a congregation of food trucks, only instead of fast food and hipster joints, they were all farm-to-table mobile establishments.

"I don't think so." He looked around and took it all in. "I looked up cool places to eat near the precinct, and this showed up as a special event."

"I wouldn't have pegged you as the type to put that much research into things. Especially not a date."

"It depends on the girl." He smiled. "There may be a part of me that wants to impress you."

"Just a part?" I teased, because it was easier than telling him that I was thoroughly impressed and got butterflies just thinking of him.

"Believe it or not, I don't do this very often. And when I do, I'm not usually sharing my deep dark secrets, so I don't have as much to compensate for."

"You shouldn't have to make up for being vulnerable and letting people in."

"In theory, I know that, but my go-to has always been to smile through the pain and take care of everyone else."

"You never got sick of it and cursed and became an asshole to everyone around you?"

"Does your sister?"

"She's better at being miserable when she feels it now, but it used to be all smiles, then a blowout every few months where she said horrible things to all of us. Those she really felt she had to compensate for."

"I hate the fact that you see me as a sick patient," he admitted, bringing me to the stand where my eyes went wide reading the menu.

"I don't," I admitted. "Sometimes I say things, then I remember, and I feel terrible. But you seem so happy, untouched, and kind of make me feel like everything is going to be okay."

"It's what I was good at," he agreed.

"That wasn't your job though."

"I'm sure I was insufferable sometimes, too," he assured me.

He let me order what I wanted, then paid before we found an empty picnic table to eat on. He made a mess of his tacos, but only smiled harder when they fell apart in his hands. "I've never figured out how to not get these everywhere."

"It's all the same once it's inside," I shared what my dad always said.

"Do you want to try one?" he offered.

I wasn't a big fan of meat, so the pork belly wasn't doing it for me, but there was an apple coleslaw on it that looked delicious. I nodded and bit into the tiny part of his taco that was still holding together.

"Look at that. You've got the skills," he said when the rest of the taco stayed in his hands after my bite.

"It took years of schooling."

"And?"

"It's not bad, but you probably should have ordered this. It's like a taste explosion in my mouth, and my hands are clean," I pointed out with a grin.

"It's not bad?" He cocked his head at me.

"Try this," I encouraged, making sure I scooped up enough noodles, cheesy sauce, wild mushrooms, and snap peas.

"Vegetables in mac and cheese?"

"It's much healthier this way." I was completely serious, which got him to laugh in a way that warmed my heart. It was so pure and innocent.

"There's so many textures and flavors, but they go really well together," he declared, slowly eating his spoonful so he could make an informed review.

"I win, right?"

"You win," he agreed.

After we were done with dinner, he brought me to a churros stand where he got a bunch of regular cinnamon churros, as well as a sriracha one that I politely declined.

"How's that tasting?" I asked, trying to hide my smile as his scrunched face showed me exactly what he thought of it.

"You know when you're like, I love chocolate, and I love mayo, but if someone offers you chocolate flavored mayo…"

"You run for the hills?"

"Well, they do put it in cake sometimes to make it extra moist…but yeah, you run for the hills."

"How does the bag fit in with the churros?"

"What do you mean?"

"You said the bag was for after dinner," I reminded him.

"Dinner includes dessert," he said like it was silly of me to think otherwise. "But I guess I can tell you what's next." He slowly opened the burlap sack he'd been carrying.

"What is…a jersey?" I asked.

"The Hornets are playing. You're very lucky."

"We're going to a basketball game?" I asked.

"You wanted to know what I was passionate about, and basketball is the closest I have."

"I've never been to a game before." I was excited, which was strange because I really wasn't into sports.

"Glad I could surprise you."

THE STADIUM WAS LESS than a fifteen-minute walk from where we ate. All we had to do was follow the crowd of people in Celtics jerseys to the TD Garden.

Although sports weren't my thing, my father watched hockey and football, so I was used to reading with Sybill or talking with my mom while my dad watched the games, rewinding it occasionally to show us something he found incredible, even if we couldn't care less about it. I thought this being a live game would help me muster enough excitement to make Tristan happy, but as soon as it started, I found myself way more invested than I thought I would be. Tristan, even if he said he wasn't that into it anymore, was super excited. He shared this enthusiasm with me, explaining what was going on and who the major players were.

I looked on the court when he pointed things out, but I also spent a lot of the game just watching the way his face lit up when something cool happened. He kept running his hand through his dark hair, pushing it back so he could see better, although I don't think it made a difference either way. To his vision, that is. It made all the difference in the world as far as how fast my heart was beating watching him.

He patiently explained all the rules to me when I asked, even if I played dumb for a few that no human being wouldn't know.

"What was that whistle for?" I asked halfway through the game.

"Traveling," he shared.

"What does that mean?" I watched his lips as he spoke, his eyes on the game, then turned to the players when he faced me.

"They found out he was in Europe last week, and that's not cool, so they called him on it."

I nodded like I had been for every other explanation, until I processed what he said. "That's not at all what it means," I argued, but he was smiling.

"You asked." He shrugged his shoulders and grinned.

"I like listening to you explain it to me," I defended myself.

As it turned out, learning the rules of basketball from him was fun, but it was nothing compared to the stories he could make up.

"None of that made any sense, but I believed every word when you were saying it," I pointed out after his explanation for a penalty shot. I was completely shocked – and a little nervous – that he could lie so seamlessly.

"The trick is to base it in truth. And add enough details to show you know what you're talking about, but not so many that you're trying too hard to prove yourself."

"I appreciate the pointers, but I'm not sure I can believe a word you say from now on."

"I wouldn't lie to you about anything important." He was suddenly serious. I believed him, but I raised my eyebrows as if I didn't, so he considered it and added, "Unless it was to protect you and keep you safe."

"To not hurt my feelings, or to hide your mafia side job so I don't snitch and get stitches?"

"I guess it's up to you. Do you want to know about my hits, or would you rather be in the dark about contract killings?"

"Definitely in on them," I said after pretending to think about it first.

"So really, there's no reason to lie to you at all, I guess."

"Perfect." I smiled, but he took my hand, and the sparks felt reproachful this time, reminding me that I was currently hiding a huge secret from everyone I cared about. It wasn't expressly lying, but I'm pretty sure lies of omission would count in this case. It wasn't that I felt we were at a stage where I should be sharing all my deepest, darkest secrets with him, but I had to tell Sybill and my parents. It was easy to convince myself it could wait until I saw them in person because this wasn't the kind of thing you told people over the phone, but I also knew it was an excuse, and I was stalling.

"I'm not really a hitman," he promised, misreading my look, but caring enough to notice that something was up.

"That's good. I wouldn't want us to have a Mr. & Mrs. Smith situation on our hands," I teased, but it was his smile that got me back into the excellent mood.

TRISTAN'S TEAM WON, but it was obviously not anyone else's. We'd gotten a few looks on the way in for wearing different jerseys from literally every other person in the arena, but there were glares and mean-spirited comments on our way out. Luckily, I felt exhilarated and couldn't care less.

"I'm sorry. I didn't mean for you to experience thousands of people hating you. I just couldn't forgive myself if I betrayed the Hornets," he apologized, grinning from ear to ear.

"I think the competition made it more fun," I assured him.

"One and done, or would you ever go again?" Tristan took my hand as we walked through the streets. I wasn't sure if he was taking me to another location, or walking me to the subway station, but I wasn't questioning it.

"I would go again if it was with you," I admitted.

"I was hoping I'd ignited a passion for basketball in you, but I would also hope you'd let me come with you. As long as it wasn't for a job."

It took me a minute to realize he meant a hit job, then I burst out laughing.

"I love your laugh," he said, which should have encouraged me to continue, but he was looking at me, and my lips, in a way that wasn't funny at all.

I tried to find something witty or sexy to say, but instead I stood there, feeling my heart beating against my chest. I wished I hadn't licked my lips when I swallowed, because it made him look at them, and then I looked at his lips. Suddenly he was moving close, with his thumb resting gently on my cheek, his fingers in my hair, urging me close.

I couldn't tell if he moved forward or if I did, but before I knew it, his lips were on mine and it was like fireworks were going off in my head, around us, and even in my lips, which tingled when we pulled apart.

I debated if I wanted to comment on the kiss or just kiss him again. The kiss was winning, but then my phone rang out with the notification I reserved for Grace.

"You should probably get that," Tristan recommended, resting his forehead against mine.

If this was work, then he was right. But it could very well be her asking what happened on our date tonight, so interrupting it to tell her would be counterproductive.

"Hold that other thought," I asked of him, pulling my phone out and seeing I had three missed calls from her, but no voicemails. I tried calling her back, but the line was busy. My best guess was that this was about Amber, given the new information we got this afternoon, but I wasn't supposed to be working on that case, so she wouldn't leave a message.

"Everything okay?" Tristan asked.

"I have to get back to work."

"It's nine o'clock," he pointed out.

"I know, but there's an emergency."

"On a cold case?"

"We do current cases sometimes. It might just be a report I didn't fill out properly, but Grace asked me to stop by."

"I'll walk you," he assured me.

The fact that I was lying left a bad taste in my mouth, but he took my hand to guide me back to the precinct and I convinced myself we just weren't ready for the truth.

CHAPTER TWENTY-SIX

We were at the fountain in front of the precinct when a woman in a black hoodie with the Celtics logo on it looked up at us and froze. She was shorter than me and so tiny that the sweatshirt floated on her, but she still looked gorgeous, like she got cold at a club, so someone gave her their jacket, but everything else was flawless.

"Oh my God," she said, pausing slightly after each word. "Are you Jason Felding?" she asked Tristan. "My sister loves you. You're like, her favorite player in the whole league. Is it a league? She's the one who's into sports, but she will just die when she finds out I met you. Can we get a selfie?" She turned to me at the end, not letting him get a word in.

I knew from the game that Felding was one of the Hornets players. Although the name was written on his jersey, Tristan didn't look like the player at all. His hair was a lot darker, and he was many inches shorter.

"I'm so sorry, but I am not Jason Felding. I would love to be, but I just bought his jersey at one of the stands."

"I could have sworn...your eyes are like, identical," she said, turning to me for support.

Tristan's eyes were a really dark brown, almost the color of his iris, while I'm pretty sure Felding's eyes were blue.

"The shape," she added when I wasn't convinced.

"If your sister is into sports, there is no way she would confuse us."

"Right. Yeah. That makes sense."

I could see how much it killed him to disappoint her and crush her smile, even if he had absolutely nothing to do with it.

"We can still take that selfie if you want," he offered.

"Really? That would be awesome."

Rather than a selfie, she handed me her phone and I took a few pictures of them together until she was satisfied her eyes weren't closed and he was at the angle that made him look most like the player.

"WHAT?" Tristan asked when the girl went on her way, and it was just the two of us again.

"It kills you to disappoint people," I realized. "Even her."

"I don't like it," he agreed. "Is there something wrong with that?"

"You probably need therapy for it. In a non-judgmental, I-totally-feel-you way. I also think it's sweet."

"But," he pressed.

"You need to be happy, too."

"I am," he said, wrapping his arm further around me so he could pull me close.

"I had a really good time tonight," I told him.

"Let's do it again."

"I would very much like that." I brought my hand up to brush away his hair so I could see his big eyes. "What time do you leave tomorrow?"

"Lucy wants me to stay for brunch. I think she's making her

own danish pastries, but then I'll head out." He sounded as reluctant to leave as I was to let him go.

"Well, drive safely. It would be a shame if something happened before you could get back here."

"It wouldn't stop me."

It was a ridiculous, macho thing to say, but the way he looked into my eyes as he did, I believed him. I gave him a sad smile, feeling silly because I knew the night I met him that he would be leaving, but I felt like we had wasted most of the time we could have spent together.

"Call me when you get home. So, I know you're safe," he said, seeing my hesitation and cutting the cord for me. I was grateful until he kissed me again, making it that much harder to walk away. Maybe Grace just needed me to sign something, or butt dialed me, and I could convince Tristan to come back and go for coffee with a walk around the park.

TRISTAN WAITED until I was inside the precinct to leave, so I looked back and waved before going to the staircase, not without noticing the desk sergeant's appreciative glance in his direction. She had clearly been sleeping, judging by the imprint of her sleeve on her forehead, but the door was extra noisy at night. Probably for that very reason.

I speed-walked to B-473 and found the light was on with a steaming cup of coffee on Grace's desk. She couldn't be far, so I glanced through the papers she had out and mostly saw our recent reports.

After a few minutes, I texted Grace, *"I'm here,"* in case she was upstairs with Malcolm, but her phone dinged in the hallway. I assumed that meant she was on her way back, but when she didn't come in, I poked my head out. She wasn't in the hallway.

The sound of her phone wouldn't carry from the washrooms, but I still headed over and found them empty. I went through a list of possibilities in my head, which included her dropping her phone in the stairwell, and me not realizing the sound came from a drawer, but also ax murderers and kidnappers. I decided to just get it over with and call her.

It rang once in my ear before the sound came from the hallway, past the point where the lights got wonky and everything felt haunted. It stopped after three rings, so I left a message. She was either hiding for some sick joke I didn't understand or...I didn't even want to think about it.

"Hey Grace, it's Alison. I'm at the precinct because of your calls, but I can't see you anywhere. I think I heard your phone, so I'm following that, but I don't think you're this cruel, and—"

I stopped when I saw busted glass scattered on the ground. I knew I should get help, but my first instinct was to find Grace. I took a few steps into the intermittent darkness, moving as quickly as I could with the terror I felt.

Grace was on the floor in a door opening. I noticed the puddle of blood under my shoes before I saw the wound on her stomach.

"Help!" I screamed at the top of my lungs. "Help!"

I pressed my hand to Grace's stomach, trying to stop the blood, but there was so much of it on the ground, and she wasn't breathing. I wasn't sure if anyone heard my screams, so I hung up on Grace to dial 911. When I told them she'd been stabbed, they said they were going to send officers, but I insisted she needed an ambulance as well. I could hear the ding of the elevator and footsteps, so the cops were on their way. Or the desk sergeant, but she didn't seem like the type to run toward a scream in a dark and scary basement in the middle of the night.

"What is your address?" the 911 operator asked me, trying to keep me calm, but her calmness made me feel like she didn't understand the severity of the situation, which only got me more worked up.

"I don't know, it's the South Boston Precinct on Broadway."

"I will get the cops to you, but you need to tell me where you are," she said soothingly.

"I'm at the precinct," I repeated, enunciating like my dad used to do with my grandma. I understood how it could be confusing to have someone tell you a stabbing had taken place in a police station when no one else had contacted anyone about it, but we weren't going to get anywhere if I kept having to repeat myself a million times. "I'm in the basement outside room...B-372." I had no idea who came up with their numbering conventions, but it wouldn't be too hard to find us if I kept yelling whenever I heard a noise.

"Are you a police officer?" she asked, sounding confused for once.

"No, I work in...sort of like data entry for cold cases," I downplayed what I did before hearing someone. "Over here!" I yelled, not sure if it was a cop from upstairs or if the ambulance was really fast. I was relieved I wouldn't be alone with her anymore. Unless whoever hurt her was coming back.

"Goncalves," the man said, sounding shocked when he got to us. He had a badge on a chain around his neck like Malcolm, but I had never met him before. Then again, I didn't know anyone on the night shift except for the desk sergeant who avoided the basement like her life depends on it. If only Grace had done the same tonight.

"She's lost a lot of blood," I said, as if the puddle I was kneeling in didn't already tell him that. "I found a pulse, but it took me a lot of tries because it's really weak. I didn't think she was breathing, but she made like a wheezing sound, so I think it's just really...really faint." I told him everything I knew, which was nothing. I knew things didn't look good, even as I looked up at him with 'save her' written all over my face. Relief flooded me when I heard sirens.

"Just keep applying pressure," he encouraged. He looked exhausted, with big circles under his eyes, but it was the fear in them that scared me.

It felt like an eternity went by with nothing but Grace's occasional labored breathing, before two paramedics arrived with a stretcher and a bunch of equipment. There were other officers by then, but all my focus was on Grace and the paramedics. I thought I would be relieved when I was finally able to stop pressing my hands into her wounds and let the professionals take over, but without the warm pressure of her body and the faint rhythm of her heart, I couldn't tell if she was still with us or not, and I got a sinking feeling that I wasn't going to see her again.

I followed them to the elevator and held her hand when we got off on the main level. Not that it did anything but lie limp in mine. I was going to ride in the ambulance with her and stay by her side until she woke up, but two officers blocked my way. Rather an officer and a detective, as one was in uniform and the other wore a suit.

"Hello, my name is Detective Kloots, and this is Officer Stevens. I'm sorry, but we'll need to ask you a few questions," the shorter of the two explained. He took out a small notepad, and I could just imagine the hat that would complete his ensemble if this were a film noir. But it wasn't. This was real life.

"I need to go with her. To the hospital. She can't be alone," I argued, wondering if Malcolm was listed as her emergency contact. Maybe it was Enrique. Or neither of them, since she liked to keep her secrets. I reached for my phone to see if I had either of their numbers, but my pocket was empty. I must have left it downstairs in the lake of blood.

"They'll call someone who can be with her once she's stable," he assured me, revealing a trace of humanity. I didn't know if he knew her too, but he took a breath to steady himself. "What is your name?"

"Alison Carmichael." I tried to pull myself together as well, but when I brought my hand up to move the hair away from my face, I saw that it was covered in blood—Grace's blood—so any hope of being 'put together' went out the window.

"And you work in the precinct?"

There was a hint of suspicion in the crease of his brow, so I took a deep breath, very aware that I had no plausible explanation as to why I was here in the middle of the night. "I have a summer internship through my university. I've been Miss Goncalves' assistant for the past few weeks."

"Did the two of you often work late at night?"

"She asked me to come by. She was working late, and I was in the area, so I guess she wanted company to walk home." I knew it was a lie, as did my body, because it started sweating, trying to betray me to the detective. I wasn't going to admit that I came thinking she wanted my help on a weird artifact completely unrelated to work, or that I used my magic powers to investigate it for her. Much better to lie.

"You were close?" he asked, raising that eyebrow again.

"We are," I said, empathizing the present tense. I didn't think I would have characterized us as such if he'd asked me this afternoon, but we did know each other's darkest secrets, and I had met the two men they might call for her, who would both back my story.

"Did you see anyone else in the basement? Was she alone when you arrived?"

"She was. I went to our office first, and I waited. Then I heard a noise, so I called her and followed the ringing until it stopped and I...I found her," I shared. This wasn't my first time calling an ambulance and describing a scene that was burned in my memory, making it hard for me to breathe. It was, however, the first time I had the cops grilling me about it, making me feel like I was the one who'd stabbed her.

"DID Miss Goncalves have any enemies that you're aware of? Anyone who wanted to cause her harm?" Detective Kloots asked after making me go through every detail of what happened.

"Isn't anyone missing from the cells?" I asked. It hadn't really entered my mind that someone had done this to her intentionally, that she wasn't just in the wrong place at the wrong time.

"Everyone is accounted for," Officer Stevens spoke. If he'd had any power in my interrogation, he would have been the good cop to Detective Kloots' bad cop, but it seemed murder investigations were above his pay grade. *Attempted murder investigations*, I amended.

"We all need to be let in by the receptionist … desk sergeant," I corrected myself. "They should have a log of whoever was in the building and shouldn't be," I tried. "Has anyone called her family?"

My question surprised them. Detective Kloots looked to Officer Stevens, then at his notes, which didn't seem to hold any answers. "I didn't think she had any family."

"Then I should really go to the hospital to be there for her. She shouldn't be alone."

"No, she shouldn't," he agreed. "But she was stabbed in the basement of our precinct, and the only name I didn't recognize on the list of people who've been in or out tonight was yours."

"Does that mean they're still in here?" I asked, a shiver going through me.

"We don't know." Kloots sighed, hopefully realizing that I wasn't likely to have stabbed Grace. Or maybe he was taking on both good cop and bad cop. "If you don't mind, Officer Stevens will get some of your DNA, so we can figure out what's what from the crime scene."

"Then I can go to the hospital?" I asked.

"Then you'll be free to go, but we might have more questions, so we would appreciate it if you stayed in town for the time being."

"I'll be here," I assured him, although a big part of me wanted to fly to California so my parents could take me in their arms and tell me everything would be okay.

Detective Kloots nodded before heading for the elevators, but Officer Stevens lingered to bring me to a room where he swabbed the inside of my cheek for DNA.

"I'm really sorry you're going through this," he told me. "Grace was always smiling and friendly. Is," he corrected himself.

"She's also really strong."

"Kloots isn't as mean and scary as he's making himself out to be. He's shocked. Everyone is. This is supposed to be a safe place where the bad guys can't get in, and the ones that do are in cuffs."

"I get it." I understood the fear, although I would never blame an innocent bystander for it.

"Do you have someone to take you home?" Officer Stevens asked, handing me a pack of wet naps.

"I, um...I can call a cab or something. But I think I'll go to the hospital first."

"She'll be in surgery for a while, and they usually don't let non-family members in the ICU."

"I'll take my chances." I swallowed against the bile rising in my throat. I used the wet naps on my hands first, but Officer Stevens motioned to my face. I didn't know if it had splattered, or if I'd touched myself before realizing my hands were bloody, but the wet nap came back red.

"I can drive you home if you want," he offered.

"Is there any chance I can have my cell phone?"

"Where is it?" he asked.

"Downstairs."

"Not until they've cleared the scene." He looked apologetic, yet helpless.

"Right. Um, this may sound weird, but could you give me Detective Cortez's number?"

"They were close," he said like he knew, even if he probably didn't know the extent of it.

"I just want to make sure someone told him," I agreed.

"You can use my phone if you want," he offered, handing it to me.

"Thank you."

I WAITED, not sure if I wanted to phone him with Officer Stevens in the room. Thankfully, Detective Kloots poked his head in, so Officer Stevens had to go deal with that and I was able to make the call.

"Stevens?" Malcolm asked, surprised. Wherever he was, it sounded windy, with people yelling things in the background. His calmness told me he didn't know what happened yet. It put a damper on my plan of calling him for information and put the burden on me.

"It's Allie," I shared.

"What's wrong? Is everything okay?"

"Grace stayed late, and she asked me to come, but..."

"What happened to her?" he asked calmly, even though he must be panicking on the inside. It was part of what made him such a good cop.

"When I found her, she'd been stabbed," I admitted.

"Was she..." His calm demeanor broke.

"She was barely breathing, and her pulse was really weak, but she wasn't gone yet. I tried to put pressure and help her, but there was so much blood." I wanted him to know what he would be walking into once he got to her. "I didn't even think that maybe I should have let her—"

"No, you did the right thing," he cut me off. "There's no way of knowing whether she's accomplished what she was meant to."

I shuddered at the thought, then took a deep breath to calm myself. Malcolm did not need me breaking down on top of it.

"What hospital did they bring her to?" he asked.

"I don't know. I keep asking to go, but they've been questioning me."

"That's protocol. They're not trying to catch you in a lie, they're just figuring out what happened."

"I didn't hurt her."

"I know," he assured me. I could hear sirens around him.

"Where are you?" I knew the obvious answer was at work, probably a crime scene, but before he registered how upset I was, there was a moment when I thought he might be expecting my call.

"Near a ravine talking to the park ranger who found Amber Dennis and Matthew Crawford."

"Are they…" I wasn't sure I wanted to know the answer, but I heard the tired smile in his voice.

"They're in bad shape, but we're hoping they'll pull through." He sighed. "I'm going to call Enrique and head to the hospital, but I want you to go home and try to get some sleep. I'll call the people in charge and let you know if they find anything."

"Are you sure you don't want me to come to the hospital?" I offered. I didn't want to beg or tell him that the last thing I wanted to do was go home to be alone right now.

"I'm sure. Try to get a friend or an officer to drive you, and I'll call you in the morning."

"Okay," I said before remembering that my phone had become evidence. "You'll have to call my home number. I left my cell with…I don't think I'm getting it back."

"Take care of yourself," he asked of me, and I remembered that Grace said he saw me as someone he had to protect, like his own daughter. Too bad he didn't realize I would rather spend the night with him and Enrique at the hospital than alone in my room, replaying what happened.

.   .   .

AFTER ANOTHER TWENTY minutes or so, I was allowed to leave, but I'd been an idiot and also left my clutch in the basement, which held my house keys. Technically, they were evidence now, but Stevens worked it out so I could get at least my house key back once they'd logged it and done all their tests. Then he would personally drive me home to make sure I was safe.

CHAPTER TWENTY-EIGHT

Stevens told me to wait for him in the atrium since it would take a while, but some of the adrenaline wore off and I felt like I was suffocating inside the building. I needed air, so I went out, getting a sympathetic nod from the officer they had manning the desk while the desk sergeant from earlier was giving her statement.

I wasn't expecting the cool night air to do much, but I took in a deep breath of it and felt all the tears I'd kept at bay since I found Grace push to the surface. I was about to let them out when I saw Tristan in the distance, watching me.

He looked different. Strange even. The sob caught in my chest and I stopped, grateful that the confusion gave me another reprieve from my emotions.

"Are you okay?" he asked, the words laced with concern and fear.

I wanted to let him take me in his arms. I was convinced they would make me feel at least slightly safer, but the voice in the back of my head wanted to know why he was still outside the precinct.

"What are you doing here?" I asked, swallowing against the dryness in my mouth. "I thought you went home."

"I…" He paused, but in this situation, embarrassing honesty was better than being vague and making me think he was a weird creeper. Especially given my previous teasing accusations. "I was hoping your boss just needed something quick, so I might have the chance to walk you home, maybe get ice cream, and…I would have left after a few minutes, but then everyone was on high alert and there were screams and sirens. You weren't answering your phone and I didn't want to leave until I knew you were okay."

I'm not, was what I wanted to say, but I wasn't sure we were at the falling apart in front of each other stage. Not yet.

"It wasn't me," I said instead. "Well, the screams probably were but…none of this is mine." My legs and arms were still covered in blood. It wasn't so obvious from a distance in the dark, but it was all I could see.

"What can I do?" he asked.

It hit me then, the reason he looked so different. He wasn't smiling. Normally, even if he was saying something completely depressing, there was still the slightest upturn to his lips, the possibility of a smile. This time, there was nothing.

"I think I came out here to fall apart," I admitted, very aware that the tears had already started, but I couldn't have stopped them, even if I wanted to.

"I've got you," he promised. He wrapped his arms around my shoulders, his hand gently cradling the back of my head, and held me while I finally let the sobs out. He repeated those words as well as calming shush noises, but his arms were the only thing holding me together.

TRISTAN BROUGHT me to the 24-hour diner across from the precinct and got me a cup of tea.

"We don't have to talk about it," he assured me.

He took the seat across from me in the red vinyl booth, his right hand holding my left. I focused on the way his thumb gently rubbed my skin, trying to soothe me, but I found myself wishing he'd sat beside me in the booth. The bright lights were too harsh, probably designed to keep the cops and waitresses awake, but I felt exposed in my bloody clothes. Not that anyone else seemed concerned by them.

As if reading my mind, Tristan pulled off his leather jacket and wrapped it around me. I felt guilty that it would be stained now, but I was mostly grateful.

Eventually, I managed to tell him everything that happened after he dropped me off. He listened patiently, even when I told him how badly I did not want to go home to be alone right now, making it clear that wasn't an invitation. I was feeling way too vulnerable for my liking, but I trusted him. Which also worried me.

"I'm so sorry," he said after I finished my story.

"It's not your fault." I said it in response to the look on his face rather than his apology.

"I think it's human nature to blame ourselves and think of all the what ifs. Not that it would have made a difference if I'd gone with you, but..."

"I kept wishing I'd stayed late with her instead of going with you or picked up when she called and been there for her. But maybe I would be lying on the floor with her, and nobody would have found us until morning. If even." I shivered, even with his jacket.

"Is it wrong of me to say I'm really happy you didn't?" he asked.

"You don't have to wait with me. I should probably get back to the precinct so Officer Stevens can bring me home."

"Is that what you want?"

"Not really." I sighed. "But I don't want any of this. I just don't have a choice."

"We can go back to the precinct if you want. And I can let Officer Stevens drive you home, ask you to call me if you need anything."

"But…" I asked, sensing he had another option in mind.

"But I'm right here, Allie, and I'm not going anywhere when you're like this. Whether that means sitting on the couch with you so you don't have to be alone tonight or waiting at the precinct until a cop brings you home, I'm right here."

"Okay," I decided.

"Which one?"

"I really don't want to be alone tonight." I was nervous, but way more afraid of what my mind would do if left on its own versus having Tristan there while I was scared, distraught, and vulnerable. "But only if you don't have anywhere else to be or…" I didn't want to remind him about his friend's house, but I knew he was supposed to leave in the morning.

"I'm not going anywhere," he repeated.

CHAPTER TWENTY-NINE

It took another twenty minutes before Officer Stevens gave me my keys, but my cell phone was covered in Grace's blood, and they wanted to go through it to see what Grace and I talked about. Somewhere in the back of my head, I knew that was a huge invasion of privacy—probably illegal without a warrant—but I also didn't care. It wasn't like she and I ever discussed our Giftedness or side cases via text. I was more worried about what they might find between her and Malcolm. Not just about the cases we weren't supposed to be working on, but it would take a lot of explaining if they called each other 'mamá' and 'mijo' in their text messages as well. Hopefully, they were smarter than that.

Tristan had taken his car to the precinct for our date, so he told Officer Stevens the ride wasn't necessary. The officer didn't argue, but he clearly didn't trust the guy who'd been lurking around for hours.

"Could I have your name and number?" Stevens asked.

"What for?" Tristan went back to his polite smile. I was impressed by how easily he could summon it, but it must be exhausting to always pretend everything was fine, when it very often wasn't.

"Miss Carmichael doesn't have a cell phone, so if we get any updates or require any more information, we need a number to contact her."

I knew I should just give Officer Stevens my home number, but I let Tristan give him his personal information instead. I felt like it was mostly to have a record of who was taking me home, possibly for his own protective instinct.

TRISTAN'S CAR was in a parking garage across the street, so I waited with Officer Stevens while he went to get it.

"If there's anything, you can just call us." He handed me his card.

"Like if I remember something I didn't say?" I was pretty sure I'd gone over every single detail with Detective Kloots.

"Or if you need us," he assured me.

"Thank you." I did my best attempt at a smile before getting into the red car Tristan pulled up in.

HE GAVE me free rein of the radio and heating, but we didn't talk outside of my turn-by-turn directions. I dreaded calling my parents. I'd hoped they might have had so much going on with Syb's dating adventures that they wouldn't realize I hadn't called tonight, but the answering machine was flashing when we walked in, boasting six new messages.

"I'll go get my things from my car." Tristan gave me an excuse so I could listen to them on my own. I wasn't sure if I wanted to call my family before he got back or wait so I could have him with me.

"Where did he take you?" Was the first thing Sybill asked when she picked up.

I paused, completely forgetting that the surprise date had been tonight, given everything else that happened. "A basketball game," I said once I remembered.

"What's wrong?"

If I told my parents I'd found someone nearly stabbed to death where I work, their response would be to freak out, get stressed, and for one of them to come and get me. And I should be with them. But I wanted to make sure Grace was okay before I left, and I didn't want my family to freak out until I got there.

"Nothing now. My boss called me to go in after the date so I could explain something in my report on a cold case they reopened."

"Staring at death can't be fun," she said like she understood. "How was the game?"

"Who won?" my dad asked in the background.

"Did the kiss cam find you?" my mom added.

I sighed and brought my hand up to massage my temples, trying to compose myself enough to answer all their questions with the necessary enthusiasm.

"The game was a lot more fun than I expected. Tristan enjoyed it so much that I couldn't help but be excited, too. Our team won, but no one else was happy about it. Some of them were actually pretty upset, but we avoided any cameras that make people kiss."

"You didn't want to kiss him?" Syb asked.

"You weren't rooting for the Hornets, were you?" Dad cut in.

"We were. And I did," I said as Tristan came back inside. I tried to lower the volume on the phone as much as I could, knowing how loud speakerphone could be.

"Did want to or did kiss him?" Sybill asked.

My cheeks reddened, but Tristan just gave me an encouraging smile, like he was completely oblivious before pretending to be busy with his stuff.

"You ladies can talk about that stuff tomorrow when I'm

running errands." I was saved by my dad, who probably didn't mind hearing it, but misunderstood my reluctance.

"We tried calling a few times on your cell phone. Your dad convinced me not to call the cops, but it was close," was my mother's way of telling me that she didn't appreciate me not answering.

"I know, I lost my cell, so I had to wait until I got home to call you."

"Want me to do that find your telephone thing?" my dad offered. It was his favorite part of the family plan, and although he would never actually spy on us, he looked forward to being able to track someone like a spy.

"That's okay, I'm pretty sure I just left it at the office." The lie was convincing because I knew exactly where it was. *Stick to the truth and don't give too many details.*

"You must be heading to bed now, it's getting late," my mom said, ever worrying about my well-being.

"Yeah, I'm exhausted." It wasn't until I said it that I realized how true it was. Not only was it late, but I was emotionally drained. I wouldn't have made it up the stairs if that was still where my bedroom was.

"We love you Allie," my mom and Sybill said loudly, but I heard my dad in there, too.

"Love you guys," I said before hanging up.

"You didn't tell them," Tristan called me on it.

"I didn't want to worry them."

"I guess I'm honored?" he tried. "And not that I'm judging, but..."

"I will tell them, but not at night when I don't have any answers and I'm susceptible to break down and make them feel terrible that they can't be there for me."

"Look who's putting on a brave face," he said sadly, not at all condescending. I closed my eyes when he took me in his arms, and rested my forehead against his chest.

"Thank you," I said. "For coming. I'm sure babysitting me from the shadows is not how you wanted to spend your last night here."

"I wanted to spend it with you, so I'm good," he assured me. "Not like that. Or like this. I just mean…I like you."

I think he exaggerated the awkwardness to make me smile, so I gave him a quick, sad one. "Do you mind if I go shower?" I asked him. "I can get you a new shirt or something comfy to—"

"I had a gym bag in the trunk," he assured me. "Kitchen is that way?"

"Yeah, I won't be long."

"Take all the time you need."

I KNEW HE MEANT IT, but I had every intention of getting in and out as fast as humanly possible. Instead, once the warm water washed over me, I let the tears fall as well. I would have stayed in for hours if I didn't have Tristan outside, waiting for me.

I came out in my housecoat to find Tristan in the kitchen, making something that smelled heavenly. I put on a thick pair of flannel pajamas and went to join him.

"My mom was always cooking my entire childhood, even when I could barely eat. Now I know why," he said, putting a chocolate chip cookie on a plate in front of me, along with an herbal tea.

"I made a lot of banana bread," I agreed. "Syb is the only one who eats fresh bananas in our family, but when she wasn't feeling up to it, they would go bad, so I baked."

"Did she eat the bread?"

"Rarely, but one of us would. And the house smelled happy and homey rather than sick and sad."

"Hence the cookies." He gave me a crooked smile.

"Thank you."

"You're welcome."

. . .

WE WENT to bed once the cookies and hot beverages were gone. I slept in my room, while he insisted on taking the couch. I kept wanting to check my phone for messages from Malcolm, but I didn't have it. And he would call the house phone if he knew anything. Rather, he would wait until morning because he wouldn't think I was staying up all night waiting for news.

I usually slept on my side, but after a half an hour spent staring at the family picture on my nightstand, wishing Sybill was here to crawl into the bed with me, I decided to sleep on my back. The ceiling wasn't any better, so I buried my head in the pillow. No matter how I positioned myself, when I closed my eyes, all I could see was Grace on the floor, looking so pale, her blood on my hands.

Eventually, I got up to make myself a glass of warm milk and honey, maybe with another cookie.

"Couldn't sleep?" Tristan asked once I was in the hallway.

"I'm sorry. I didn't mean to wake you."

"You didn't. I've been listening to you toss and turn for a while now."

I was going to apologize again, but he raised his arm that held the blanket, very clearly inviting me to join him.

"I'm not—"

"I know," he assured me. "But when your mind is racing. I think it's easier to sleep when someone's there to hold you still."

I debated it, knowing this was another line I was crossing that would make it harder when he went back to where he came from. But I was exhausted, and I wanted to stop shaking.

I went over and cuddled next to him on the couch, letting him put his arm around me. I still couldn't sleep, but the steady rhythm of his heartbeat made my whole body relax and feel as safe as I could, given the circumstances.

CHAPTER THIRTY

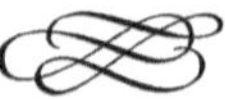

By the time I woke up the following morning, Tristan was no longer on the couch with me, but the smell of bacon and eggs wafted in from the kitchen. It took me all of a nanosecond to remember why I wasn't in my own bed and why he was in my house, but it was comforting to not be alone. And with him cooking and taking care of me, if I wasn't careful, I was going to fall for him even more than I already had.

"Good morning." His face lit up when I walked into the kitchen. "I'm an early riser who wakes up famished, and we've established food is our comfort language. I hope it's okay. And that you like bacon because I made a lot," he shared, bringing me a plate with toast and scrambled eggs.

"You're really going above and beyond," I said, taking a seat.

"It's all a part of my master plan of sweeping you off your feet."

"You're doing an excellent job." I'd woken up feeling like I wanted nothing more than to wallow and feel sorry for myself, but he was the perfect amount of banter and light that didn't make me feel like I was being inappropriate, but like I might eventually be okay again.

"All the credit is owed to my mother," he said like he hadn't spent his night trying to calm me enough to sleep or his morning making me a feast. "I'm assuming you want to go to the hospital this morning?"

"I don't think I'm expected at work. Malcolm hasn't called yet?"

Tristan raised an eyebrow at the name. I wanted to reassure him, but I wasn't sure how I could explain who Malcolm was – and why I called him by his first name – without revealing who he *really* was.

"There have been no phone calls," Tristan assured me. "I can drive you if you want. Assuming you're not sick of me yet."

"Are you sure? I took over your whole night. And morning. You're supposed to be having brunch and going home."

"I called my friends, and they completely understand. Even said I could stay at their place as long as I want." He smiled at the shock that realization brought me. "You're not used to people taking care of you, are you?"

"I'm more familiar with the opposite," I agreed. My parents obviously took care of me and raised me to always feel loved and never want for anything, but Sybill had been the priority we all made sacrifices for. Even if we both had the flu, it was a given that she would need more attention and come first.

"As someone who spent most of their life being taken care of, you have no idea how happy it makes me to be able to give the tiniest bit of that back. I would offer to spend the day there with you, going to get you food and coffee as needed, then make sure you got home okay, but that's probably a bit much." His wording and the look he gave me implied the offer still stood, and he would gladly do just that.

"I'll be fine once I get there, but I would definitely appreciate a ride."

His master plan was working.

. . .

WE LEFT AS SOON as we were done with the dishes, which he insisted on helping me with. He took my hand in his, resting them on top of the middle console for the entire drive. He was serious this morning and kept looking over as if he wanted to offer to stay with me again, but he was getting good at figuring out what I wanted. Or at least needed. He dropped me off with the promise that he would call me, and that I would call him if there was anything he could do to help.

I WALKED through the huge glass doors into the hospital I knew too well. My mom had worked in their neonatal unit for as long as I could remember. She used to bring me to the daycare before I started school, and then we spent so much time here trying to figure out what was wrong with Sybill, running every test imaginable. Mom even convinced the daycare to take us during the summers after we aged out, to be close to the doctors if ever something happened to Sybill, which it always did.

"Don't tell me Sybill's here?" Amy, one of the veteran nurses, asked before I even made it to the front desk. She looked exhausted, probably at the end of her shift.

"No, she's in California doing really good," I assured her, putting on as big a smile as I could muster. "I'm here to see a friend, Graciela Goncalves. She was brought in by an ambulance last night. I'm hoping this is the right hospital."

"It is. She's on the fifth floor. Room 516," she told me after typing it into the computer. "Make sure you give your family my best."

"Will do. Thanks, Amy."

I usually took the stairs if I wasn't with Sybill, to get to her faster, but I didn't mind delaying what I might find in room 516. I stopped by the cart in the atrium and got three black coffees with a combination of creamers and sugar on the side. Then I took a deep breath and headed for the elevators.

. . .

"Carina." Enrique was there as soon as the elevator doors opened to the fifth floor. I was surprised when he took me in for a hug, but he looked like he'd been awake for days.

"I brought coffee." I motioned to the tray I was trying to keep balanced.

"You're an angel," he told me. "You find her, and you bring coffee."

"It's nothing," I assured him. "How is she?"

"She's in a coma." He sighed, trying to put on a brave face. "Malcolm had to pick some stuff up at the office, but he should be back soon."

"Is she going to be okay?" I felt like such a child.

"I think so." It was an exhausted smile, but it was real. "She lost a lot of blood and they had to fix a bunch of stuff on the inside, but they're optimistic. We'll know more when she wakes up, but they don't think that'll be today."

"Thank God," I said, fighting back the tears. I'd been so worried that she wasn't going to make it.

"They said she wanted you to walk her home?" he asked me while walking into a hospital room. I hardly recognized the woman in the bed as Grace. She was so unbelievably pale, with tubes coming out of her arms and nose.

"She had questions about a case I was helping her with." I wasn't sure how much he knew about her. Or me.

"Yeah, she said she found something and would meet me at home instead of at the bar." He sat and took her hand in his, giving it a kiss, then rubbed it like Tristan had done to mine last night.

"I'm so sorry," I apologized for not getting there sooner, for not being there with her.

"As far as I'm concerned, you saved her life. You have nothing to apologize for."

A nurse I didn't know came in and checked Grace's IV before taking her vitals. We stayed quiet while she worked, but I couldn't help but notice the way she looked disapprovingly at Enrique before leaving.

"What was that about?" I asked, even though it probably wasn't my place.

"I think Grace put me down as her uncle for the emergency contact thing," he said like he couldn't care less who thought he was being inappropriate.

"Have they told you anything?" I didn't want to pry, but so far, they acted like I was their primary suspect.

"No one is telling me anything. I've run over it a million times. It has to be an escaped prisoner, or she caught someone trying to do something they shouldn't because she had no enemies or…everyone loves her."

"It's hard not to."

"Nothing," Malcolm said, walking into the room. Then he spotted me. "You came." He sounded surprised.

"I can't imagine being anywhere else."

"Of course. Thank you," he said.

"What was the nothing?"

"They've gone through the hallway and there are no hairs or fingerprints that don't belong to you, my mom, or the paramedics."

"What does that mean?" Enrique pressed.

"It means we have no idea who did this to her, and it's unlikely someone just stumbled upon her in the precinct's basement."

"You mean it was planned?"

"I mean someone had the presence of mind to cover their tracks."

I let out an involuntary shudder.

"Alison brought coffee," Enrique changed the subject.

"Thank you," Malcolm said, but the unspoken truth was that he wasn't going to leave her bedside, because chances were someone did this to her on purpose.

CHAPTER THIRTY-ONE

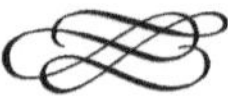

When Tristan dropped me off again the following
morning, Malcolm looked more confused than
anything. I guess I wouldn't be coming every day if Grace had a
scheduled surgery or the flu, but there was something about
seeing her so close to death that made me not want to leave her
side until I knew she would be okay. And a couple of weeks
with a colleague isn't normally enough to form a meaningful
bond, but she knew things about me that no other human being
could know. Except for Dr. Richards, but he basically sent me to
her. I'd emailed him to let him know what happened, but he
probably didn't check his work email that often during his holi-
days. I knew this meant I should call him, but I did not feel
ready for that yet. It was best to try again once we knew she was
going to be okay.

After Enrique brought us the stale, watered down coffee
from the machines, I volunteered for all subsequent coffee runs.
Some of the cafeterias were good, but I needed the fresh air that
came from going to the cart outside.

. . .

THE CART WAS BUSY, so I walked around while the line died down, then ordered my three coffees and went back upstairs. In the ICU, most of the rooms had glass walls so the nurses could see what was going on, but I spotted a man with red hair and did a double take. I slowly took a few steps toward him, trying not to be creepy, but it was Matthew. In the flesh, not just a memory. On closer inspection, he was handcuffed to the bed, which meant the cops I thought were watching over Grace, were probably there for him.

"ARE Amber and Matthew on this floor?" I asked Malcolm, handing the guys their coffees.

Enrique looked confused, but Malcolm sighed. "There were enough inconsistencies in Hunter's story that I convinced them to let Matthew stay here until he recovers, but as soon as he's stable, they're sending him to the prison ward."

"Even if he's innocent?"

"They're advising against waking Amber up from a medically induced coma, so there is nothing but Hunter's word against two unconscious people. With Hunter's father being a highly respected prosecutor..." he reminded me.

"But once they wake up..."

"As long as Hunter doesn't convince a jury that Amber was brainwashed, her word should be enough to clear Matthew. It works in our favor that Hunter was too proud to admit she was trying to leave him."

"Any luck arresting Hunter?"

"I'm hoping Matthew's testimony will help, but he was severely dehydrated and on the brink of starvation when we found them. I tried to ask him what happened, but he was focused on Amber."

"I'm surprised they didn't bleed out."

"So was I. Apparently, they got their hands on a hiking backpack, and he macgyvered a system to give her a blood transfusion."

"Of his blood?" Malcolm nodded. "I thought Matthew was a soldier?"

"Army medic, I believe."

Matthew could have known Amber's blood type was the same as his, but I couldn't imagine him surviving his own blood loss, let alone giving her some. Even if Hunter missed every artery when he stabbed him, he would still be too weak to donate blood.

"What's wrong?" Malcolm asked me.

"I know this probably breaks a lot of rules…but is there any chance I could talk to him?"

"I doubt it. They'd be worried he might hurt you."

"There's only one cop in front of his room. He has to take bathroom breaks."

"What do you think you'll accomplish?"

"Don't you want to find out what happened?"

He looked at me, not liking it, then looked to his mother in the bed and slumped his shoulders.

"Five minutes," he gave in. "And not a minute more."

"Thank you." I gave him a hug, mortified the second it happened, but he just shook his head at me and sighed.

My opportunity came in the afternoon when the cop watching Matthew asked for a bathroom break, and Malcolm covered for him. I knew it was coming, and that I would have more than five minutes, because the cop had cafeteria chili for lunch. But I didn't want to betray Malcolm's trust.

Once I was in the room, I realized that I had no plan and nothing to make Matthew trust me. I wasted precious seconds by slowly walking up to his bed, but he was sleeping, and I had to figure out a game plan.

"Who are you?" Matthew asked, slowly opening his eyes to look at me sideways. He did not trust me.

"I worked on your case." I chose honesty.

"You're a cop?"

"Not really. I go through cold cases to see if any evidence was overlooked, but they asked me to look at the necklace and knife when they had nothing but a little boy's story to go on."

"You have her necklace?" he asked.

"We *had* it, but they did a number on it, looking for clues to find you. The whole amber necklace for Amber was cute. That's how we got her name, realized she was missing, and started looking for you. I heard they think she'll be okay." I was blabbering, wasting my five minutes on nothing.

Matthew looked away from me as he brought his hand to his chest, tugging at the neckline of his hospital gown. I didn't understand how he could survive after giving Amber the blood he was already struggling to replenish...but then I couldn't see a wound.

"Where is it?" I asked him. Was I wrong? Did I mix up the memories? Or did Hunter want so badly to stab Matthew that I felt it, even if he didn't actually do it?

"Where's what?" Matthew let go of the gown and struggled to sit up. I panicked when his hand went to the call button, but he didn't press it.

"You were stabbed," I said with certainty. Even if I didn't understand my Gift, I trusted it so far.

As soon as I said it, his eyes darted to me in fear, and I knew I was right.

"I don't know what you're talking about."

I looked down at my watch. I didn't have time to come up with a story that made sense, or to ease him into it, so I was blunt. "Hunter's story is a load of crap. You didn't abduct them because you were jealous, and you would never hurt Amber, no matter what she did to you first." He was with me until I added, "But you were stabbed. In the chest."

I pointed to where I assumed it would have happened. Instead of telling me I was crazy, he looked at me with wide eyes like I was a witch. Or a God. Maybe an angel, but definitely not human.

"How do you know that?" he asked.

"How did you survive?" I turned it on him.

"I have no idea," he admitted. I waited, so he let out a breath, then told me his story. "I knew Amber was in trouble, so I went to their place. Her head had this gash on it that...I wanted to go after Hunter and kill him myself, but I had to get her out of there first. I was in the closet getting her suitcase when Hunter came up behind me. I didn't hear him until he had this fishing wire around my neck. I struggled and tried to fight him off, but I couldn't breathe, and everything went black." He took another breath, but it was an excuse to gauge my reaction.

"I woke up in the woods under a pile of dirt and leaves, like a half-assed, shallow grave. I heard Amber scream and I just ran to her. I had no idea that it had been two days, or that I'd been dead." Matt looked like he'd been waiting to tell the story to clear his name, but he knew that anyone who heard it would lock him up in a psych ward.

"Amber was stabbed when I got to her. He'd just left her there with a kitchen knife planted in her stomach like she was nothing. The S.O.B. actually thought that if I was dead and he nursed her back to health, that she would take him back. I took the knife out and did what I could with the limited supplies, but I was so focused on her that I didn't even notice Hunter until he took the knife and stabbed me with it."

I listened to his story with my jaw on the ground and my hand on my heart, too horrified to interrupt him. I'd felt some of the moments he was mentioning, but it was something else to look him in the eyes as he relived it.

"Hunter ran off into a cabin and I couldn't wait around for him to come out with a rifle and do more damage to Amber, so I helped her to her feet, and we ran. We were slow and clumsy, so he would have caught up to us in no time, but we fell into this hole. It was too deep to climb out of, even if we had the energy, but unless Hunter fell in, he was never going to find us. We heard him looking for us, and I died praying the bears would eat him.

"When I woke up, Amber was wrapped around me, dried tears running down her face, barely holding on. She convinced herself she was hallucinating, but my wounds were gone. Not healed, gone."

He waited for me to be as shocked as he was, but I let him know I believed him and didn't think he was crazy. "You died and came back to life. Again."

"It didn't make any sense. But Amber needed blood, and I figured I came back to give it to her. When she was freezing and I somehow made a fire with my bare hands and nothing else, I didn't question it. I spent days just trying to keep her fed and warm and alive, and to claw my way out of that hole. I nearly collapsed when I reached the cabin, but I convinced the park ranger to follow me to Amber. The last thing I remember was making sure she had a pulse when they pulled her out, and then I woke up here."

"I'm so sorry you went through all that," I told him, knowing it wasn't nearly enough, but we were running out of time. "I only had a few minutes until your guard came back, but there is a detective outside who believes you're innocent. I promise I will get you free." I headed for the door while he looked at me in shock.

"All I care about is Amber."

"I know." I sighed, before admitting, "I can't explain it either, but when I touched the necklace, I saw some of its memories.

And the knife's. I know he stabbed the both of you, and I know how you feel about each other."

"Did he tell you anything?" Malcolm asked once I was safely back in the room.

I looked over to Enrique, who was asleep in the chair beside the bed, then told Malcolm everything Matthew told me, finishing with, "We have to help him."

"Of course. I'll see what I can do," he assured me.

He went out to talk to the other officers, leaving me alone with the sleeping couple. It still felt surreal to see Grace like this, and it terrified me that she hadn't woken up, but the doctors assured us it was normal, and that being asleep was helping her heal. None of it was comforting, but I was used to days like this, so I concentrated on the steady beep beep of her heart machines.

CHAPTER THIRTY-TWO

On Sunday, Tristan made pancakes and offered to spend the day with me, but I sent him home. I went to spend a few hours at the hospital with Grace, although there was no change. With her, at least.

"Did they move Matthew?" I asked when I got in, replacing Grace's daisies with fresh ones. I was hoping it was just to another room, but yesterday he'd seemed lucid enough to be moved to the prison. Maybe telling people the truth – at least a version of it – would have been a good idea to buy him some time.

"I assume he's in the room next to it. Amber's," Malcolm told me with a smile creeping onto his worn-out face.

"They're letting him see her? Is she awake?" I was cautiously optimistic, but not ready to get my hopes up. We needed a win.

"I looked into the domestic abuse, and it turns out Amber wasn't the first woman Hunter hurt. His high school girlfriend's testimony was on my boss' desk this morning when I got the news that Amber was awake. She skipped the parts about Matthew dying multiple times, but she otherwise told them exactly what happened, so they released Matthew. And as of twenty minutes ago, Hunter is in police custody."

I let out a breath and felt like a huge weight had been lifted as I sat down in the chair on Grace's other side.

"Now if my mother could wake up, I might finally be able to get some sleep." He gave me a tired smile, running his hand through his hair. He looked much older than his forty-five years.

"No change?"

"They don't tell me much unless I flash my badge. Enrique is her emergency contact, but I'm getting the impression they think she should be awake by now. They don't say that, but I can see it on their faces."

"Or you're exhausted and afraid, so you're expecting the worst," I suggested before Enrique came in with an assortment of take-out boxes from his bar.

"Apparently I'm not eating enough," he said, putting the boxes in front of us without touching them.

"You can't live on coffee alone." Malcolm sighed, reaching into one for an apple turnover.

BY THE TIME I was ready to leave, there was hardly anything left in the three boxes, and both men looked slightly less exhausted after hours spent telling me fun stories about Grace, including the many times she almost burnt houses down while trying to make roast pork. Apparently, she wasn't very good at flambéing things, but was determined to figure it out. I couldn't picture her going home to attempt fancy recipes, but there was a lot I didn't know about her.

I also got to spend more than those initial five minutes talking to Matthew, who was fascinated by all the 'Gifted stuff' Malcolm told him. Grace apparently knew someone from the army who was Gifted, and Malcolm arranged a meeting so

Matthew could have a better understanding of what happened to him.

"I think it was saving her. My purpose," Matthew confided in me near the end of our conversation. "I spent years staying away from Amber because I thought it was what was best for her, but in the end, it nearly killed her. I should have just done what made me happy." I could see that she was, and would always be, the thing that made him happiest in the world.

At around four o'clock, Tristan was waiting downstairs for me. He'd been there the first night without me asking, because he knew I needed it. We made dinner together, watched a movie in the living room, and then I fell asleep on the couch with his arms around me. The bed somehow felt more serious than I was ready for this to be, but it didn't get much more intimate than holding me in his arms so my trauma couldn't prevent me from falling asleep. What worried me was that the couple he housesat for had been back for almost a week, and there was only so long you could crash at a friend's house before you wore out their hospitality and had to go home. Or officially stay at my place.

I may or may not have pretended I was still sleeping when he'd gotten a call from Delia and told her he couldn't leave yet. I was torn between not wanting him to feel obligated to stay, and not wanting him to leave.

Tristan usually picked me up in his car, but I wanted to walk by Dr. Richards'. I'd given in and tried contacting him about Grace again, but he had yet to return my calls. His replacement at the museum reminded me he was on his summer sabbatical, which meant it was none of my business where he was. His house looked empty from the outside, so I figured he was gallivanting around Europe without a phone plan and would come home once Grace was already back to normal.

"When do you have to go back?" I asked Tristan while we walked home from Dr. Richards'.

"That's kind of up in the air." He shrugged with that smiley nonchalance I knew so well. "How long do you want me to stay?"

"I'm serious," I pressed, smiling in spite of myself.

He looked at me like he was considering it before he sighed and reached for my hand. "How about some tea?"

He brought me to a cafe without waiting for my answer, but it was chilly out today, and I loved a hot tea when it was cold and rainy. But I also felt like he wanted to tell me something while we were sitting face to face.

"London Fog, or do you want to try something new?"

"I'll stick to the usual." I could feel myself smiling, because people didn't often notice stuff like that about me. There was a coffee shop by the museum that I went to at least four times a week for years, with mostly the same staff, and the last time I went, not a single person there could tell me my name or 'my usual' that I ordered every single time.

"I'm thinking hot chocolate." Tristan pulled me close and checked out the menu.

"That's very different from black coffee," I pointed out, leaning back into his chest.

"It is." He kissed the top of my head and all I could think was that I wouldn't mind if he stayed forever.

Tristan ordered and paid for both drinks, then found us a table by the window with cushions and a warm, cozy feeling. It was the kind of seat that was probably empty all summer, except for days like today.

"We used to bring a thermos full of hot chocolate to my little sister's soccer games. Serena," he shared. He held my hand across the table, but his eyes were on his cup. "I always had to be bundled up with a dozen blankets, and I could tell my parents were nervous wrecks the whole time, but I loved watching her play. And I thought it was important for me to be there, for her to look over to the sidelines and see me, something she could remember after I..."

"It must have meant a lot to her." I gave his hand a squeeze.

He gave me a sad smile, but then his face went somber. Like the night I found Grace, only this was more internal.

"It did. Every time she scored a goal or did anything awesome, her first instinct was to look over at that spot where I always sat. It still is." He said the last part to himself, then swallowed. Whatever came next was why he brought me here. "I didn't really come here to house sit. My friends just let me stay at their place because they were going out of town." He sighed. "After the cancer went away, I...I became different, and our relationship changed. I still tried to be there for every game and every big moment in her life, but I could tell it wasn't the same. It upset her when she saw me there, so I kept sitting further and further away, so she couldn't see me...but she always found me. Like a sixth sense, telling her where I was."

I wanted to ask him what happened that changed their relationship so drastically, but I knew better than to go there until he told me. *If* he told me.

"Just before I met you, Serena told me that I was hurting her more than helping, and she would rather I stay away."

"I'm sure she didn't mean—"

"No, she definitely meant it. And I can see your brain working, trying to come up with solutions and reassurances, but that's not why I'm telling you. This isn't something I can fix if I give her time or talk to her. It breaks my heart, but I know that. So, I came here. To give her space. To get away from all the places she would otherwise have to see me. I do have another family of people who are waiting for me to come back…but I can't do that yet. Because I don't know who I am when I'm not that person. Serena's brother. My parents' son. And I've always been this happy, easygoing guy, but I don't know if I can be him there, and I don't know who else to be."

"So, you'll stay for a while to enjoy all of my happiness?"

"Diminishing the serious stuff with a joke is usually my job. Although I try not to make it so morbid."

"Well, now you get to see what it's like to not be that person."

"There's a lot going on right now, but I like making you smile." He brought his hand to my face and brushed it against my cheek.

"I like that, too," I agreed. "And I love your smile. But it means a lot that you were honest with me. Vulnerable. Not smiling for once."

"I have many hats."

"I look forward to getting to know them all."

CHAPTER THIRTY-THREE

I spent Monday morning at the hospital with Malcolm and Enrique, but when Suzie took the afternoon off to sit with Grace, Enrique and I made ourselves scarce. Enrique said he had to rush off to take care of something at the restaurant, but it was obviously an excuse to give them some alone time, which he made clear when we stopped by a taco truck to kill time before he drove me home.

I hadn't gone back to the precinct since the night I found Grace, assuming I wouldn't be needed, but it was still a blow when the message on my answering machine confirmed it. The cold case lab was closed indefinitely, and the summer program was cancelled. Which meant I no longer had a reason to stay in Boston.

I felt like such a failure, but to be honest, I wanted to go to California so my mom could take me in her arms. I could get into our summer routine and forget about what happened. Not that I would be able to, but it would be easier there, where worrying about Sybill and trying to distract her could take up more of my brain space. Or not worrying about Sybill because she seemed to be doing wonderful there. But we could go to

Disney and take advantage of this bout of normalness in her otherwise unhealthy life.

Malcolm would keep me updated, and I could make sure he called me as soon as Grace woke up, so I could apologize profusely and the tightness in my heart would subside. The only thing holding me back at this point was Tristan. It wasn't like he could wait for me to come back, because by the end of the summer, he would be gone. Maybe it was better to rip the Band-Aid off now, before it got to a point where I couldn't function without him, rather than just couldn't sleep?

IF I WAS LEAVING, I had some stuff I would need to get from the precinct's basement, so after abandoning an online perusal of flights to California, I rode my bike to town.

I guess it was silly of me, but I expected the precinct to be surrounded by yellow crime scene tape, with officers and detectives standing around, looking for clues. Instead, everything was business as usual.

I gave a smile and a head nod to the desk sergeant as I walked by, but he came out and stopped me.

"I don't think we're expecting you anymore."

"I'm just coming to get my things. If the internship is done for the summer, I'll need my raincoat," I explained.

"Was it in the hallway or…"

"The room. B-473." I was glad he said hallway instead of the crime scene, although my standard image for a hallway now included Grace bleeding to death on its floor. I'd given up on anything I'd brought with me to 'the hallway'.

"I think they're done with that one. I'll send an escort with you."

"An escort?"

"We haven't technically released the crime scene yet. Since it's right here and that room would be a nightmare to go through thoroughly, they've sort of just been going back to it. We couldn't have you tampering with anything."

He said it politely, and it was all very logical, but I got the impression that they didn't trust me, and that I was possibly on trial. Or at least on their list of suspects. You would think a police station would have security footage in their haunted hallways to prevent this sort of thing, or better security guards so murderers couldn't get in.

I DIDN'T WANT to cause trouble, so I stood there and waited for him to find someone to babysit me while everyone else went about their day, as if someone hadn't been attacked and left for dead one floor down, less than a week ago. It was unnerving and made me want to scream.

"Miss Carmichael."

I turned around at the voice and found, "Officer Stevens." I gave him a grateful smile, especially when he suggested we take Grace's secret staircase. He didn't say it, but I knew it was so we could avoid the crime scene.

"Have they found anything?" I asked as we walked.

"I'm not a part of the investigation, but I don't think so. There's no APBs, no one they want to question…so far, I think they have no idea what happened."

"That's comforting."

"It happened in their house, and Detective Cortez has taken a vested interest in it. They'll find whoever did it," he assured me with a confidence I admired.

The room was locked, but Officer Stevens had a keycard. Again, I was surprised by the lack of crime scene tape. It made me wonder if the hallway itself would be completely back to normal by now as well.

I'd brought an empty backpack, so I filled it with the knick-knacks I'd accumulated over the last couple of weeks. It was surprising how much junk I'd managed to leave behind in so little time. Although, to be honest, other than the raincoat, there wasn't much I wanted to keep. A coffee mug I'd received for free from a mall promotion. An old phone charger that had so much tape and holes it was a wonder it still worked. Mostly, I wanted to come to see if they had figured anything out yet, but they hadn't.

"Do you have everything you need?" Officer Stevens asked after I sealed my bag and looked around. I considered doing some snooping. I could tell Stevens I was making sure I hadn't left anything behind, and he wouldn't suspect a thing. But I had no clue what to look for, and it would feel like I was betraying Grace. Those drawers were hers. She was nice about me finding the artifact in her secret hiding spot, but I'd felt terrible.

"I think so." I tried to give him a smile, but I saw a handprint on the wall behind him and froze.

He quickly turned around to see what startled me, instinctively reaching for his gun. He dropped his hand and slumped his shoulders when he saw the bloody print. "I'm sure it'll all be clean by the time you come back."

"I'm not coming back." I hoped the program wouldn't be dropped, but if or when it reopened, I wouldn't be a part of it.

"That's a shame," he said, though I wasn't sure if he was flirting or just being polite.

"I'm sure someone new will take my place."

"Not likely. Miss Goncalves didn't just run this program; she *was* the program. If she doesn't come back—to work here—I think they'll drop it."

"*That* would be a shame," I said, but I didn't feel strongly enough about it to do anything.

Officer Stevens walked me all the way to the front doors and offered me a ride home, but I assured him I was fine. I wasn't, but I felt like walking around and feeling normal would do me more good than riding in the back of a police car. I wanted to call Tristan, but I didn't want to be clingy and vulnerable all the time. Plus, I deserved some ice cream after everything I'd been through. Ever since Dr. Richards decided I was Gifted and invited me to meet Professor Mallory. Not that I explicitly blamed him, but my life was a lot simpler before he got involved.

Instead of soft serve, I got a sugar cone with two scoops of their caramel crunch ice cream, the one with chunks of brown sugar inside. I had to convince the girl to add sprinkles after she told me it wasn't the best combination, but I was doing everything in my power for this ice cream to make me feel happy. It was a lot of pressure, but it had always lived up to my expectations before.

IT TURNED out she was right, and peanuts might have been a better topping, but even the ice cream wasn't living up to the hype. Everyone else around me was in shorts and skirts, enjoying the gorgeous summer evening, but there was a chill that I couldn't shake, and the ice cream wasn't helping.

I was almost at the garbage can when I felt lightheaded. I stumbled the rest of the way to a bench so I could sit, but when I did, I saw a man in a hoodie and sunglasses walking toward me.

My vision went blurry, but I kept thinking how weird it was for the man to be bundled up when it was so warm out. Then I realized that it was so he wouldn't be recognized. The chill turned into a cold sweat as the fear took over me. I tried to get up and run away, but I just made it easier for him to sweep me up in his arms, like I was a friend who wasn't feeling well, rather than someone he was trying to kidnap. I assumed he wasn't going to kill me in the middle of a public space, but then again, this was probably the same person who stabbed Grace inside a police station.

I went to scream, but he put a gloved hand over my mouth. We were between buildings, and it seemed like everyone in them must have already gone home for the day, because no one was stopping him. My arms and legs felt like they weighed a ton, so my feeble attempts to escape didn't even slow him down.

I wanted to be the type of person who was strong and fought to her last breath, never giving up, but I caved and started crying. Every last tear I'd been holding in. I was going to be dead soon, so what was the use?

"Boston PD, freeze!"

Just as I was giving up, I heard a voice that sounded like Officer Stevens. I thought I was imagining it, but it still gave me the extra motivation to fight back again.

"Let the girl go and put your hands where I can see them."

The man who held me had stopped walking, but he made no effort to let me go or even to face them. It was like he was debating if he was going to fight or flee, but his grip tightened, implying that neither option meant releasing me.

"I repeat, let the girl go and put your hands in the air or I will shoot." Stevens' voice was nervous, but steady. He was well-trained, and I believed he would take the shot.

I didn't want to be in the man's arms when that happened, so instead of trying to fight him, I focused all my energy on rolling away from him, hoping my weight would do the rest. I lunged just as the man spun around and threw a knife, which gave me the momentum I needed, especially since he was down to one arm holding me. I fell to the floor just as I heard gunshots.

The man hesitated before running off down the alley, followed by other officers, but Stevens was on the ground a few feet away from me with a knife standing up out of his bullet-proof vest like as if his chest was the bullseye.

CHAPTER THIRTY-FOUR

"What do you mean *they're* after me?"

Officer Stevens promised me the knife barely pierced his vest, and the wound looked a lot worse than it was, but Detective Kloots was the bearer of bad news.

"IT got back to us that last Thursday someone hacked into one of our servers. The only things they looked into were Graciela Goncalves, room B-473, and you." Which explained how a dozen officers had mobilized in the less than five minutes since the man took me. They'd been looking for me.

Panic built as my heart raced in my chest. I reminded myself that whoever did this chose to go in the middle of the night when the room should have been empty. But then again, maybe they lured Grace there and used her phone to do the same with me. Maybe she was already in a pool of blood when someone else made those missed calls.

"There's no reason to panic. We've got you. We believe that the person who came after you just now was the same one who attacked Mrs. Goncalves, which means you're not safe here, but we're handling it. I'll have an officer drive you home, and we'll keep two patrol officers stationed outside your house until we catch him." Detective Kloots tried to be reassuring, but it felt weird given how he'd treated me like the prime suspect up to ten minutes ago.

"I'm in protective custody?" I asked, the concept so foreign in my mind. None of this made sense.

"For the time being," he agreed.

"Do you have any idea who's behind this?"

"Not currently. But since both incidents happened so close to the precinct, we must assume it has something to do with a case you two were working on. We're looking into her reports and the files she left on the desk. Hopefully one of them will give us a clue."

"How would anyone even know what we were working on? We go through old cases everyone has forgotten about, and nothing happens unless we find something, in which case the damage is already done."

"One of our techs mentioned he found you with Detective Cortez in his lab. Was that for one of your cold cases, or were you helping out on something more recent?"

"Detective Cortez was nice enough to show me around the precinct when I told him I'd only ever seen the basement," I lied, hoping Malcolm would as well. I was pretty sure they wouldn't do anything to me for looking at the evidence, as long as he didn't mention my Gift, but Malcolm might get in trouble for showing it to me. And I would get in trouble for lying during a police investigation.

"That's what he said as well, but I don't remember him giving tours to any other interns."

The implications about Malcolm and I would have made me laugh if the Detective wasn't looking at me with all the suspicion he could muster.

"I didn't think you ever had other interns," I pointed out,

trying to sound calm and in control of the situation, but I really wanted to run away from him and this whole mess.

"We'll get to the bottom of it, don't worry," he assured me, but only half of the promise was meant to be comforting. The other half was a threat.

THEY BROUGHT me to an interrogation room to take my statement, 'for my safety'. When I told them how weak and dizzy I'd felt, Detective Kloots had them draw my blood so they could see what I'd been given, while another officer went to the ice cream stand. Just to be on the safe side, I called Malcolm from the precinct to make sure everyone else was okay. He sounded horrified by what happened to me and called back for Detective Kloots as soon as I hung up.

ONCE I WAS 'FREE TO GO', I was actually only free to be put in the back seat of a cop car so they could drive me home and wait in my driveway. I offered them to come inside where it was cooler and comfier, but they weren't supposed to get comfortable.

I didn't like being alone with my thoughts in the house, where my heart kept racing and making me feel like I was going to faint. Once I'd packed a suitcase and booked a flight to California in the morning, there wasn't much for me to do other than wallow in my fear, so I made some coffee, put the fresh batch of cookies Tristan made last night into a Tupperware, and headed out to the cop car in my driveway.

"Is everything okay?" the cop with a mustache, Officer Hill, asked me. The other one, Officer Jones, was clean-shaven and looked younger than Officer Stevens. He came out of the car when he saw me approaching.

"Of course, I just thought you might like some coffee and cookies," I shared, showing them the treats.

"I probably shouldn't," Officer Hill said, looking like he wanted to.

"I definitely should." Officer Jones was undeterred by the calories as he came close. "Did you make these?" he asked, biting in.

"My friend did," I shared. "Are you staying out here all night?"

"Another team will come in a few hours. We'll be back tomorrow."

"Or they'll catch the guy, and you can sleep at a normal time in your own bed," I suggested.

"Your driveway or out on patrol, it doesn't really make a difference," he assured me.

I smiled, but they both tensed, bringing their hands to their guns as I heard someone walk up behind me.

"Is everything okay?"

I recognized Tristan's voice before I turned around to face him.

"Yeah, I'm..." I tried to say the words, but I couldn't lie to him. Especially not when my face was telling him the truth. Instead, I smiled apologetically and shook my head.

"Do you know this man?" Officer Hill was back to business.

"This is my friend, Tristan Davis. He made the cookies," I explained.

"You gave them away?" Tristan pretended to be hurt, trying to make me smile, but I was so not there.

"I would have eaten them all otherwise."

"I'll just have to make you something else. In a smaller quantity." He smiled, and I wanted more than anything to let him come inside and make me comfort food, to fall asleep feeling relatively safe in his arms, escape into our little world and try to forget everything that was going on. But there were cops in my driveway to make sure a man couldn't break into my house and kill me. Tristan would make me feel safer, yes, but it wasn't safe for him. He didn't have anyone who wanted to hurt him...not unless he stayed here with me.

"It's probably best if you went home," I argued. I think my cop friends wanted to run his ID and make sure he wasn't a threat, but they took a step back when they realized I was sending him away. Tristan was slower to accept it.

"Why are there cops here?" he asked what should have been his first question.

"Someone tried to kidnap me a few hours ago." It sounded ridiculous, like I was lying, or telling him about something that happened to someone else.

"How...are you okay?" he asked, trying to take me in his arms, but I wouldn't let myself melt into him. I couldn't let him make me feel safe. Because then I would never be able to send him away.

"He drugged me and tried to carry me off somewhere."

"Is it the same person who—"

"They think so," I agreed. "It's the only reason they were able to stop it. They were already looking for me because they realized the person was after me, too."

"Then you should come with me to Lucy and Gabriel's. No one would think to look for you there and...I can keep you safe." He reached for my hand. I felt the sparks, and the butterflies in my stomach, but I couldn't.

"I think you should go there. Alone," I added.

"Allie..." he warned, understanding where I was going with this.

"I couldn't live with myself if you got hurt because of me." I ignored his protest.

"I can take care of myself," he assured me. "And I could never forgive myself if anything happened to you."

"That's what these guys are here for." I looked at the two men in front of me, their uniforms implying they were better suited to the job, but I knew the uniforms didn't make them invincible or bulletproof.

"Then let them protect both of us," Tristan tried.

I didn't know if that was even allowed, but I knew that I wanted to minimize the amount of people who could get hurt because of this. Because of me.

"You should go home, Tristan," I repeated.

"Because you want me to leave or because you don't want me to get hurt?"

"They're the same thing," I said, even though I knew exactly what he was asking.

"Allie…"

"Sir, we're going to have to ask you to leave." Officer Jones stepped forward.

"That's okay," I assured him. I didn't want this to be the kind of thing where Tristan was arrested or forcibly removed. I just didn't want him to get hurt. "You haven't done anything wrong, and I wish I could let you come in, but I need you to go. So at least one of the million scary things in my head won't come true."

"And what about you?" he asked.

All I could do was shrug because I didn't know what was going to happen.

"I'll call you when I get home," he decided, eying the cops.

"It's better if you didn't."

"You just said…"

"That I don't want you to get hurt. If they're after me, that puts you in danger. You were supposed to have left days ago. So just go home." I tried to stay strong, but I knew there was no way I could convince him if he looked into my eyes. "Goodbye,

Tristan." I turned and went inside while I still had some resolve.

THE HOUSE SEEMED TOO BIG, too quiet, and too scary when I was awake, so I went to bed and spent hours staring at the ceiling, trying to make sense out of my current situation. But none of it made sense. We had no secrets worth killing for, nothing to silence us about that wouldn't live on from the reports we'd already sent out. Hunter was behind bars, and the artifact was back with Dr. Richards. That thought should have been reassuring, but then why wasn't he getting back to me?

I tossed and turned a while longer before giving in and calling Malcolm.

"Are you sleeping at all?" I could hear the hospital machines in the background. I knew he spent his days at his mother's bedside, investigating the incident, but I assumed he went home at night.

"I'll sleep once she comes home," he dismissed me.

"I'm calling because I was wondering if you ever reached Dr. Richards. To tell him about Grace."

"I thought you left him a message."

"I did, but he hasn't gotten back to me."

"You're worried?"

"I wasn't, but then I kept thinking that the most dangerous thing I've worked on was the artifact because it was worth so much money, and I know your mom gave it back to him, so...I don't know if you guys do Wellness Checks?"

"I can send one of my guys to look into it," he assured me.

"Thank you. It's probably nothing, but I'll feel better knowing he's okay."

"Of course."

I told him about my California plans, and although he said they'd miss me at the hospital, he thought it would be good for me to be with family. Although he did make me promise that I wouldn't go anywhere except for the hotel and the hospital.

EVEN WITH MALCOLM looking into Dr. Richards, I still tossed and turned until the first rays of sunshine came up, when I finally accepted that I was not going to get any sleep.

CHAPTER THIRTY-FIVE

It was a whole other battle to get Detective Kloots to let me fly to California, although I wasn't sure if he was more concerned about my safety or one of his suspects leaving the state. I had a new cell phone with my old number, so I assured him I would be reachable 24/7, and I wouldn't need police protection if I was thousands of miles away. Or at least those were my arguments, but I think it was Malcolm's support that helped me more than anything.

The officers on my protective detail drove me to the airport, but with all the debating, we were caught in rush hour traffic. I had intended to get there early and grab a bite in one of the coffee shops, but instead we moved at a snail's pace and listened to the radio, interspersed with hundreds of cars honking. It wouldn't be so bad if we had good music to listen to, but Officer Hill had it set on a news of the world program that mostly stuck to stocks and finance, which was an absolute bore.

"The artifact was taken from the exhibition in London. It is reported that this is the most expensive museum heist in history. Although most art is priceless, this object is made of solid gold and

covered in gemstones, the smallest of which would fetch half a million dollars if sold on its own."

"So, the item as a whole would be worth how much, approximately?"

"Usually, you say the artifact is priceless based on its historical value. If it was created by a renowned artist or if it's a cup that was once used by the first Queen Elizabeth, but in this case, it has very little historical significance, as far as we know. They've dated it to sometime around the fifth century BC, but archeologists are baffled as to what its use could have been. Even today, it is worth more broken down."

"The theft also made headlines because no one has any idea how the thieves managed it. There is no sign of forced entry, no disturbances...the museum's curator said it was like it just vanished from thin air."

It was radio, so it wasn't like I could see the object they were referring to, but if I had any money, I would bet on it being the gold artifact Grace and I looked at that contained something to get rid of monsters.

My first thought was that I was glad I was getting away from all of this, that I could leave it all behind and seek refuge in my family, maybe without even telling them what was going on until it was settled. But then my second, much scarier thought, was that if I was right and they were talking about that object, then the thieves had no problem smuggling it across an ocean from England. How far would they go to find me? If they organized the untraceable heist of a priceless artifact, surely, they could figure out where I had gone. It didn't make sense to me that they would leave no trace for the robbery and then make a mess of the precinct, but then again, stealing something might be easier than getting someone like Grace to talk.

The idea terrified me, but if I was right, there was no way I was going to lead them to my parents and my sister. I debated if I should tell my protective detail what we were up against, but I was being ridiculous, right? And it would probably seem like I was hiding something if I suddenly remembered that Grace asked me to check out a priceless artifact for her. It wasn't like I could play dumb and pretend I didn't know how valuable it was.

"Will my family be safe if I go to them?" I asked instead.

"You'll be in a different state, so that's not our jurisdiction," Officer Hill explained.

"I wasn't asking you to come protect me. I just want your opinion."

"It depends," he said after considering it. "If they're after you because you're working on something they don't want you to be, then yeah, removing yourself from the situation will neutralize the threat and you'll all be safe."

"But if they're after me because they think I know something…" I tried, not wanting to reveal too much. I didn't know anything useful, either about the artifact, or where it was. This could even be completely unrelated to that and be about the flashlight, or the vase…but I had a sinking feeling that I was leaving with things unfinished, and the last thing I wanted was for this danger, whatever it was, to follow me to California. To them.

"Then it all comes down to who is after you. It's possible they've already forgotten all about you…or they might find you no matter where you go." I could see he felt bad for saying something he knew would scare me, but I got the feeling he could have said a lot more.

"Your suggestion would be…

"If Detective Kloots offered me protective custody, I would take it and keep using it until he told me I was safe," he said with a shrug.

"Would it be terribly inconvenient if…"

"We would love to spend the night in your driveway," Officer Jones assured me as his partner got off at the next exit. I doubted the airline had 'someone wants to kidnap me' insurance, but it was a small price to pay for my family's safety. And while I trusted the cops to do their job, it would be hard for them to figure it out without all the information I wasn't telling them, which I still felt very strongly that I shouldn't.

I HADN'T TOLD my parents I would be coming, figuring I could avoid a lot of awkward questions if I just surprised them with the news that my internship was cancelled, so I didn't have to tell them I wasn't coming anymore. Officer Hill called Detective Kloots on the drive home, and although he had ultimately approved me leaving the state and implied it would be a good riddance, he sounded relieved that I'd changed my mind.

I wanted to call Tristan, but that would defeat the purpose of staying away from people I cared about to keep them safe.

Instead, I let the officers take me home, where I took out my old studying supplies; notebooks, post-its, a whiteboard, and markers. I started by writing down everything I knew about both incidents and attempted to draw what the golden artifact looked like. My artistic abilities left much to be desired, but it was more than enough for my purposes.

I wrote down all the possibilities I could think of as to what might have happened, including the possibility that Grace's stabbing and my attempted abduction were unfortunate yet completely unrelated events. That was the only one I felt confident crossing off. I didn't know what the odds were, but I didn't believe in that kind of coincidence.

Once I had all my theories laid out, as well as a list of things to investigate, I called Malcolm.

"I hear you changed your mind?"

"I heard something funny on the radio and didn't want to risk bringing all of this to my family," I said simply, though it was anything but. "Is anybody looking into the artifact Dr. Richards brought your mom?"

"I don't think they know about it."

"Don't you think they should? I mean, I trust Dr. Richards with my life, but do you know whoever gave it to him? Can we trust them?" I asked.

"A lot more than I trust a random guy I met on the subway," he snapped.

I was taken aback by his comment, and his tone, but reminded myself he was sleep-deprived, and Grace wasn't waking up like she was supposed to.

"Not that it's any of your business, but I ended things with him yesterday. He doesn't even know I'm still here."

"I'm sorry, I shouldn't have...that didn't come out right. Detective Kloots was concerned....and after Isaiah's —"

"What about Dr. Richards?"

"I had officers check in on him. From the outside it looked like he was just gone away for the summer, but I insisted they break in to make sure, and...we weren't the first ones to do so."

"Is he okay?"

"He wasn't there, but there was enough to make us consider him a missing person."

I brought my hand to my chest, trying to digest the information and not think about what might have happened to my surrogate grandfather.

"And Detective Kloots thinks it was Tristan?"

"No, but I can't blame him for being concerned about a guy who showed up at the precinct immediately after my mother was stabbed and waited outside until you came, then showed up at your house and wouldn't leave. He was also in the visitor's log a few days before—"

"He brought me soup because I told him I was sick. And he was outside the precinct because he dropped me off right before I found her, and I thought it might be an in and out thing."

"You asked him to wait?"

"No, but…didn't Officer Stevens look into him after he took down his info?" I let him know I knew why they asked.

"They did, and he was clean. But maybe too clean. Or maybe I'm exhausted and grasping at straws."

"Maybe," I agreed, deciding it would be best to move the conversation away from Tristan. "So, you're looking into the friend who gave Dr. Richards the artifact?"

"You sound like you want to interrogate them yourself?"

"More like Google. I'm 99% sure the artifact was recently stolen from a museum in London," I shared. "That's what I heard on the radio."

"Stolen? That's not—"

"Not at all like Dr. Richards, which makes me think he didn't know. I'm not judging whoever gave it to him, but if I'm lying to the cops, I want to be sure his *friend* isn't the one who broke into his place and attacked us."

Malcolm sighed, considering it, before a second, resigned sigh told me he agreed. "It's a professor at your school," he admitted.

"What department?" I asked.

"Archeology, I think. The last name is one of those girl's names, but my mom always called her Minnie."

Grace had mentioned Minnie before, but not with a last name. Then it hit me.

"Dr. Philomena Mallory?" I asked, convinced that couldn't be it.

"That sounds about right," Malcolm agreed. "She often brings things from her digs to Isaiah, and he'll get my mom to figure out what's inside," he explained.

"She told Dr. Richards she found the artifact on a dig?"

"I don't lynow. But she also has a lot of museum connections. If you say it was stolen, I would guess a colleague asked her for help without telling their boss, and someone noticed."

"You have that much faith in her?"

"I trust that she would never hurt my mom," he said with certainty, but the wording stuck with me.

"I guess I'll go back to the drawing board."

"How are you feeling?" he asked as an afterthought. "After the attempted kidnapping," he specified.

"I'm getting better. Although I won't be having ice cream for the foreseeable future." I tried, and failed, to make a joke to lighten the mood.

"They didn't tell you?" he asked.

"Tell me what?"

"Detective Kloots said your blood tests came back and there was nothing in it. Nothing in the ice cream either."

"It was an untraceable drug thing?" I'd heard about them on TV shows and hoped they were just plot devices.

"You weren't drugged."

"Maybe it was undetectable, but I definitely had something. I nearly passed out in his arms and couldn't see straight."

"I'm not arguing with what happened. I'm just telling you it wasn't drugs."

"Plants?" I tried.

"Not any of the ones we know about."

"Are you thinking—"

"I don't want to, but your symptoms lasted from the moment he spotted you to the moment he ran away, right?"

It was true. As soon as I got out of his arms, I wasn't light-headed anymore, and my limbs went back to normal almost immediately.

"Can you think of any Gifted who don't like your mom?" I asked.

"No, but I've heard stories."

"Of what?" I asked, but all I got was silence. "Aren't Gifted kept alive so they can do something to benefit humanity?"

"Ideally, but I think some of them do terrible things, too."

"Thanks for the heads up," I said, swallowing against my suddenly dry throat. I had a lot to learn.

IT WAS GETTING LATE, but I had a million thoughts running through my mind. Professor Mallory being Gifted raised a lot of questions, especially if Malcolm thought whoever tried to kidnap me was Gifted. None of the ones I knew could make someone feel the way I felt or fill out that sweatshirt. Whoever it was, they were a lot taller than me, and strong.

I closed my eyes and tried to remember details of the man who took me, but I couldn't. He'd been blurry, I was woozy, and I kept going back to Malcolm's comments about Tristan. I knew it wasn't him. I couldn't remember what my potential captor looked like, but I would have recognized Tristan's smile and his smell, like vanilla scented candles and Oil of Olay soap mixed with grass. It was an interesting combination, but I'd noticed it the first night on the couch. Maybe Malcolm was right that I didn't know a lot about Tristan, but for some reason, I trusted him. Just like Grace trusted Minnie. Only I was assuming they knew each other for longer than a couple of weeks.

Tristan had shown the appropriate amount of interest in my work when I talked about it, but he never asked for details. His questions were more about how I felt about things and what I wanted. Yes, he'd stopped by to visit without me inviting him, but that was swoon-worthy, not creepy. It wasn't like he suggested we eat the soup down there where he could search through our files. We probably would have given him the Grand Tour of our basement if he had.

I didn't know much about Tristan, especially not recent things, since we usually talked about his teenage years, but I knew in my gut that he wasn't the one who tried to take me. Not just because I didn't believe he would do something like that, but because every time I'd touched him, he had given me sparks and made me feel safe. That didn't sound like the type of person who wanted to hurt me. If he did, he would have had ample time to do whatever he wanted to me while I literally slept in his arms. I thought of maybe calling Malcolm to point that out, but I felt just as awkward telling him about the boy I let into the house as I would my father. Plus, none of it mattered now that I sent him away.

Tristan kept messaging me to see if I was okay. I stuck to one-word replies so I wouldn't lead him on or give him the wrong impression, but it was nearly impossible to fall asleep without him.

CHAPTER THIRTY-SIX

The following morning, I woke up with a Game Plan, so I texted Sybill and asked if she could go somewhere she wouldn't be overheard. She called me back almost immediately.

"I'm hiding in a closet surrounded by hotel robes. What is going on?" Her voice was muffled, but I could hear her curiosity and excitement.

"Do you think you would be able to use your laptop without Mom and Dad noticing?"

"Is this a porn thing?"

"No, of course not. It's more of an illegal hacking thing." I wasn't sure which was worse, but she did frequently offer to put her skills to good use.

"I'm not looking into Tristan so you can find an excuse to get rid of him instead of finally being happy."

I winced, painfully aware that I had already found an excuse and lost him for it.

"Glad to hear what you really think of me, but this doesn't have anything to do with Tristan."

"That makes it a lot less interesting," she warned.

"It's for a case. I don't want to go to my superiors without anything concrete, but I have some theories."

"Hacking into police records for security checks is one thing, but case files…"

"It's only one case file. And some hospital records. Maybe a bit of security footage."

"Hospital records?" She liked that even less.

"On the victim. Graciela Goncalves," I agreed.

"What about her?"

"Anything and everything they have. Even if it's just a note a nurse made after they took care of her, something she said in her sleep…"

"What's your theory? It might help if I know what I'm looking for."

"Well, my mentor thinks that if you go in with a theory, you'll find things to confirm it rather than looking for the truth."

"But you have a theory? Or you're hoping I'll find something that gives you one?"

"Both." I smiled. It was easier to pretend that she caught me than to admit that it was my mentor who got stabbed in a precinct surrounded by cops. She would realize Graciela was Grace as soon as she looked into it, but I needed her to grill me after she found the information and got invested, rather than now, when she would probably convince me to give up on it and go into hiding.

"And what's the case file?"

"I'll send you everything I need you to look into."

"We convinced Dad to go golfing today, and I'm sure I can get Mom to go shopping or something if I tell her I'm hanging out with Damian. He might be useful." I could hear the smile in her voice when she mentioned him.

"But Syb, you have to be careful. Cover your tracks so no one knows you got in." She'd tried explaining to me how it all works once. I'd listened intently and tried to follow, like she did when I talked about Archeology, but I didn't understand half of the things she said.

"Of course. We're not amateurs."

"And I need you to promise you won't tell a soul. Not Mom and Dad, not anyone else, about anything you find."

"I definitely don't want Mom and Dad finding out."

"Syb, I need you to promise."

"I promise."

I let out a sigh of relief. They were just words, but she would never go back now that she'd said them. "You're the best."

"And don't forget it."

THE LIST I sent her had Grace's hospital records on it, but also both of our case files, Dr. Richards' missing person report, who accessed our report logs, security footage from the precinct, Professor Mallory…anything and everything.

IT TOOK Sybill an hour to get rid of our parents, but the second she opened the case file, she video-called me, fuming.

"This is why you sound so weird when you call, and always have to run off before we can talk about anything?"

"We talk about you," I reminded her.

"What the hell is going on?" She was more upset than I had ever seen her, even worse than the outbursts that brought us to the shrink's office.

I tried to tell her as much as I could without freaking her out, but she would find out more than I did from the case files. I tried to be incredibly reassuring about my police protection, but she wasn't buying it.

"We have to tell Mom and Dad. You need to come here, or we need to go home, and—"

"No, Syb, this trial is finally working for you, and I don't want anyone else to be in danger because of this. Plus, you promised."

"I hate you."

"I know, but it's a mystery to solve and the faster we figure it out, the sooner the nightmare will be over."

"And you'll come here?"

"There's nowhere else I'd rather be."

"We're on it," she said reluctantly.

SYB SPENT the rest of the day calling me with whatever information they found that might be useful, but every time, she sounded more scared for me. Thankfully, the anger she'd started off with built up until she finally decided she was more worried than angry and developed a determined resignation that made her incredibly efficient.

It made me smile when I saw the way Damian looked at her when she talked to me, but the footage and photographs she sent me crushed it immediately.

The girl who'd stopped us for a picture after the basketball game had been hanging around the precinct for at least fifteen minutes before we got to the fountain, like she was waiting for someone. Syb used facial recognition software to find out who she was.

"I think it's broken. It says her name is Mai-Ling Cao, but she died almost a year ago."

"I'll ask Detective Cortez if he recognizes her," I assured them, but cold shivers ran down my spine. While they assumed there was an issue with the technology and its markers for Asian features, I assumed this meant she was Gifted. She was way too tiny to be the one who tried to kidnap me, but she could easily have been in on it.

. . .

Everything else came back clean except for Dr. Richards' office. Sybill sent me the crime scene photos, and his filing cabinet had been rifled through, picture frames were smashed, and there was a huge pile of sand or ash in the middle of the floor, probably from an urn. My only comfort was that there wasn't a single trace of blood or bleach. I was still hoping he was off on a phone-free vacation.

I looked at all my files and felt like such a silly child, running around like I could solve the case before the cops did. In truth, I had way more questions than answers. This was one of the very many reasons why I did not want to be a detective. I also really didn't like people trying to kill me. Or guns. I liked helping people, but that was where the similarities ended.

I kept going back to the drawing board, making lists and trying to find connections. Did Grace know her attacker? Did I know mine?

My thoughts were interrupted by my phone ringing for the dozenth time today, Tristan's face appearing on my screen. I alternated between pressing ignore and letting it ring. I had told myself I wouldn't listen to his messages, but that lasted until about two minutes after he left the first one. Tristan was safer if he stayed away from me. Sure, I would feel better with him here, but I would never forgive myself if anything happened to him. And, as much as I hated it with every fiber of my being, there was the tiniest part of me that couldn't let go of what Malcolm said. Tristan had shown up out of nowhere with no real past and didn't volunteer much about his present either. I reminded myself it was because I didn't ask, but in the scheme of things, I was probably more trouble than I was worth. Him sticking around, even after I sent him away, was curious to say the least. And I'd been so grateful when he was there outside the precinct that I hadn't considered how weird it was. How long would he have waited for me to come out? And what lie would he have told to justify it? Or would the truth have been enough? Then, that scary voice in my head said that maybe he wouldn't have told me anything at all. Maybe he was just going to follow me home and...

I shook my head as the phone stopped ringing, which meant the answering machine picked up and I would have another message to listen to. I trusted Tristan. He was literally the only good thing I had going on right now, even though I'd sabotaged it. I wasn't sure of much these days, but my heart would break if Tristan was behind any of it.

CHAPTER THIRTY-SEVEN

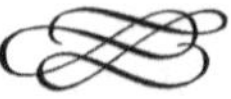

I wasn't sure how much I was allowed to go out with my protective detail, so my trips outside mostly consisted of bringing them food and coffee.

Eventually, I convinced them to let me spend a few hours at the hospital, checking in on Grace. Officer Jones came with me under the guise of keeping me safe, but he did take the time to give Grace's hand a squeeze and tell her they were all pulling for her. He gave me a look when Malcolm and Enrique both greeted me with hugs, but then Enrique hugged him as well. Hopefully he chalked it up to a Latin thing, not that I knew what we were hiding anymore.

Suzie came over after work, and it looked like she and Malcolm had finally owned up to their feelings. Luckily, she knew Officer Jones, so I finally got the chance to ask Malcolm about my investigation while they caught up in the hallway.

"This girl was outside the precinct on the night your mom was attacked. I looked into her, and all I found was a death certificate." I showed him the picture Sybill sent me. It was from a security camera, but Damian photoshopped it to look like it could have been from a social media account. Enrique pretended he couldn't care less about the cop side of things, but he stood by the door to keep watch, and leaned over Malcolm's shoulder to see the picture. I knew Tristan looked nothing like that basketball player.

"She's not Gifted," Malcolm shot me down. "Or at least I don't think she is."

"Time traveler?" It was sarcastic, but I didn't see how else we talked to a dead girl.

"Twins," he corrected me. "We looked into her at the time of her sister's death, but we couldn't find anything to suggest it wasn't just a car accident. Poor girl looked like she would rather we send her to the electric chair than make her live with her survivor's guilt."

"I can't imagine…" I brought my hand to my chest, feeling it break in solidarity.

"You say she was at the precinct?" he asked, bringing it back to the investigation.

"We saw her at the fountain across the street."

"That's a pretty wide net…how did you find her?"

"She talked to us that night. About the game. We were also wearing jerseys," I explained, but he wanted me to explain the photograph, and I was not going to give up my sister. "I can't sit at home, alone, waiting for someone to possibly come after me."

"I'm not judging; I just don't want you to put a target on your back, or get hurt in the process."

"The target is already there. I'm just trying to figure out who put it."

"Be careful." It was as close to him giving me permission as I was going to get.

"Just out of curiosity, do you know what Professor Mallory's Gift is?" I asked, careful not to sound like I suspected her.

"Not knocking people unconscious." He was confident in her innocence, but I got the impression he didn't know what she was capable of.

. . .

SUZIE CAME in with Officer Jones, so we were going to head out, but the doctor came in right after them.

"Dr. Black?" I was surprised, but also happy to see him. He was our surgical consult when I brought Sybill into the ER a few years ago, and he knew more about medicine than any doctor I'd met before. He couldn't figure out what was wrong with Sybill, no matter how hard he tried, but he fixed all her symptoms at the time. Definitely one of my favorites.

"Miss Carmichael." He smiled, checking his chart to make sure he was in the right room.

"I'm visiting a friend," I assured him, but I saw Enrique's eyebrows go up. He didn't know as much about Tristan as Malcolm did, so he frequently tried to set me up with the doctors and nurses he met while waiting in line for coffee. Sybill often referred to Dr. Black as Dr. McDreamy, but I had it on good authority that he was madly in love with his girlfriend, who was also a doctor. Or was studying to be one, but Mom raved about her when she was doing her neo-natal rotation.

"How is Sybill? Is the millionth time the charm?"

"It seems to be. She's going to Disney and having a lot of fun."

"I'm glad to hear it," he told me before turning to Malcolm.

"You must be Mr. Goncalves?" he asked.

"Detective Cortez," he corrected, extending his hand for Dr. Black to shake.

"My apologies, I thought I saw a resemblance."

I tried to hide my smile that the doctor thought Malcolm was Grace's father, but he caught me and pretended to be offended before smiling as well.

"I'm her partner, Enrique Castile."

"Pleasure to meet you." Dr. Black cleared his throat. "I'm sure you've been told that we expected her to be awake by now, but that isn't a reason to be concerned yet. Bodies heal at different rates, and I am sure she will wake up when she is ready." He looked to the empty doorway, then back to the guys. Even though they made it seem like Enrique was next of kin and Malcolm was just working a case, Dr. Black sensed that wasn't the whole story and talked to them both. "That being said, we would like to run some tests this evening and see what's going on."

"Of course, whatever you think is best," Enrique told him.

"Do you think this will help her?" Malcolm asked.

"It's just a few tests, but I hope it might."

I would have stayed all night to find out what happened, but Officer Jones looked at me and nodded to the door.

"I'll call you the minute anything changes," Malcolm assured me.

I gave them hugs before following Officer Jones out, nearly bumping into a nurse I didn't know with raven hair and dark eyes like Tristan. On paper I feel like she would seem creepy, like Morticia Adams, but she was beautiful, and those dark eyes looked kind.

"Yes, Nurse Etta, come on in," Dr. Black called her over, so I gave her a smile and moved to the side so she could go in.

"I TAKE it you spend a lot of time here?" Officer Jones asked me while we drove home with Officer Hill.

"You have no idea," I agreed.

"Grace is tough. She'll be out of there in no time," he told me, more to fill the silence than because it was true.

I nodded and spent the rest of the ride looking out the window while they talked about what they were going to do with their night off.

. . .

ONCE HOME, I made a pasta dish and brought two portions out to my replacement detail, then settled in for the evening. I was going over everything I had when my phone buzzed with a video call from Sybill.

"What's up?" I asked, as cheery as I could be in case this was a group call with our parents.

"I looked." There were tear tracks on her cheeks, and her eyes were red and puffy. "I knew I shouldn't, but we were looking at everything else, so I figured why not, but…"

"What are you talking about, sweetie?" If she'd called on the home phone, I would have used my cell to text my mom, but I didn't want to leave Sybill.

"The trial was double blind, but we were looking into hospital stuff for you, so…"

Double-blind trials were when some participants were given the actual drug while others were given a placebo, but neither the doctors nor the participants knew which were which. It prevented biases and people improving just because their brain thought they should be, but it also meant you could spend weeks or months taking sugar pills without any chance of getting better.

"I'm in the placebo group."

"That's great, Syb."

"No, that means I'm imagining that I'm getting better, but once my body realizes I'm not getting any medication, I'll be right back where I started."

"Maybe it's something else that's making you better, and the warm weather kicked your immune system into high gear, or—"

"Maybe," she cut me off.

"I'm so sorry," I told her.

"Don't be." She sighed and wiped away the tears she wouldn't be able to explain to our parents. "At least I got a summer."

"And it's not over yet," I reminded her.

"When are you coming?"

"Soon." I hoped I wasn't lying.

"Did any of it help?"

"I'm still trying to figure that out."

"I looked into Dr. Richards' credit cards and passport. None of them have been used."

"He might be staying with a friend somewhere. He mentioned something about Greece."

"Maybe."

"Are you okay?"

"I will be," she assured me.

"I love you. And I miss you."

"Miss you too," she told me before we hung up, leaving my heart even more torn than before.

CHAPTER THIRTY-EIGHT

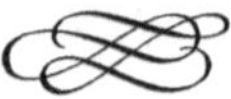

I woke up to my phone ringing. I was annoyed that Tristan would call me this early, but when I went to ignore his call, I saw it was Malcolm.

"Hello?" I tried to sound like I wasn't still sleeping.

"I'm sorry to bother you so early in the morning. God, I thought it was later."

"Don't worry about it. What's up?"

"She's awake," he shared. I could hear the smile of unbridled joy.

"Like awake awake?" Sybill had surgery once and they said she was awake, as in she'd woken up from the anesthetic, but she still slept for the rest of the day.

"After I brought her some water, she asked Enrique and I why we weren't at work. The doctors are with her now."

"Thank God," I said, his enthusiasm taking over me. She was awake, her brain seemed to be okay, and she recognized them.

"I don't expect you to come now. I don't think visiting hours even start until nine, but I knew you would want to know."

"I'm really happy you did."

"The doctor wants Detective Kloots to let her rest, but he'll be here to get her statement as soon as he's allowed. Then we can hopefully put this mess behind us."

"That sounds so good."

"You can go back to sleep. I'll call if there's more news, or you can check in when you wake up," he offered.

I hung up and considered going back to bed, but there was no way I would be able to sleep now. I got up and made coffee, as well as some turnovers. Grace probably wasn't allowed to eat yet, but Malcolm and Enrique would appreciate it.

I put the rest of the coffee in a thermos and went to get my bike. I had everything packed so it wouldn't be a problem for me, but I was aware that it would seem like I was trying to get away from my protective detail if I lost them on the subway platform.

"Morning," I said after banging on the window, offering them the thermos and the extra turnovers. I used the cherry flavored Pillsbury ones and added cheese because it made them seem healthier and more like a breakfast food, if that made any sense.

"Everything okay?" The sun was up by now, but it was still very early to be awake.

"I was going to head to the hospital, which involves biking to the station and taking the subway. Are you good to follow or…"

"Or we could drive you," Officer Hill finished for me.

"I feel like I'm using you as a taxi service."

"I doubt we'll stay on you much longer, but you might as well enjoy it while you can," he assured me.

"I appreciate it," I told him, getting into the back seat. They listened to the radio, switching between pop stations whenever it got to talking, except when their scanner would go off. I assumed they would abandon me if there was a big incident close by or if no one else responded to something, but they barely even reacted to the codes being reported. As a civilian, I didn't know many, but every time I heard one I recognized, I shivered, because it was either a murder, a kidnapping, or a rape, some dangerous crime that warranted all the evidence being saved for decades.

"Tell her we're all thinking of her, and the basement is a miserable mess without you two," Officer Jones said with an encouraging smile.

"I TOLD you not to come right away," Malcolm reproached when I handed him the turnovers. Grace's bed was empty. "They're doing a scan. Enrique went with her."

"Did they do something after the tests last night?"

"No, the nurse brought her back and said Dr. Black would find us with the results in the morning. When I woke up around three this morning, my mom asked me for a glass of water, and I nearly had a heart attack."

Enrique came in, followed by a nurse wheeling a gurney. An orderly helped her get Grace into the bed, then they exited the room, leaving me staring at Grace. I didn't know why I expected her to look like herself so quickly. I had more than enough experience with lengthy recoveries, sharing a hospital bed because Sybill was skin and bones and couldn't keep herself warm. I shuddered at the memory.

"She looks better when she's awake," Enrique assured me before taking me in for a hug. The smile was not leaving his face, and I could practically see the relief all over it.

"I heard that." I nearly jumped out of my skin when I heard Grace's voice. Her eyes were still closed, but she adjusted her position like when you're super comfy in bed and didn't want to wake up just yet.

"You're awake," I said, not expecting the rush of emotions I felt. I bit the inside of my cheek to stop myself from crying like a weirdo.

"Barely," she argued. "Why are you in this boring room instead of playing hooky with Tristan?"

"I brought turnovers," I said, not sure how to respond.

"Where was your baking before I got stabbed?" She tried to get us to smile, but it was too soon.

"Are you allowed to eat?"

"Not fun stuff," she argued, nodding to the bag that fed her the nutrients she needed while she was in her coma.

"Do you remember what happened?" I asked cautiously.

"Malcolm said you have a protective detail?"

"I do," I agreed. "But that doesn't answer—"

"Stay with them," she warned me. "Stay with them in as public places as you can."

"Who was it?"

"I don't know. I never saw their faces, but they were Gifted."

"What were their Gifts?"

"I grabbed a mop from the supply closet. It was a stupid idea, but I thought I could...I don't know... he turned it to sand."

"The mop?" I asked.

"He could have turned me into sand, too. He told me he would. I don't know what stopped him, but the other one stabbed me instead."

I looked to Malcolm to see if this was news to him, but he just looked apologetic that he hadn't warned me beforehand.

"I just had one man. He didn't turn me to sand, but I felt so weak," I shared. "You think they'll come after me again?"

"They had questions about the artifact. When I couldn't answer them, they realized I wasn't the one who had the memory."

"They knew it was me?" I asked.

"They had your name, but I didn't tell them anything, I swear. I said it was me. I tried to repeat everything you told me and everything you wrote down, but they kept asking if she was wearing a necklace, and I couldn't remember."

"I can't either." I tried to think back, but that night with the artifact felt like months ago. "I didn't see the woman because it was her feelings, and his power was focused on the gold, but... maybe?" I guessed.

"You can't say those things, Allie. You can't ever admit to any of it. You can't trust them."

"Who are they?" I pressed.

"You can't tell them what you saw, and you can't tell them what you are."

"Gifted?" I asked, at the same time as Malcolm.

"The other thing. I asked Isaiah if he knew, but—Isaiah." She stopped herself and looked at us, her eyes wide with terror. "Have you seen him? They said they went to him first, but he wasn't helpful, so they...I have to talk to him. I have to make sure..." She was so insistent that I didn't even notice the machines beeping until a nurse pushed me out of the room while two others tried to calm Grace down. "I need to find him. He won't come back, so I need to make sure..." She kept trying to get out of bed while they held her down.

"There are no visitors allowed right now, and that woman needs her rest," the oldest and sternest of them reproached Malcolm and I after he ushered us out of the room, all the way to the elevators. Malcolm was dressed like a detective, and a woman could only have so many sexy uncles waiting by her bedside.

"What happened in there?" I asked Malcolm once we were on our way to the ground floor. I wanted nothing more than to go back up. Every bit of relief I'd felt at seeing her awake was completely replaced by the image of her being held down while she screamed frantically. It made me shudder all over.

"I don't know, but she's right. Until whoever did this is caught, you need to be with your protective detail at all times." I expected him to look afraid, but he looked guilty, like he was hiding something bad from me.

"You think Dr. Richards..." I tried to give the impression that I could handle it, but all I could think of was that pile of sand in the photos of his office.

He hesitated, then said, "There was a pile of sand on the floor in his office. We assumed it was from a timer or a bag he brought on a dig, or..." he stopped, because we both knew where the sand came from. "I'll have Kloots post officers inside your house as well," he decided.

"Even if the people after me are Gifted?"

"Especially if they're Gifted."

"But the cops aren't," I pointed out.

"They have vests and guns. You have neither," he reminded me. "And don't let any strangers get close enough to touch you."

"I wasn't planning on it," I assured him.

"Take care of yourself Allie," he said, adding weight to it, before doubling back to another entrance.

CHAPTER THIRTY-NINE

Officers Hill and Jones didn't ask too many questions once I got to them, not after their first were met with shrugs and one-worded answers. I let them know Grace really was awake and seemed to be doing okay, but I didn't have answers for anything else they asked. I still didn't know who attacked her, or me.

"Detective Cortez said he was going to send more people, so you'll be able to hang out inside from now on," I said as we walked to their car, trying to sound optimistic. I didn't like the reason behind his decision, but I was glad I wouldn't have to be alone.

"You'll probably get senior officers inside, but you can come out and have a chat to make sure we're still there whenever you want." Jones misread the why, but knew there was something wrong.

"I was thinking grilled cheese for lunch. Maybe with some bacon bits?" I suggested.

"I wouldn't say no." He gave me a warm smile, which I tried to return.

. . .

By the time we got to my house, the other squad car was waiting. We were walking over when Officer Hill stopped and motioned for Jones to stay with me while he went to greet the new members of my team. I was about to ask what was going on when I felt him. Or at least, my heart beat faster, so I looked up and saw Tristan walking toward us.

"What are you doing here?" I asked him.

"I heard you were still in town."

"You shouldn't be here."

"I don't scare that easily."

"I do." Even as I said the words, I knew that I didn't want him to leave.

"I know you're afraid, and that makes perfect sense, but if they think you're safe here, then I'm sure I'll be safe here with you. And I've told you, I can take care of myself."

"I don't want you getting hurt."

"Then let me be with you." He attempted a smile.

I could see Jones was ready to remove him if I asked, and Hill kept glancing over, but I noticed neither of them had their hands on their guns this time.

I looked over as if they could help me make the decision, so Jones said, "He's no longer on our list of suspects."

I looked from him to Tristan, wondering what changed. "I spent a few hours in interrogation. And was at the hospital when they came after you."

"Are you hurt?" I asked, looking for an obvious wound. I had to physically stop myself from checking to make sure he was okay.

"No, I just…check in on the chemo kids sometimes."

"Like you talk to them, or…in costume?"

"Whatever helps," he agreed.

"That's what you do when you're not with me?" I asked, before realizing how it sounded.

"Among other things. It means a lot to some of them."

The prospect of falling asleep in his arms tonight made my heart sing, but I'd just found out the threat on my life was way scarier, and nobody was safe.

"How are you?" Tristan asked instead of trying to come inside. Officer Hill went into the house with one of the new officers while the other talked with Officer Jones, who pretended he wasn't listening in on our conversation.

"Grace is awake, so that's a relief."

"I heard. That's great news," he told me. "But I asked about you."

"I'm okay."

He raised his eyebrows and gave me a sideways glance.

"Given the circumstances," I amended. "I can't believe Detective Kloots told you Grace was awake. And that I was still here."

"My friends at the hospital have been letting me know how Grace was doing. In a general way, not breaking confidentiality," he assured me as an afterthought, although anything they told him about a patient would have been confidential.

"That makes more sense. I don't even think Kloots trusts me half the time."

"It was Detective Cortez. He ran my whole interrogation. I don't have any experience being questioned by the cops, but it definitely felt weird."

"Weird how?"

"Like he was just as curious about whether I stabbed a woman as whether I had any intentions of hurting you. I felt like I was with your sister again."

"Do you?" I asked instead of addressing Malcolm's overprotectiveness.

"Never." He added way more weight to it than I was expecting, with not even a hint of teasing.

I took a breath, about to tell him things were more complicated now, but I realized I couldn't hear Officer Jones anymore. I looked away from Tristan and tried to find him, dread already building inside my chest because I knew they wouldn't leave me unprotected. Tristan turned around to look at the house as well, putting his arm out to stop me right before I saw the blood and froze. Our front door was black, but the trim was white, and there was a very obvious handprint, along with a crumpled form on the welcome mat.

Three men barged through the door, all dressed in hoodies and wearing sunglasses. The one in the front held a knife. I couldn't be sure because of his dark clothing, but it looked like he was covered in blood.

"Get in my car," Tristan told me, full of authority. It took me a minute to see his red sedan parked in front of my neighbor's. I wanted to run toward the house and try to help, not that I would be much use, but Tristan shot me a look that told me not to argue.

I ran as fast as my legs would carry me, reaching the passenger side door in what felt like an instant, but also a century. I heard what sounded like lightning striking an electrical box, but when I looked back, the sky was blue and clear. One of the hooded figures was on the ground, but the other two kept coming, completely unfazed.

"Get in!" Tristan urged me, rushing to the driver's side.

I barely had time to shut my door before we were moving. I felt dizzy, just like last time the hooded man was near. Tristan shook violently, like someone trying to fight off exhaustion, but he kept driving away at full speed and eventually, we must have gotten far enough away that their powers didn't work. It was a relief to know there was a limit to Gifted powers, but it was a tiny consolation after what we'd just seen.

CHAPTER FORTY

We both stayed quiet as I tried to regulate my breathing and Tristan concentrated on the road. I tried to process everything that had just happened, but it felt like I was in a nightmare and needed to wake up. I pinched myself, but while it didn't wake me up, I barely even felt it through all the numbness.

"Are you okay?" I asked Tristan, my heart still pounding in my chest.

"I'm fine. How are you? Did they get you?" he asked, switching between the road and me, full of concern.

"I'm good," I assured him. "Where are we going?"

"I'm bringing you as far away from them as possible. The friends I was staying with can keep you safe while we figure it out."

"What kind of friends?" I asked, recognizing the tightness in my chest as fear.

"The kind who are used to helping people in need when they can't necessarily go to the police." My heart broke when my brain was able to process the fact that Hill and Jones were gone, and it was entirely my fault. Grace had said to be out in public, but I thought she meant to avoid dark alleys and secret meetings. Not that my house wasn't safe.

I looked at Tristan, wondering how he knew that we shouldn't go to the cops and whether he'd realized that the dizziness was caused by one of the hooded figures back at my house. "I need to call Malcolm," I decided. "Detective Cortez."

I wasn't sure how Detective Kloots would react to me losing my protective detail and running off with someone who was one of his prime suspects until this morning, but Malcolm would hear about it and be worried. Part of me also wanted to know what Tristan said to convince Malcolm to trust him. Most of me did, but part of me was very concerned by how well he was taking this.

"I must have dropped my cell phone, but you can use the phone when we get to the plantation." I could tell there was more, that he was arguing with himself over whether he should say it. "You shouldn't tell him where we are."

"Are you kidnapping me?" I tried to make it sound like a joke, but our teasing banter worked better a couple of stabbings ago.

"I'm not trying to keep things from you or to keep you from the people you feel safe with. I'm trying to protect the friends I'm hoping will help us. If you'd rather, I can bring you to the police or drive off in the distance and never look back, but I think this might be our best bet."

"Never look back?" I asked. At first it was because he was implying that he would leave his life behind to go on the run with me, but then I realized that would mean my life and my family as well.

"Until it's safe," he specified. "I don't plan on spending the rest of my life on the run, and I don't think you should either."

"What is your plan? Hide out there, get fake identities and black-market weapons, rage a war, and come home once we've won?" I was still trying to be light and teasing, to make myself feel better, but I also had no idea what he was planning.

"How much of that is a serious question?" he asked, turning to face me. He had a confused smile that made me think we might get through this, which was silly, but I'd missed his smile.

"Fifty percent?"

"I can work with that." He shook his head, but the smile grew.

"I think a normal person would have panicked and ditched me a while ago," I pointed out.

"That would have been the smart thing to do," he agreed. "But I barely graduated high school, so…" He shrugged with a smile.

"I'm serious," I told him, although I'm pretty sure I was smiling as well.

"I told you, Allie, I'm not going anywhere."

"Why?" I asked. "Nothing to do with my own self-confidence, but I have to question your sanity or at least your sense of self-preservation."

He looked over to me, considering it, and said, "Death doesn't scare me. I resigned myself to it a long time ago. And it feels like everything is changing and falling apart these days, but being with you…I start to believe that maybe I'll be okay."

"You've noticed the scary men chasing us and trying to kill me?" My heart was pounding with fear, but also something else.

"I'm much more afraid of something happening to you than anything happening to me."

"Beating cancer doesn't make you superman," I warned.

"Oh, I'm terrified and nothing like superman. But I know what matters, and I'm not going anywhere," he said again, taking my hand when we got to a red light.

I knew this wasn't the time for it, but I was afraid and shaking and I wanted him to take me in his arms, so when he looked down at my lips, I took it as an invitation to lean forward. He brought his hand to the back of my head and pulled me close in a kiss, tentatively at first, but then I felt fireworks, electricity, and magic.

We pulled apart when the car behind us honked to say the light was green. I wasn't ready to tell him about the Gifted thing and scare him off, but I wanted him to know what we were up against.

"There's something I need to tell you," I told him after taking a deep breath.

"Do you mind if I go first?" He looked guilty, which worried me.

"Are you secretly married?" I tried to lighten the mood, but my heart was pounding in my chest. I couldn't handle a heartbreak on top of everything else right now.

"No, nothing like that." His laugh was easy, if a little relieved, but he still looked nervous. "I wouldn't add it to your plate on top of everything, but once I bring you in, you'll find out. I'd rather tell you about it myself so I can try to answer any questions you might have or will have because there will definitely be questions."

"Is this a cult?" I asked. Part of me cursed my habit of babbling nonsense when I was nervous, but I also really needed to not be let down again, so I didn't mind delaying the inevitable.

"I hope not," he said like he was considering it. "I mean, Jaz is usually a part of a commune, which is like a cult. But they don't have the whole messiah leader who's married to everyone. They're all free to come and go as they please."

I looked at him and realized that he was nervous too, but his heart was in the right place, and I trusted him. I didn't know if my interruptions were helping or making it worse, but I decided to stop and let him speak.

"When I was seventeen, my cancer got really bad. They

wanted to amputate my leg as a last-ditch effort to save me, but before they could do the surgery—"

I'd heard the story before, but I was going to listen patiently until I felt dizzy. Tristan clearly felt the same and had to swerve to avoid a pedestrian when he woke himself up. His car smashed into a stop sign and wouldn't listen when he put it in reverse.

He gave me a look like he wanted me to stay inside, or maybe run away to safety, but I could not forgive myself for leaving him behind. Not that I had weapons or anything that could help us get away.

"Tristan, don't!" I warned when he put his hand on the door handle.

"It's okay," he assured me.

He got out of the car and got into a fighting stance he must have seen in a movie or a video game because his hands were wide open instead of being in fists. I got out of the car as well and watched as he swung, nowhere near making contact.

Two of the men in hoodies were in the distance, and one of them had an arm pointed toward each of us, making me feel like I was about to pass out. Tristan was concentrating with all his might on some kind of wushu where he waved his arms in great circles and pointed his hands at the men. Whatever he was trying to do wasn't working.

"Allie, run," he told me. There was a pleading in his voice, but I wasn't rooted to the spot by choice. I'd tried many times to get to him, but my legs refused to move.

I was going to reply, as I made another effort to run to him, managing to throw off my balance and land against the car rather than falling flat on my face, but before I had the chance to try again, the second hooded man walked up to Tristan.

"We just want the First Lifer," he told him. "You're free to go."

Tristan looked over to me, shocked, but before he could say

anything, the man attacked him. Since the wushu stuff wasn't working, Tristan made actual fists and fought him like that.

I didn't know much about martial arts, but it looked like Tristan did. Every time his fist made contact with the hooded figure, he doubled over or spat blood until he finally managed to block one with his bare hand on Tristan's forearm. Tristan froze, making me think the hooded man might have been holding a knife or a syringe with a toxin, but then he used Tristan's distraction to reach up for his cheek.

Before he could make contact, Tristan pushed him off, onto the car. It was weird. One minute the figure leaned against the car, but the next, the car disintegrated into a cloud of dust, and the man stumbled, catching himself just in time. I'd heard Grace describe it, and I saw the sand on Dr. Richards' floor, but nothing prepared me to actually witness it. I blinked, as if that would somehow make the car reappear, but all I saw was the hooded man and a pile of sand.

I was so focused on the car that I didn't notice the other hooded figure had come closer until he twisted his fist in a way that made Tristan keel over and fall to the ground.

"I had him," the one who had been fighting Tristan growled.

"So did I," the other replied with a heavy accent.

I ignored them and ran to Tristan's side. I tried to wake him up, but I couldn't feel a pulse. I started doing compressions, holding off my meltdown as the man who turned things to sand walked toward me. From up close, I could see his face. I was shocked when I recognized Logan, Professor Mallory's teaching assistant.

"We've been looking for you," he told me, reaching his hand forward. I expected to vanish like the car, but instead of killing me, he scooped me up into his arms. Then the world went dark.

CHAPTER FORTY-ONE

I woke up in a car driving on an abandoned highway in the middle of the night. Nothing looked familiar, and there were no businesses or road signs to locate myself.

"And she's awake," Logan said, looking back at me from the rearview mirror.

My hands were bound together by zip ties, as were my feet. I tried to move around but someone had fiddled with the seatbelt, so it was constantly in that restrictive setting it goes into when you try to make a sudden movement.

"If you're uncomfortable being bound, Kazimir can lower your heart rate and make you weak again. We're just not sure what the long-term effects would be, or if he can sustain it without killing you."

"Where are you taking me?" I asked.

"What fun would it be if I told you?" he countered. He still looked like the cute and helpful TA he'd been the night of the get-together, but I could see there was a darkness behind those eyes. In fact, they were completely black.

"I don't have the artifact. That's what you're after, right?"

"Oh, sweetheart, it's delightful that you've been trying to

piece it all together, but you're out of your depths here." At the party, he'd sounded like an average college student, maybe a couple of years older than me, but now, behind the taunting and sarcasm, he had the airs of someone much older talking down to a child.

"Care to enlighten me?" I suggested.

"We know you don't have the artifact. But what you do have is much more valuable." He didn't sound like he was joking, but I had an idea of what the artifact should be worth, and my life didn't compare. "I'm guessing someone saw your Gift and told you all about the Gifted. How wonderful it was that you found your community. You probably bonded with Dr. Goncalves over your need to protect people and keep them safe." He spoke like those ideals were childish and immature, but his next words chilled me to the bone. "How shocked were you when you found out that all the other Gifted were dead?"

"I don't know what you're talking about," I argued. It was too late to deny any of it, but I wasn't going to be like those criminals on TV who reveal their entire master plan and give away everything. Not that I had a master plan, other than to keep him talking and explaining things until someone came looking and found me. I fought back tears when Tristan was the first person I thought of. Then I remembered Jones and Hill back at my house and wasn't so sure I wanted anyone to find me. I bit the inside of my cheek so I wouldn't give them the satisfaction of seeing me cry.

"I'm sorry. I don't mean to come off as cruel. It was not our intention to hurt anyone, just like we don't want to hurt you now." If they wanted to make sure I wouldn't believe a word they said, this was the way to do it.

"How do you unintentionally stab a woman multiple times in the stomach? Or kill a sweet, innocent old man?" I clenched my teeth, willing myself not to cry.

"Hey, Dr. Richards was my friend, too. It wasn't my fault he wouldn't give you up and tried to stop me from touching his things. And Grace...well, we needed a sample of her blood. And to make sure she couldn't tell anyone what we were doing. But Ted got carried away. He's a bit of a loose cannon if I'm honest, but your boyfriend—"

"What do you want from me?" I cut him off. I had no interest in reliving Tristan's death.

"Your Gift," he said simply. "I've been around quite some time, and you're the only First Lifer I've ever seen who has it."

"First Lifer?" I asked. It was also what Grace had called me, but if he could give me more information, I was going to take it.

"Unless you died since we looked into you, you're a rare breed of Gifted who was brought back to life before you truly died. Your Gift was activated, but you never fully transitioned."

"Why do you care? I can relive traumatic memories. It's not going to further your agenda," I said without any knowledge of what his agenda might be. All I knew was that when Grace realized I was a First Lifer, she told me to keep it to myself.

"I knew you didn't know," Logan gloated. "My friend here was terrified of snatching you because we didn't know if you could use it once you took it, but based on our conversation with Grace, I had an inkling you had no idea."

"Use what?" I knew I was playing right into his plan, especially the way his smile got big when I asked the right question. But if there was something about me that scared a man twice my size—who could stop my heart without laying a hand on me—then I wanted to know about it.

"You suck the essence out. That's your Gift. When you touch an object, you get the most traumatic or emotional moments from when someone poured a piece of themselves into it. For regular humans, you literally suck out their soul, bit by bit. But for Gifted..." He shook his head and let out a breath. "You suck away our Gifts."

I knew I should concentrate on that information and find a

way to use their powers against them, if that was possible. But I was focused on the middle part of what happens when I touch normal people.

"What do you mean about souls?"

"Oh, I was waiting for you to catch on. Soul as in life-force, what keeps people in the land of the living. We have excellent researchers, so it wasn't hard to figure out. We weren't sure if you actually hated your sister or were just too clueless to realize you'd spent her entire life slowly killing her."

I didn't want to react, but I let out a gasp, shocked by his words. They couldn't be true. I would never hurt Sybill, intentionally or not. But this was the first time in forever that I wasn't constantly by her side, and against all odds, she was getting better on the placebo.

CHAPTER FORTY-TWO

We eventually arrived at a run-down warehouse that must have made pies or jams at some point because there was a lingering, sickening sweetness as soon as we got inside.

Logan and Kazimir had secured my hands in a way that I couldn't reach out to touch them. I wasn't going to let them know that it wasn't only my hands I could use my Gift with, but they were bundled up and wearing gloves anyway. They put me in a chair and tied my arms onto the armrests, then left me alone.

I studied every corner of the room that I could see, trying to find an escape route, but most of it was filled with old machines, empty mason jars, and wooden crates. Other than the door we'd come in by, which was behind me, they all had sophisticated-looking locks. Possibly alarms as well.

"This wasn't necessary. She isn't a prisoner."

I recognized her voice immediately, but I had been hoping she wasn't in on it. For Grace's sake more than my own, because of how strongly Malcolm trusted her.

Professor Mallory came and started to untie one of my arms, but Logan reminded her, "They said they stay."

"It's just a precaution until they see you're not going to hurt us," she assured me, pulling up a chair to sit across from me. "Did the boys fill you in on the way?"

"I'm a freak of nature who's been killing my sister and I could have been home by now if I'd just taken the time to touch them," I resumed what Logan had shared, trying to sound annoyed rather than terrified, which was more accurate.

"That's their theory, but I'm not sure you could use it. Just like I don't think you get any stronger from making your sister weaker. You're not a parasite."

"Thanks, I feel much better." Sarcasm and anger for the win.

"I mean it, Alison. You are not a prisoner. You are here because we need your help."

"You've got a funny way of showing it."

"Logan went rogue when he found out about you, but it was imperative that you hear us out. We can't imagine you would turn us down once you do."

"Then you lack imagination. And common sense."

"I'm sure you guessed that the artifact contains the blood of a Gifted woman taken centuries ago? You see, humans are fascinated with power. Using it, acquiring it…people without powers want to get them. Those with passive powers want more. For as long as there have been Gifted, there have been people trying to exploit our powers to become Gifted as well."

"I'm sure there have also been Gifted telling them to die and see what happens."

"That is an option that many have taken," she agreed. "There's an entire organization we call the Fanatics. They've made promises, started projects and refused to finish them, hoarded information…it's pathetic, really."

It was unnerving how she could sit there so calmly, like this was a polite conversation among colleagues while I was literally tied to a chair in front of her. Her henchmen had murdered five innocent men for getting in her way. Six, if you counted Dr. Richards, which I didn't want to, not to mention Grace.

"Were any of them successful?" I told myself it was just to keep her talking, but I was also curious to know. So much of this Gifted stuff was a mystery to me, and I was looking for any explanations she could give.

"That's debatable. I think some of them have been, but most did it for personal gain. No one succeeded on a large scale."

"Is that what you're trying to do?" I asked, based on her disdain for those selfish people.

"No, that's where I'm different," she argued. "I don't want more power, and I certainly don't want to give it to a bunch of people without a purpose who will just use it to further their own agendas."

It took so much self-restraint not to roll my eyes at her and her self-aggrandizing diatribe.

"I believe we should even the playing field in a different way. What I want is to take away Giftedness. And I would like you to help me do it."

"How?"

"Your Gift already takes it away. Temporarily, of course, but I believe that we can synthesize a serum so a single injection would cure a person of not just their Gift, but their Giftedness as a whole."

"You talk about it like it's a disease."

"Isn't it? Like a cancer, it develops inside you, but doesn't show signs until it's too late."

"I guess you have a passive, boring Gift?" I tried to make it sound like I wasn't fishing for information on what I was up against, but the death glare she shot gave me pause.

Luckily, she took a deep breath to regain her cool before speaking. "The Gift isn't the issue, so much as everything that comes with it. You have no idea what it is like to die time and time again, only to wake up, cold and alone, to start all over again with a new identity, new friends...a completely different life."

"I don't," I agreed. "So why would you choose me? I'm sure there are others who have my Gift. Is it because I'm easier to control when I don't know how to work it or—"

"Perhaps I should have started with why you are so important. First Lifers are very rare. Most Gifted don't find out about their Gift until they have died and come back to life, at which point their body is in stasis. They will come back to life every time they die, but they will not get older...their bodies are frozen in a moment in time, at which point their Gifted gene, for lack of a better term, was depleted. Once the Giftedness has been fully activated, your body carries the Gift, but not the potential. You are not our first First Lifer, nor the first who can take away people's Gifts, but you are the only First Lifer with your particular abilities."

"You can harvest my Gift because it's still active in my DNA." I was nonchalant, but I swallowed hard. If Henrietta Lacks was any indication, I wasn't getting out until they bled me dry.

"With your help and the use of your DNA, we can break down the molecular structures needed to create a serum that will remove Giftedness," she agreed.

"And why would I want to help you do that?"

Grace might dislike the fact that she looked like a child compared to her son and lover, but would she rather have died before meeting Enrique, or watching Malcolm grow up? If the books were right and Gifted existed to accomplish important tasks that the world shouldn't be without, then removing Giftedness could alter the course of history in terrible ways I didn't want to think about, given the atrocities that still happened with Giftedness safely in place.

"Because I don't think you hate your sister. I assume you

would rather she not die slowly from the nearness of you." She was blunt, but her words hit me straight in the heart. I bit the inside of my cheek to hide it from her, but she had me. If the choice was to help her or be responsible for the death of anyone who got close to me, how could I say no?

CHAPTER FORTY-THREE

As soon as I agreed, Professor Mallory retreated so the others could run tests on me. I felt a renewed sympathy for everything Sybill had to go through on a regular basis.

I had to help them so I wouldn't hurt her anymore, but my brain still tried to find a way out. I watched the Gifted they brought to me, trying to figure out their Gifts and how I could potentially use them in a battle if needed. Not that any of them came close enough for me to touch.

"Lola," Logan called, nodding to me.

The shortest of them, a woman with bleached blonde hair and amethyst eyes, stepped away from the others. She closed her eyes and held her palms out toward us.

"Fifth…Twelfth…" She paused for a really long time, tilting her head like she was concentrating. "One hundred and eighty-sixth?"

"One hundred and eighty-seventh," Logan corrected her.

"Is that how long you've been Gifted?" I was glad when someone else asked, a woman in a lab coat with a very large needle, patiently waiting her turn to prod me. I thought she might be German based on her accent, but it didn't help that she looked scary and stern.

"Lives," Logan shared, his face hard. There was an overwhelming sadness to him in that moment that would have made me feel sorry for him if he hadn't been pivotal in killing people I cared about and kidnapping me.

"Are you five for five?" Lola asked the woman, which implied that the guy who could stop my heart, Kazimir, was on his twelfth, although I had no clue how long each life lasted. Did Gifted drop dead of old age every hundred years, even if it didn't show?

"Not once per year, if that's what you are asking. Two times my first week, and then the…the mishap." She turned to Logan with the tiniest of sighs, but he looked away from her. I had no idea what she was talking about, but everyone else understood. The more she talked, the more I leaned toward Russian, since she pronounced her Ws like Vs. None of it would help me escape, but it could help the police catch them if ever they released me. Although unless they came up with a formula that worked, prison cells wouldn't be able to hold them.

"And the girl?" Logan pressed. It worried me how he distanced himself from me, never using my name, though I knew he knew it. Every paranoid cell in my body told me he was making me less than human so it wouldn't be hard to kill me, but the non-paranoid cells agreed.

"First." She shrugged. "Doesn't even look Gifted."

"You can tell?" I asked.

For a second, my eyes burned as if I had opened them in the ocean. Everything was blurry, but then it went back to normal. No one else noticed or cared.

"Lola finds Gifted. It's truly fascinating to hear her explain it. I believe the Lives are like tree rings?" Professor Mallory came in and turned to Lola for confirmation.

She nodded, which explained why it took her so long to count Logan's, and how she could have made a mistake.

"Let her touch you."

No one was as surprised as Lola, who looked back to make sure Professor Mallory was talking to her.

"You hired me to confirm she was in her First Life," Lola argued.

"And you did excellent. Now we need to test other things."

For all their criticisms of Giftedness, Lola did not want to give hers up.

"It's temporary, and yours is the least dangerous of everyone in this room in case she can take them."

There had been the tiniest trace of fear in Kazimir's face, but it disappeared after that. His Gift worked from a distance, which wasn't something they wanted me getting my hands on. I wondered if his Gift working from afar meant I could also remove it from afar, but I was pulled from my thoughts when Lola came and put her hands on mine.

I felt like a wave passed through me. I expected to see everyone in the room transformed into circles with many rings, but everything looked the same. I closed my eyes and tried to get my palms facing someone, but for all the struggling that took, it changed nothing.

"Anything?" Professor Mallory asked me.

"Nothing," I told her.

"But you felt it?"

"It's not working," Lola said before I could answer. "I can't feel anyone." She sounded panicked, like she had lost a limb. Or maybe she was worried I sucked the Giftedness out of her, and she was going to drop dead. As much as I wanted to find a way out, I did not want to be responsible for any more deaths.

"Let me know when it comes back."

Professor Mallory left the room, not even remotely concerned by Lola's distress.

. . .

THE RUSSIAN WOMAN wore thick gloves to turn my arm over for a blood test, but with my palm facing upward and her arm so close, I was able to touch it while she clumsily searched for a vein with her gloved hands.

As soon as I made contact, I concentrated on sucking her Gift out, taking it into myself, which terrified me since I had no clue what her Gift was. I felt lightheaded for a moment, but that was it.

She said something in a language I did not understand, speaking directly to my arm.

I had tried to give blood when I turned eighteen. They made me drink bottles of water and play with a stress ball for at least twenty minutes before the nurse could find my vein. This woman was no better.

"We don't have all day, Hilde, just stab her." Logan took to tapping his foot and glared at her with his arms crossed.

She stopped with the needle and looked from me to him, horrified, speaking more of what must be her mother-tongue.

"What's wrong?" Logan asked.

"She touch you," Kazimir stated, then repeated it in whatever language she was speaking.

Hilde ripped her arm away from me and let the needle fall to the floor. She kept talking, gesturing frantically, but Kazimir was the only one who understood her, and he wasn't the best at English either.

"Get human nurse," he told Logan before bringing Hilde out.

Logan looked at me like he wanted to stab me and get it over with, but he didn't trust me. For all he knew, I could have all their powers and be pretending. Not that seeing rings or being a human translator would make me any more threatening than I currently was. I did my best to make my face go blank while he analyzed me. Let him think I was dangerous. Let him be afraid of me.

"Bring her to her room," he told Lola.

"Me?" she was shocked.

"You're already broken," he said with disdain, leaving us alone.

LOLA BROUGHT me up a temporary wooden staircase to a room which must have been an office back when the plant was operational. There was only one window, a horizontal rectangle beside the door through which I could see the inside of the warehouse. Or I could have if it hadn't been painted over in black. The glass looked thick, the kind I probably couldn't break without causing serious damage to myself, not to mention what the twenty-foot drop would do to me.

There were some leftover safety posters on the wall, warning about overheating the equipment, but the room itself was freezing. They'd 'furnished' it with one of those foamy exercise mats, a pillow, and a throw blanket. I wondered if they had lots of prisoners, if they knew I was coming, or if this was just how everyone working here lived. I could have asked Lola, but I preferred to let her silently stew over her hatred for Logan. Her rage would have been directed at me otherwise, since the Professor seemed untouchable, but Logan was fair game.

She didn't say anything before slamming the door behind me. It had been retrofitted with an exterior lock, and it sounded like Lola removed the staircase once she got down.

It might be better for everyone if I just froze to death before they found me in the morning.

.   .   .

ONCE I WAS BUNDLED UP, I moved the tiny mat closer to the opposite side of the room, to avoid an orange-red stain on the dark green carpet. At least it was farther from the large vent the cold air was coming from. There was a smaller hole in front of me, just big enough for a mouse, but I didn't feel a draft coming from it.

I sighed and finally let myself think about everything that happened today. Everything had gone by so fast, or I was unconscious for it. I hadn't processed the fact that Officer Hill would never give me that disapproving look that always turned into a smile, Officer Jones would never rave about anything and everything I made, and Tristan…I shook my head and focused on the officers, not ready to go there yet.

Officer Hill had mentioned a daughter once, but I didn't know anything else about him or Jones. I didn't even know their first names, except that both started with R. They probably thought they were safe sitting in my driveway, their wives relieved they weren't out dealing with criminals, just eating baked goods from a lonely intern. Then they were killed without a second thought, an obstacle Logan had to get rid of to get to me. The anger boiled in me at that thought because Kazimir could easily have put them to sleep instead of allowing that third one, Ted, to leave them a bloody mess with the other cops I never got the chance to meet.

Tristan was different. I pushed him away for a reason, but he showed up at my door and I what? Decided I would rather let him die than be alone? It was pathetic. I was so selfish.

Tears burned my eyes, but at the same time, it didn't seem real. One minute Tristan had been standing there, winning his fight, and the next he was gone.

I could tell myself he was sleeping, but I hadn't found a pulse, and he wasn't breathing. If someone found him and called an ambulance, they might have been able to save him, but there'd been no one around. I had an aching, broken feeling inside my heart that made me want to cry and never stop.

All these lives lost because of me. So, I could live and what? Give them exactly what they wanted? Tristan beat cancer and lived to make people smile, yet hanging out with me got him killed.

I knew I was working myself into a migraine, so I tried to breathe and calm myself down, but none of the thoughts I usually told myself worked. None of this was in my head. It was my fault.

I deserved what was coming for me, and the people I cared about were better off without me.

CHAPTER FORTY-FOUR

ello?

H I thought I woke up because I was so cold, but then I heard it again. A voice, coming in loud and clear.

"Hello?"

"Thank God, I knew I heard someone," the voice replied. She sounded familiar, but too muffled to be sure.

"Who are you?" I tried to find where the voice was coming from.

"The prisoner to your left. Or behind you. I guess it depends how you look at it."

The sound came from the mouse hole, which made me think there was another room on the other side of that wall, leading to the other half of the building, where the machines were.

"How long have you been here?"

"I lost count, but probably a year."

"A year?" My stomach dropped. "Isn't anyone looking for you?"

"I'm sure they will eventually. Unless they think I died. I don't blame them." She added the last part as if she was worried

I would think badly of her parents, but the rest of it she was definitely rolling her eyes for.

"Are they keeping you because you won't do what they want?"

"More like they still want me," she corrected. "I have a Gift that makes me very useful to some powerful people, so they like to keep me around. What are you in for?"

"They think I can help them get rid of Giftedness." I sighed. I didn't know if I believed I could do what they said, but the more I thought about it, the more I worried whether they would let me go once I did.

"You're the chosen one. They've been talking about you nonstop ever since they realized what you were."

"Did they mention what they plan to, um…"

"Do once they're done with you?" she finished for me. "They don't really think that far ahead. They have all the time in the world, but they live day by day, which is super annoying. Once they get it to work, I'm sure they'll figure something out."

She talked about them not so much like jailers she was afraid of, but like parents she was annoyed with. She was either much younger than me or grew up very spoiled.

"Have there been a lot of prisoners before me?"

"They have test subjects at the other facility, but I've only ever seen animal trials here. Nothing ever works." She sighed. "I'll be glad when it does."

"You're anxious to get the cure?"

"I'm anxious to not be useful to them anymore. To finally be free." That time, the annoyed teen sounded more like a defense mechanism.

"You must be glad I'm here."

"I'm glad for the company. And for myself, if it works."

"But," I pressed.

"I shouldn't say."

"Please?" I got nothing but silence in return. "I'm Alison," I told her. "They murdered people I really care about right in front of me so they could get me here. Now I feel like helping them is betraying those people. But on the other hand, I found out that my Gift has been slowly killing my sister every time she gets close to me, so it would be nice to not do that anymore. If you know something, I would really appreciate you sharing." I said Gift through clenched teeth because it was clearly anything but.

"It's like anything else," she said after a while. "Some things sound too good to be true, and they are, but you're okay as long as you read the fine print and know what you're getting into. I know what I would be giving up, and I don't care. It's a curse if you ask me, and I want it gone."

"Is your Gift something painful?"

"Only when they want it to be."

The way she said it sent another chill down my spine. She sounded so violated. I wanted to reach across the wall and take her in my arms.

"It might be selfish, but I don't care. I'd rather not be the one doing things against their will," she said quietly, almost to herself.

She did care, but I needed answers way more than I wanted to call her on it.

"Who are you talking about?"

"Everyone. All the Gifted."

"I thought you wanted it gone?" I remembered the way Lola looked when she lost her Gift, and the way Logan called her broken.

"I want it gone, but that's my choice. Logan can be a dick, but he's earned it, you know? After what happened to his family..."

"I don't know."

She hesitated, and I was convinced she wasn't going to tell me, but then she let out a deep breath. "I don't know what year it was, but he was working for his father in Egypt, so his family came to visit him. I can't remember if it was two or three kids, but one of them was like a tiny baby, so they rented a car and drove around until they were stopped by whatever bad people live in Egypt. The way Hilde tells it, they were going to shoot the baby, so he jumped in front and took the bullet. She kind of worships him, like gave up her life to test one of his theories, so not sure how much you can trust her, but the point is he died of his injuries and woke up to his family starving to death with multiple degree burns. He tried to get them help, even tried letting them eat him and drink his blood by the end of it. He watched them die, one by one, while he kept coming back. By then he didn't care about being rescued – he just wanted to die – so he kept starving to death, waking up, bashing his head in with a rock, waking up...over and over until the Professor found him. They've been researching Giftedness and trying to find a cure ever since, but if you ask me, it's made them a little crazy."

I gagged multiple times during her story, which she told like it was happening to characters on TV. On some level, I understood how that could turn someone into a monster. Especially if there was no way out, no chance of meeting them in heaven or hell, or whatever you believed in.

"I mean, everyone deserves to be able to give up and quit when they don't want to wait for their elusive purposes to show up anymore..."

"Which is what the cure would give them," I agreed.

"In an ideal world, yes, but some of those higher ups..." She paused. "It's not really pro-choice if instead of closing abortion clinics you force mass sterilization."

"Are there babies involved?"

"No, I'm…I'm just saying there's a difference between giving people the option to do something and forcing them to."

"They would give it to everyone," I understood.

"And then who would stop them?"

"Lights out!" an angry voice demanded, probably from outside her room, but she didn't speak again, no matter how much I whispered.

I WAS ALREADY on the fence about trusting Professor Mallory when it was just creating an option for people who didn't want the burden of Gifts that were more like curses. It would be wrong to strip the Gifts away from the people who wanted to keep them, to end the lives of people who might want to keep living, even if they were on borrowed time. I kept thinking about their purposes. If some higher power created an entire race of humans with special abilities as an insurance policy to make sure important events could occur, what would happen to the world if we took them away? How many lives would be lost? How many discoveries wouldn't be made? How many disasters would ravage the earth if the insurance policies were gone?

When I looked at the big picture, there was no way I could be a part of this. When I looked at how it affected me personally, it was a little more complicated. I loved my sister more than anything, and would do everything in my power to not hurt her. But what if my purpose was to help her child who got kidnapped someday like Amber? Or to save someone's life?

The sacrifice of moving out and not getting too close to anyone was worth it if God, or whoever, wanted it to be that way. To be honest, I didn't think Sybill would forgive me if she knew what I took from other people so I could cuddle with her.

The final strike was the fact that it could take years for them to come up with a formula that worked. And who knew if they would ever let me go, even if they did figure it out? Tristan, Dr. Richards, Officer Hill, and Officer Jones did not give their lives so I could give up and give in.

I had no idea how, but I was either going to get out or die trying.

CHAPTER FORTY-FIVE

I looked at my watch and saw that it was four o'clock. I figured I had at least until sunrise before they came for me, which gave me a couple of hours. I would need to overpower whoever they sent in to draw my blood, to the point that I could escape into the warehouse and hopefully find an exit. It was a terrible plan with absolutely no specifics, but I didn't have anything better. The poster on the wall was too old and brittle to even cause a paper cut. I halfheartedly tried to lift the carpeting, but while it was old and smelly, it was glued on like they were expecting a tornado.

BY THE TIME the staircase slid into place outside, it was almost six o'clock, and I was waiting behind the door with my throw blanket.

"I hope you enjoyed it, because you'll never be seeing that again."

I heard Lola's voice, so I got ready to throw the blanket over her head and run out the door, but the man who rounded the corner was roughly seven feet tall. His lab coat was bursting at the seams from all his muscles.

"You can touch him all you want, but it won't get you anywhere." Lola wasn't taking any chances herself. She stayed at the top of the staircase, refusing to pass the threshold. "Fill as many as you can." She handed him a tray full of empty syringes.

"Until she dies?" He sounded horrified, which I took as a good sign.

"Until she passes out or whatever happens when you give too much blood. We need enough to be able to test and do trials, but we'll eventually need more, and her blood is useless if she's dead."

Lola left, leaving the man looking uncomfortable about his task.

"What's your name?" I asked him.

"Fred," he shared. "I'm a nurse, so I know what I'm doing," he assured me of the needle he was assembling.

"My mom's a nurse, too." I got him to smile. "Do you do a lot of home visits?" I tried to treat him like a friend or a fellow prisoner rather than blame him for my predicament. So far, he was responding.

"They mostly come to me with people who are bleeding or dying, and I do what I can. My dad was like you, so I get that it's hard to go to a hospital, but you shouldn't have to kill yourself if it's something easy enough to fix."

"You said was?" I asked.

"Cancer. A few years back."

"I'm so sorry," I told him, my first reaction whenever someone told me of a loss, but the mention of cancer reminded me of Tristan, and I had to look away and bite the inside of my cheek while Fred tied a rubber band around my arm and gave me a ball to squeeze.

"He knew it was coming. They found the tumor and gave him

a year to live, so he took us out of school and we spent a year traveling the world. He died jumping out of an airplane, but by the time they found him in the jungle, he was alive and didn't have a scratch on him. They called it a miracle, but apparently, he was like you and just stayed alive long enough to send an asshole to jail. You know, the kind that doesn't get caught because the witnesses disappear, and he doesn't care about perjury? Well, my dad became a human lie detector after he died. No, it was not fun growing up, but it was even less fun when my dad managed to be the only witness they couldn't kill." He talked while he worked, but he looked up at the end, full of pride for his father.

"He sounds like a really great man."

"He was. Although once the guy was behind bars, my dad started aging again, but kept smoking two packs a day. Which led to the cancer." He said it matter-of-factly, but I could tell it hurt. "He never said no to helping anyone. He brought me my first Gifted fixer-upper, and you guys don't seem to quit."

I couldn't tell if he thought I was there by choice, or if he would help me escape if I just asked.

"I never knew that there was a curse on people like you. To have your blood be the cure and to selflessly donate it like this. Mad props," he told me. "Take a deep breath now and look at me, not the needle."

I looked at him, then down at the syringe he filled with my blood. I wondered if it was Logan's or Lola's cruel joke to have Fred stab me repeatedly instead of giving him a butterfly needle that could have ensured a constant flow.

I wanted to take the chance and ask Fred for help, to tell him what was going on, but there was too much at stake.

He wasn't Gifted, but he was way stronger than me, so they assumed I would be easy for him to control. However, according to them, I was killing my sister without meaning to. I could only imagine the damage I could do if I intended it.

Fred didn't react when I put my hand on his arm, other than

to look up at me sympathetically, thinking I was afraid of the needle. It wracked me with guilt, and I felt the tears sting my eyes, but I let my Gift dig into him like I'd done countless times with objects at the precinct. It worked the same, but also felt nothing like it normally did. Instead of emotions and memories, it felt like I was sucking the life right out of him. I hoped it was reversible, but I didn't have a clue what I was doing.

"I'm so sorry, I feel..." Fred clutched his chest, then collapsed into my lap.

CHAPTER FORTY-SIX

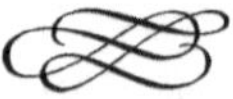

The first thing I did was make sure Fred still had a pulse and was breathing. I took the needle out of my arm and brought it with me in case I needed a weapon, along with the vial of my blood I didn't want them to get their hands on. The fact that the last thing Fred did was apologize made me feel even worse.

I crept down the makeshift staircase into the empty warehouse, but I had no idea if they had guards or people patrolling. And it wasn't like I was just going to stab anyone I ran into with the needle. It was more to be used as a threat, but who knew what Gifts the people in this building controlled. The ones I knew about went both ways; Lola's rings and Hilde's translating skills were harmless, but Logan could literally turn me into a pile of sand, and Kazimir could stop my heart if he felt the need to. I'd also seen firsthand what they could do without their Gifts to anyone who got in their way.

I crept along the wall, hiding behind defunct equipment whenever I thought I heard something, until I got to a set of double doors. They led to a long, empty hallway, but it looked like there were glass doors at the end. Even if they were locked, I was sure I could find something to break out with.

I walked as fast as I could without making noise, but footsteps sounded behind me when I was halfway through.

I ducked into the first doorway I could find. The door was obviously locked, but I was good as long as they didn't know I was missing. And didn't have good peripheral vision.

I waited in the tiny alcove, my heart pounding in my chest so loudly I was sure everyone could hear it. I held the needle by my temple, ready to bring it down on whoever it was if they looked my way, but I knew there was very little chance I would be using it, especially not before they managed to scream and alert everyone to my presence.

"I was hoping we could avoid this," Professor Mallory said as she rounded the corner and looked right at me. She used a blast of what felt like wind to knock me off my feet, then towered over me. There wasn't an ounce of fear that I would touch her and steal her Gift, or that I would stab her with my needle. But there was a hint of…humanity? Regret?

Her eyes were black, which I'd never noticed before. I could have sworn they were green, to match her red hair, but they almost reminded me of Grace's.

"I know we got off on the wrong foot, but I don't have time to coddle you and convince you right now. You simply can't leave."

"You can't keep me here against my will. It isn't right," I said, swallowing hard. She clearly could keep me, but it wasn't legal, or even remotely okay. I made my way back up to a standing position, but she looked at me like I should have stayed down.

"There was a time when that would have stopped me. Where I might have risen up to protect you from the oppressor, but that was a long time ago and I am exhausted. You were brought here against your will, yes, but you agreed to stay because you know as well as I do that this is the right thing to do. It isn't natural for normal people to come back to life like Gods. Or to wield destructive powers. Do you want to spend the rest of your life keeping everyone at bay so you don't kill them like you're doing to your sister? I mean, I hope the damage is reversible, but what kind of Gift hurts the people you love like that? Robs them of a childhood and possibly even their life? How long do you think she would have lasted? Suffering and growing weaker every day?"

Professor Mallory voiced all the fears that were ever present in my mind. I knew she was right. I didn't want to keep killing my sister, and I truly believed the world would be a better, safer place without Logan in it. Grace might even be okay with dying if it helped people…but what would happen to the rest of us? To the world without them?

More importantly, how could I trust a group of people who stabbed my friend, tried to kidnap me, killed four police officers and a young man before succeeding, then held me prisoner while they tried to come up with a cure? If this was a legitimate organization, or if their motives were pure, they would have come to me and asked for my help. Let me come every week to donate blood or something. I would have been excited to help people if that was the case. This was just trading a God for a dictator, and I didn't approve.

"I can stay away from her. Or learn to control it. But there are people who would be dead today without my Gift. People who would spend the rest of their lives rotting in prison," I pointed out.

"You would sacrifice your own happiness?"

"Better the one than the many." I knew I was quoting some-one; I just hoped it wasn't Machiavelli. Or Hitler.

"I really was like you once, Alison. Full of dreams and ideals, believing the world was a wonderful place."

"What happened?"

"I died, and it was heartbreaking. I was so young with my life ahead of me, children who would be motherless, a husband who would never get over me..."

"Until you woke up."

"I did. And mine isn't a sob story like Logan's. I had a wonderful first life, and second. I got to be Aunt Minnie to my grandchildren. And great-grandchildren. I watched many generations grow up and die. But they all stayed dead while I kept coming back. Time and time again, no matter how hard I prayed I wouldn't."

"I sympathize with that. I would love to help you find a cure for this curse and your pain. But I can't let you take it from everyone. And I won't let you lock me up in a room to waste away while you slowly drain my blood."

"You won't let me?" I expected her to make fun of me, but she sounded like she felt sorry for me. As sorry as she could feel while also demonstrating her Gift. I tried to take a step, but a blast of air—or maybe pure energy—pushed me back against the doorway, immobilizing me until she put her hands back down. "Oh, dear, there is very little any one of us has any control over. It's easy to care about what's right and giving people choices. Being Gifted might even seem like a gift to someone like you in their First Life, using it to save people and right wrongs. But it's a curse. You'll understand once you've watched everyone you love die. Your parents. Your sister. Your children. Their children. Every single person you've ever met will die while you live on, unable to do a single thing about it."

"This isn't the answer," I argued. "How many people have died from you trying to find this cure? In the past week, I can name six people who died for your mission, and not a single one of them deserved it."

"I just want it to be over." Suddenly, she didn't look like a cruel captor. She looked so human and vulnerable that I wanted to stay just so I could take away her pain. "I've been searching for a cure for over a hundred and fifty years, but I never meant for anyone to give up their life so I could end mine. I was following the research, but Logan wanted to go to the source. I didn't tell him who my contact was, but he figured it out and…" She looked horrified. My guess was at the memory of what Logan did to get to me.

To Dr. Richards.

To Grace.

To Tristan.

"Can Last Lifers come back?" I asked.

She shook her head, her face hard, keeping the emotions at bay. "Isaiah was one of the kindest, smartest men I've ever met." She smiled, but her eyes were watering. "And Grace never once turned me down when I asked her for help. You have no idea how sorry I am."

"Then why don't you do something about it?" I tried not to be reproachful, because I felt like I was maybe getting somewhere with her, but I didn't care how bad she felt if she kept hurting people.

"I'm not the only one involved. Neither is Logan. We answer to a whole group of people who are counting on us. They would never let you go, now that we know what you can do."

"I don't mind giving you a vial of my blood so you can find a cure," I tried. "I would love to not be killing my sister every time I hug her. But you can let me go. And let other people decide whether they want it."

"We don't just need a single vial. We need to study it, identify its properties, find a way to replicate it in a serum, and test the serums until we find one that works."

"You're going to keep me here forever?" I asked. "What if I sent you a vial every week or—"

"Live test subjects go to headquarters; we only work with samples here."

"I'll never get out of there alive, will I?"

"Even if I wanted to, It's not my decision. They know you

exist, which means they won't give up until they get what they want."

"Which is me. Dead like Isaiah or kept alive by machines like Grace." I knew I was pushing, but I could see that she didn't want those outcomes either.

"They'll be here by this afternoon."

"So let me go before then," I suggested.

"If Logan saw…even once you're out, they know who you are. They will find you." She stressed every word of the last sentence.

"At least I would have a chance." I needed to get out, but I had no idea what I would do after that. I was taking things one at a time and hoping I could figure it out.

Professor Mallory bit her bottom lip and sighed. "Your best bet—"

I jumped back in shock when Professor Mallory melted into a pile of sand in front of me, revealing Logan.

"Sleep well, my friend. I pray I'll never see you again." He completely ignored me and said an emotional goodbye to her, kissing his thumb before turning to me. "Alright, back to your cage."

"No," I argued, frozen in place with fear. Logan didn't need supernatural powers. If he did that to a woman he loved and admired, I could only imagine what he would do to me.

"No?" He laughed to himself.

"I told her I'm not going back."

"She'll see reason when she wakes. She always does."

I stood my ground, lifting the syringe in what I hoped was a menacing way, even though I was completely cornered.

"What are you planning to do with that? Stab me? Because for you to get that close…" he let the thought linger, showing me the tips of his fingers because that was all he needed to ensure I would never bother him again.

"But you need me alive, don't you? Unless the sand carries

my DNA, but Lola said I'm worthless if I'm dead." I had no clue where the confidence came from, but I couldn't just surrender and let him put me back in a cage. If I wasn't a prisoner under Professor Mallory's leadership, I definitely was one now. Or rather a test subject, fit to be experimented on.

A flash appeared behind him, so I squinted, trying to identify the shape. As it got closer, I froze. My breath caught in my chest and the needle fell to the floor with a resounding shatter.

Logan lunged for it while Tristan used a bat to knock him out, then snapped his neck like it was nothing.

CHAPTER FORTY-SEVEN

"Tristan?" My first instinct was to run into his arms, because his being there had to mean I was saved. Until I watched him snap someone's neck. Then my brain kicked in and reminded me that I watched him die. This either wasn't Tristan, or he had some serious explaining to do.

His face broke out into his smile when he saw me. "I came to find you as soon as I woke up." He came close before stopping himself, probably because of the uncertainty on my face.

"You woke up as in…" I went off a hunch, which either terrified me or explained everything. I wasn't sure which.

"What I was trying to tell you before was that I'm Gifted. That's why I kept pulling away every time you got too close; I didn't want you to get hurt when you found out I was nothing like I seemed, and I wouldn't be good for you. I didn't know what you were or who you were up against. Otherwise, I would never have left your side. I thought I could keep you safe, but—"

"You didn't know Logan turns people into dust and Kazimir can stop your heart from a good fifty feet," I guessed.

"Logan would've had to touch me to do it, but that other one…I tried to stop him, but nothing worked."

"Nothing as in…" This probably wasn't the time or the place, but I needed answers.

"I can usually control electricity."

"Like Thor or like a socket?"

"More like Thor, but on a much smaller scale." He smiled at my comic book reference. "I'd been feeling these sparks with you, but I don't use my Gift that often, so I didn't realize they were you taking it."

Finding out the sparks were caused by my Gift hurt way more than I wanted it to.

"I didn't mean to. I'm still figuring things out."

"You have nothing to apologize for," he assured me. "Can you use the Gifts when you take them?"

"No, I suck the life out of people just to watch them suffer." I was exhausted and overwhelmed. I wanted to go home.

"I want to hold you in my arms right now and kiss you until you don't look so sad, but I'm going to stay back until we get out of here, okay?"

"Okay," I reluctantly agreed, but it would be dangerous for him to touch me then, too. "Did you bring backup?"

"They're on their way," he said. "But I'm hoping we'll be long gone before they get here."

"None of your friends can teleport? Or fly?" I was mostly teasing, but Gifts seemed to be the most random things. Even mine. It could do damage, as I was unfortunately finding out, but they weren't superhero powers.

"No, one of them can run pretty fast, but he's performing open heart surgery. He might not even be here by the time the others arrive."

"How will they know where we are?" I asked. "How did you?"

"My sort of adoptive kid sister saw it."

"She saw them bring me in?" That either meant that she was

close, or more likely that she was in league with the bad guys. A double agent?

"She saw the machines when you were in the factory. There was apparently a clock shaped like a strawberry, so…she's really good at puzzles. Seeing patterns and things that aren't there."

I thought back to who was in the room with me when I was in the factory. Logan, Hilde, Lola, Professor Mallory, Kazimir…

"Which one is she?"

"I can guarantee you didn't see her. She'll want to apologize for using your eyes without asking, but I didn't give her a choice."

I had about a million questions I was going to ask, but we rounded a corner just as Kazimir came out of a door to our right. Either because he saw me first, or just because I was their target, he immediately got to work slowing my heart. This time I didn't just feel woozy. I was about to pass out.

Tristan shot his hand out and a bolt of electricity jumped from his palm to Kazimir's chest before I felt normal again, and Kazimir fell to the ground.

"That's what you tried to do." I remembered his wushu. "Is he…" I couldn't get the words out, but Tristan knew exactly what I was asking.

"We don't want to be here when he comes to."

Lola was in the next hallway, shouting into a walkie talkie, but Tristan's Gift was weak. I didn't know if it was because he died or from being so close to me, but he couldn't have done permanent damage even if he'd tried. I walked up behind her and focused on sucking out her Gift, and any energy I could, before Tristan knocked her out with his bat.

"Did I touch you?" I asked of his inability to conjure up the same electricity he had for Kazimir.

"No, it just takes a while for your Gift to come back to its full potential after you die," he explained. "Days for full capacity, but maybe ten minutes before I can knock someone out with it again."

WE WENT ALONG in silence for a few minutes. Finding two of them so close together made us think there must be more, but the next person we found was Hilde, working with a microscope in a small room with a glass wall.

"We don't have to do anything to her, right?" I asked. "I think her Gift is just knowing a lot of languages."

"No, but we don't want her coming after us." He went to the room across from her, which looked like a broom closet. He emerged less than a minute later with a mop and its bucket, filled with dirty water. "This should give us a head start," he said after looping the mop through the handle and spilling the bucket's contents onto the floor, making it slippery.

WE GOT to the glass door exit, which was locked, but a few well-placed hits with Tristan's bat shattered a pane, creating an opening large enough for us to crawl out of. Into what, I didn't know, but I could figure that out once I was out of the building. Then I could find a police station, or whoever was equipped for dealing with supernatural beings like us.

I CRAWLED through and breathed in the fresh air, which had a hint of fermentation, but never tasted so sweet. I looked back and smiled at Tristan, making sure he was following.

I was so busy rushing to freedom that I didn't see Logan step out in front of me until I ran right into him, bounced back, and landed on my back with a thud.

CHAPTER FORTY-EIGHT

To make sure I couldn't touch his skin, Logan wore gloves and many layers of clothing. I doubted that would have stopped him from disintegrating Tristan if he'd been the one to bump into him, though, so I was grateful I was in the lead.

"A benefit of dying so many times is that you regenerate very quickly. Though I didn't expect to see you again." He cracked his neck and glared at Tristan. "I thought you'd agreed, Alison."

"To help people, not to force everyone to give up their Gifts because you want them to."

"It's not natural. The very concept of being Gifted takes away their free will. All we're doing is restoring the balance."

"But you would die," I pointed out. Logan was talking to me, but his eyes kept going back to Tristan, who was clearly trying to summon more of that electricity, but hiding it for the time being. "You're not in your First Life, so losing your Giftedness would kill you."

"And I welcome it with open arms. I've excelled at everything my entire life, and then the one time it matters, I fail so spectacularly that I still haven't figured it out decades later. But now I know where to look."

"Why not keep it for yourself and anyone else who wants it?" Not that I wanted to give him what he wanted, but it would be better than being a prisoner responsible for killing all Gifted.

"Little kids grow up imagining how much fun it would be to have powers. To fly or be invisible. They use the story of Midas to warn you, but it doesn't come close. You don't understand what actually happens when you're immortal. When a moment of anger can cost you someone you care about. When you can kill yourself over and over again, die a thousand painful deaths, but it never works."

One hundred and eighty-six, I thought to myself.

"I'm sorry for your losses," I said, trying to keep him talking, tentatively taking a step closer.

"It's none of your business, and it doesn't matter now. I'll be with them soon enough." He took a step forward, cautiously preparing himself to use his Gift on Tristan, but I stepped between them, knowing he wouldn't use it on me. Logan was a lot stronger, so I couldn't break free, but he couldn't hold me in his arms and prevent me from touching him at the same time. I felt an intense, dry heat when my hand reached his face, and then nothing, before Tristan shot a bolt of electricity to Logan's chest.

It was tiny compared to what he'd used earlier, just enough to make Logan release me.

"I came prepared for you," he practically spat at me. "The needle gives us a more pristine, larger sample, but I'm sure we can figure something out even if we have to collect your blood from the floor. As long as you don't die, we can always get more."

He took a long blade out of a scabbard, a cross between a sword and a knife. I'd used the only weapon I had, so I had nothing to stop him from chopping into me.

Then Tristan stepped between us.

He was weak. He couldn't even build up an attack, but his

hands must have been like an electric fence because Logan flinched every time he touched him in their hand-to-hand combat.

I watched, my hand on my chest, as Logan sliced into Tristan's ribs. It wasn't a deep cut, but the blood splattered across the white cement. I had to stop myself from vomiting as I felt it in my own gut.

I screamed when Logan went to do it again, this time more of a stabbing than a slicing motion. Tristan feinted before taking control of Logan's arm, and the two of them struggled against the blade.

I had absolutely no combat skills, and would get myself killed if I tried to get involved. We needed something that would prevent Logan from attacking us, but wouldn't kill him. We couldn't have him keep coming back to life, powers intact, to hunt us down again and again.

Logan gained enough control of his weapon to shove the handle part into Tristan's forehead, knocking him out. I screamed and ran off, hoping Logan would follow me instead of finishing Tristan off.

I was faster than him, thanks to years of jogging and the fact that he'd very recently woken up from being dead. But I had no clue where I was going.

In addition to the warehouses, the jam factory had a rundown greenhouse, tiny fields, large metal vats, and what looked like a well, but it was much larger than any wells I'd seen. I headed through the field to hopefully lose him in the greenhouse, but it was overrun with raspberry and strawberry plants.

While I tried to avoid the large branches and hazards in my way, Logan had a complete disregard for his own life and safety. When I chanced looking back, he ran right into a lattice, cutting his left eyelid. Blood appeared almost immediately, but Logan didn't even slow down.

The greenhouse was locked, and I didn't have time to bust a window for whatever cover it might have provided me.

I went for the well instead, which was covered by an old, moldy piece of wood with a metal bar on top, from which the bucket on a rope hung. I could lay down about three times across the diameter. I had maybe ten seconds before Logan caught up to me, so I tried to remove the wooden cover, but as soon as I disturbed it, the whole thing fell apart in my hands, crumbling to the depths below.

I climbed onto the metal bar and slid myself across as fast as I could while still being careful. I didn't stop until I was in the middle, out of Logan's reach.

"Come any closer and I'll jump," I warned.

"You expect me to believe you would kill yourself?"

"To prevent you from doing it slowly over years? Yes, I do."

"Then I can kill your sister. Your parents. Everyone you love. Sparky should be waking up soon, and I doubt you'll stay up there when I have my blade to his throat."

"For someone who is killing people for the privilege of dying, you sure treat death like a terrible threat."

"I would have given anything to save my family from it once upon a time. There's a difference between a life cut short and putting an end to immortality."

I breathed a sigh of relief when I saw Tristan walking over slowly, but I was careful not to alert Logan to his presence. I didn't want him to make good on his threat or finish off what he started.

I inched myself ever so slowly toward the far side of the well, causing Logan to move forward.

"That's a good girl." He encouraged me to come down, but I was moving out of the way.

I nodded to Tristan, hoping he could see what I had planned. He shot his arms out, sending a blast of electricity into Logan's back, the impact pushing him into the well.

I panicked when Logan hung on to the rope from the bucket, climbing his way up to me. Tristan rushed over to hand me the blade Logan had dropped when the blast hit him.

I grabbed the handle with every intention of cutting the rope to trap Logan at the bottom. But the second I touched it; I saw a bloody, gory scene I wished I could turn away from. The pain in my chest was agony. The images of a massacre played in my mind; Logan wielding the blade in desperation to avenge his loved ones with no remorse, none of it filling the void in his heart. The pain drove him to madness as slash after slash failed to bring his family back.

With one fell swoop, I cut the rope, flinching when I heard Logan hit the depths below.

CHAPTER FORTY-NINE

I thought one of us would need to keep watch while the other went to find a phone, but I barely made it off the pole before I heard sirens. I expected cop cars, but they were government issued black SUVs that carried agents in suits. A team in SWAT-like uniforms entered the main building while the guy who looked like he was in charge came straight to us, followed by a woman in her early twenties, dressed in jeans and a lace blouse, wearing a backpack.

I was shocked when she ran right into Tristan's arms, something I had a lot of difficulty not doing myself.

"How did you—"

"I've been on the phone with Jackie. She said she thought you got them all, but would need backup ASAP," the woman explained.

"How did Jackie know...she's the one with the eyes?" I turned to him.

"She does have those," the woman agreed.

"She's a First Lifer, too. Rosehill, where I've been living, actually has a few of them, and it's made to keep them safe," Tristan told me. "But since Jackie wasn't allowed to come, she's been checking in like an annoying presence in my brain. Rather my eyeballs, but she means well."

"You must be Alison." The woman turned to me after giving Tristan a reproachful glance.

"Delia?" I had no idea why Tristan's sister-person was tight with the FBI.

"Lucy, actually, but that's a very good guess." She made a step toward me, possibly for a hug, but I took a step back.

"She temporarily removes peoples' Gifts," Tristan explained.

I wasn't used to talking about it openly, with him or with federal agents.

"Noted. Not that I think it would make a difference for me, but to be on the safe side, I'll stay back and deal with any unexpected visitors while you give her a much-needed hug."

I was grateful, but wondered what I looked like for her to know how badly I needed that.

I still had my eyes on Lucy when Tristan took me in his arms for what felt like the best hug of my life. It was so hard to stay away from him after I literally watched him die. He was kissing the top of my head, telling me everything would be okay now, when I heard someone run over.

For a split second, I panicked that it was Kazimir, or that Logan somehow made it out of the well, but I definitely didn't expect, "Dr. Black?"

"You can call me Gabriel."

"I told her not to page you." I was shocked when Tristan went over and took him in for one of those guy hugs where you hold each other close but also slap each other's backs so no one doubts how manly you were. Tristan winced when they pulled apart, the movement aggravating the wound on his side.

"She waited until we were closing. I let a resident finish."

Gabriel came over and lifted Tristan's shirt. Lucy also went closer to see, taking a mini surgical kit out of her backpack.

"You're the one who runs really fast?" I put the pieces together, but my brain was having trouble processing them.

"Among other things," Dr. Black agreed. "Etta's at the house. I can stitch you up here or—"

"Just patch it up for now," Tristan assured him, holding my hand against what must be intense pain when they disinfected his wound. I was fairly certain that this 'Etta' was the nurse who came to Grace's room. It also sounded like she might be responsible for Grace waking up. "Thanks for coming."

"Don't mention it," Dr. Black assured him before one of the SWAT guys came over to give him a report.

I wanted to ask Lucy and Tristan a million questions, but I also wanted to let Tristan take me in his arms again so I wouldn't have to think of any of it.

WHEN DR. Black returned to us, he put an arm around Lucy. "We got three Gifted and a very disoriented nurse from inside the building, as well as a woman mid-regeneration. We'll pack up all the research we can find and see what we can do with it."

"There was a girl being held captive. She was in the room behind where you might have found a big guy named Fred… the nurse. I don't think he was a part of it, by the way. He thought he was helping."

"He'll be questioned and dealt with accordingly. I'm told both rooms up there were empty. We'll do an extra sweep, but she probably escaped with all the commotion."

"I hope so," I agreed, thinking of how damaged she was. "I don't know how you're going to hold them all when they get their Gifts back." The sun hid behind the clouds, but my shiver had nothing to do with the weather.

"That's where I come in. We have a special place for people

like…like us." I sensed a type of penance in Dr. Black grouping us together with the bad guys.

"Is it a medical facility where you'll experiment on them?" It wasn't that I didn't think they deserved it – a taste of their own medicine – but it made us as bad as them.

"No. During a break from being a doctor, I was a Special Agent. It was many lifetimes ago, but my old friends still come through with containment vans and these talented people who are used to dealing with Gifted who misbehave." Gabriel gestured to the agents scattered around us.

"Misbehave?"

"The really bad ones that deserve to be locked up so that they don't hurt more people," he explained.

"How do you make sure they can't? Do you sedate them or—"

"Sometimes. Especially during transport. Once there, we have top security cells that should contain any Gifted we put inside. But if we know what their Gift is, we can tailor it to them."

"His touch makes you disintegrate into a pile of sand," I shared.

"I've seen that before." He looked at Lucy, who shivered.

"How do you plan on containing him?"

"Are you curious in an academic way, or worried he'll come after you?"

"A bit of both," I admitted.

"We will study him. Not by cutting him open, but we have someone we can call whose Gift is to see other people's Gifts. And we have people like Lucy, who can create rooms where Gifts and magic don't work, or only work within those walls."

"The FBI has an entire division that studies Giftedness?"

"No, they have a couple of agents who oversee a few dangerous people. I set it up way back when, so if they need something, they reach out and I do my best to find them someone who can help. I'm also not the only Gifted who joined the bureau."

"As in the U.S. government is aware that they exist?"

"Some of them are. It's on a need-to-know basis," Gabriel shared. "My point is that Logan isn't their first monster, and he probably won't be their last."

"He just wants it to be over," I surprised myself by defending him. "They're trying to find a way to get rid of their Giftedness so they can die and rest in peace."

"I've been there," Gabriel understood. Darkness lurked behind his brown eyes before he snapped out of it. "Like I said, we'll go through their research. If we do find a cure, we wouldn't keep it from whoever wanted to take it."

"And Professor Mallory? I think she might have let me go."

"You like to see the best in people, don't you?" He sighed. "It's not a torture facility. We can't exactly have public trials, but there are sentence hearings. Gifted prisoners are treated with the same rights and respect as normal prisoners. They just have individual cells tailored to them."

GABRIEL'S PEOPLE did an excellent job of turning regular cops away, but we were questioned and debriefed by a handful of men and women in suits from various branches of law enforcement.

I'd seen Malcolm's car drive in and nodded for Gabriel to have his people let him through. His hug reminded me of how much I missed my dad and couldn't wait to see my family again.

"After my mom calmed down enough to tell me everything she remembered, we spent the entire night combing through Professor Mallory's affairs, her TA's, anyone who ever knew her...I found a blueprint of the lab in Logan's apartment and matched it to here."

"Thank you," I told him. "For everything."

"Detective Cortez," Tristan acknowledged him when he came over, but there was absolutely no love lost between the two of them.

"I think I owe you an apology." Malcolm extended his hand.

"You were just trying to keep her safe."

"Always," Malcolm agreed. "But I should have given you the benefit of the doubt. I had no idea you were Gifted."

"But you knew I was hiding something, which worried you. I would expect nothing less. God help whoever tries to hurt one of my sisters."

"Wait until you have kids." I could tell they were just exchanging similar experiences, but I wanted to take them both in my arms. Malcolm because he'd gone through the worst imaginable, and Tristan because he wouldn't be able to do anything once his sisters started to date. All my advice about giving them time and never giving up went out the window when I realized they'd lost him, and probably thought he was a figment of their imagination that they couldn't get rid of.

"Where to?" Tristan asked once we were finally free to go. He took my hand and brought it to his lips so he could kiss it as if this was any other day, and we were trying to figure out what to do on a date.

"Is it safe?" I asked him. I appreciated what he was doing, but the adrenaline had not left me yet. I wanted to figure out where I could go to be safe without putting anyone else in danger.

"It will be in a few hours," he said with a smile that was entirely for my benefit. He was reacting very well to the fact that every once in a while, when he touched me, we each felt a spark that ripped his Gift away.

"Tristan," I warned.

"This isn't me putting my emotions aside to make you feel better. I have never been more scared in my life. And I died of cancer." It was a terrible, cheap shot. "I don't know if you're safe. I don't know if they have more people out there who will be looking for you. What I do know is that I will not leave your side unless you send me away, in which case I might have to become the creepy stalker we joke about. You tell me where you want to go, and I will follow."

"Is it safe for me to go see my family? Is anyone still trying to use them against me—"

"I asked Delia to send people to California to keep an eye on them, so they're—"

I cut him off with a kiss. "I think I love you," I told him.

"Where did that come from?"

"You sent people to keep my family safe."

"They're your everything." He shrugged as if anyone else would have done the same.

"I love you." I knew it to the depths of my soul.

"I love you, too," he said before kissing me. "Let's get you home."

"As in…"

"California, so you can be with your people. Because you won't feel safe until you do."

"I'm aching for a hug from them, but I'm afraid to go near them knowing what I've been doing to Sybill." I got a sick feeling in my stomach just thinking about it.

"If you want, Rosehill doesn't just keep us safe, they also have classes and teachers to help us control our Gifts. It took me a while to stop zapping everything I touched." I couldn't tell if he was teasing or if he really walked around like a live wire at first.

"That might be a good idea." I wasn't sure how much I wanted to go to another facility to study Gifted powers, and Tristan picked up on it.

"But we can figure out our next steps when we get back from California," he assured me.

"We?" I asked.

"You didn't think I was letting you out of my sight, did you?"

"You'll put your life on hold to follow me?"

"To the ends of the earth."

"That's a little creepy."

"Am I scaring you off?"

"Not even a little." I smiled and leaned in for another kiss.

WE LEFT the following morning after packing our bags and letting Etta—the same one who pretended to be a nurse—heal Tristan's wound. He was right; I wouldn't feel safe until I was back with my family and everything returned to normal. But riding shotgun in his car with the wind blowing in my hair and his hand in mine...I believed everything would be okay.

EPILOGUE

"Which one do I send in first?" the bald man asked Monica, following her around like a bodyguard. Or jailer, she wasn't sure. He did everything she asked, but also a lot of things she didn't. Maybe he was more of a personal assistant-slash-babysitter.

"I'll take Van Bergen. You can tell the others to wait."

"Wait a few minutes or—"

"I may not need them."

"The mission has a much better chance of success if we send them all at once."

"If our goal was to rip her to pieces, I would agree with you. But we still need her blood. As much of it as possible. If she dies, we have to start back at the beginning and find a new First Lifer. Or be completely reliant upon the artifact, which may or may not let us in."

"We're working on it, Ma'am."

"But clearly not fast enough. Please send in Mr. Van Bergen."

"As you wish."

WHEN MONICA SAW James Van Bergen, she couldn't help but bite her bottom lip and drink him in. He was tall and muscular with sandy blond hair and the rugged look of someone who could kill you with his bare hands. He was all confidence, but not cocky, like someone who was the best in their field but didn't have to tell you about it. He was entirely her type, but she made herself stand tall and unmoved.

"Mr. Van Bergen," she said in an ominous voice.

"Miss Cao?" he asked.

"You can stick to Ma'am."

"Why am I here?"

"I've heard of your skills."

"I mostly use them against you," he pointed out.

"You do, but this time is different. I need you to find this woman." She threw the blanket at him, knowing he could get more from it than the others would get from their computers.

"Who is she?" James asked, sniffing it like a hound.

"Alison Carmichael." Monica smiled, but there was something ominous about it.

"Carmichael?" He gritted his teeth and clenched his fists, ready to punch something. Or someone.

"One and the same."

"What do I do when I find her?"

"Bring her to us."

"Alive?" he asked, as if he found the concept confusing. The closer he got, the more she could smell the alcohol on his breath. It was strange; he didn't look drunk, but he smelled like a bar.

"We need her blood for research. If she dies, it's useless to us."

"You want me to hunt her down, but let you have her?"

"I do. But she won't thank you for it. And when we are done with her...she's all yours." Monica shrugged like she didn't care, but she knew Alison wouldn't survive what he would do to her. That is, if she made it out of their labs.

"How long do I have?"

"As long as it takes. But I am not a patient woman."

"How long before you send the others? They're all outside."

"None of them have your predisposition, so the hope is that you'll get to her faster. I don't think it's beneficial for any of us to have the lot of you fighting over her, wasting time on each other instead of the mission. That's why you got her scent. I doubt you would have used the internet."

"None of that answers my question," he warned.

"Just make sure you're out of there before the others arrive."

"I'll try my best."

"You don't think you can find her?"

"I'm not sure I can give her up once I do." She liked his honesty.

"Which is why I'm sending the others."

"Fair enough."

"ARE YOU SURE MR. Van Bergen was the wisest decision? His father was—"

"I know who his father was."

"And he was with—"

"I know."

"I'm just saying."

"Are you questioning me, Howard?"

"Never, ma'am. Just ensuring you have all the facts."

"I do. James Van Bergen will find her long before the others figure out where to look. And if he tries to keep her to himself... I have a backup plan."

"Of course, ma'am." She could tell he had his reservations, but he would never voice them. "What do I do with the others?"

"Bring them in."

***

Find out what happens next in
Second Chance

***

And sign up to my newsletter for Tristan's POV!
www.amandalynnpetrin.com/tristanpov

ACKNOWLEDGMENTS

This book would not have been possible without the instrumental contributions of many people:

My dad, who makes sure the cover is consistent and legible, and who shares all my posts (sometimes before I even know they're out there).

Lissa, THE ABSOLUTE COOLEST BETA READER IN THE ENTIRE WORLD, who not only gave amazing feedback on this book, she supports me and constantly inspires me to be better.

Paul, the absolute best brother in the world, whose attention to detail and knowledge of the genre were second to none.

Rikki, who BETA reads like a fan, revealing plot holes and issues I never even considered.

My mom, who is my constant sounding board/editor/motivator/superwoman. She does everything. I'm not even exaggerating when I say that she's read the books more than I have.

My editor, Victoria (Edits by V), who saved me from misleading readers about something I knew nothing about.

And all of you who read the book, review it, share it, and enjoy it. It is so much more exciting to write when you're not the only one reading. Every one of you means the world to me. Thank you.

ABOUT THE AUTHOR

Amanda Lynn Petrin is the YA author of *The Giftedverse,* which comprises *The Owens Chronicles* and *The Gifted Chronicles.* She studied History and Psychology at McGill University so she could write compelling heroines going on magical adventures in the past, and hopes to turn these paranormal books into movies she can act in. She currently lives in Montreal, where she enjoys spending time with her family and living vicariously through the characters in her urban fantasy series.

Find her at: www.amandalynnpetrin.com

Shards of Glass

<u>The Owens Chronicles</u>

Prophecy (Book One)

Destiny (Book Two)

Legacy (Book Three)

Etta: A Gifted Chronicles Novella

<u>The Gifted Chronicles</u>

First Life

Second Chance

Third Eye

Find out more at

www.amandalynnpetrin.com

AMANDA LYNN PETRIN

SECOND CHANCE

THE GIFTED CHRONICLES
BOOK 2

CHAPTER ONE
DELIA

"Those don't go there," Penny said when we got back from picking vegetables in the garden and found our delivery man placing our order right on the threshold. She could squeeze her tiny frame through and put her basket on the kitchen table, but I would have to open the other French door to get inside.

"If Miss Hill wants me to put them somewhere else, she'll let me know," Mr. Bosworth told the six-year-old as he continued piling my groceries in the most inconvenient way. It was a shorter distance for him and spared my floors his muddy boots, but the door would have to stay open until we put everything away.

This was my opportunity to stand up for myself and tell him exactly where I wanted everything to go, but he looked over at me with a smirk, like he knew I would never tell him how to do his job – or anything – and he was taking full advantage of it.

"I'm sure Mr. Bosworth knows what he's doing and considered every option before choosing to put a mountain of bulky, fragile items in the doorway. Rather than on the table, in that corner, beside the pantry..." I gave a multitude of better options.

"I've been doing this for thirty years," Mr. Bosworth shared, though he'd only been coming here for the last two, since his father retired. He'd seen where the order was supposed to go, yet it took a year to even get him to bring the groceries inside, rather than leaving them in the driveway.

I wrote Mr. Bosworth a check and sighed when he left, staring at the mess of my kitchen. An old student had remodeled it for me, so everything had its place, but the floor in front of the door was not it.

"I'll get help," Penny decided, before she skipped down the hallway to track down other Rosehill occupants, her golden pigtails bouncing as she went. My pride wanted to tell her not to bother, that I would take care of it myself, but I knew that if Ben or Chris saw I was still letting Mr. Bosworth walk all over me, I would never hear the end of it.

I knew exactly who she would come back with, so I went out of order and put away whatever would make the most damage if dropped; a carton of eggs, glass jars, bruisable fruit...

"Do you need help, Miss Delia?" Charlie asked as he burst into the kitchen a few minutes later.

Without waiting for my answer, he stared at the pile of groceries and made a loaf of bread travel across the room to land softly on the counter beside the toaster.

There were no rules against using your Gifts at Rosehill – Jackie used hers whenever she wanted, as long as she had the other person's consent – but until you could control your Gift, you weren't supposed to use it inside the house, or around other people. Charlie's telekinesis wasn't the end of the world when it got away from him, but there were a few close calls when students nearly burnt the place down.

"That's very kind of you boys," I said as Brandon followed his younger brother and used his Gift to put away a box of canned soups. The two of them were so alike, with bright blue eyes, dirty blond hair, and matching Gifts, but Charlie's locks were almost at his shoulders, while Brandon kept his in a buzz cut.

"It's our pleasure," Charlie assured me, tucking a loose strand of that sandy-blond hair behind his ear so he could have a better eye line of his target. His eagerness – both to help and for an excuse to use his Gift – was heartwarming, but it also made me nervous.

"The cereal boxes are a lot lighter," I pointed out when I realized Charlie was going for an industrial-sized bag of flour, which belonged all the way across the kitchen, inside the pantry. I was careful not to tell him to stop, or not to lift things he couldn't handle. I knew they could both lift even the heaviest of my groceries, and I wasn't the least bit worried about Brandon, but Charlie was easily distracted, and once he lost his concentration, everything he had up would fall to the ground.

"He's got this," Brandon assured me as I opened the door to the pantry so Charlie would have one less thing to worry about.

The flour landed softly in its place, while Brandon sent the laundry detergent out of the kitchen where he could no longer see it, listening to make sure it landed on the shelf in the laundry room. His Gift was stronger than any telekinetic I'd encountered at that age, and his brother had the same potential, but I often had a case of monkey see, monkey do, that ended terribly.

I washed the produce from the garden while they worked, careful not to get in the way of flying grocery items. Penny sat on the beige marble countertop and sampled everything, occasionally giving the boys orders and suggestions.

"A little more to the left," she guided Brandon with her mouth full of snap peas.

At seventeen, he was more graceful at putting things away in tight spaces, but Charlie was braver and faster, carrying way more than his fair share with the untouchable confidence of a fourteen-year-old boy who excelled at everything he tried.

Things were going smoother than I'd expected, until Lena came in through the open French door just as Charlie was adding a jar of cloves to the spice rack. I watched in a panic as Charlie lost his hold on the cloves and they crashed down onto the rack, launching a chain reaction that had dozens of glass jars falling to the ground – until Brandon caught them all with his Gift, leaving the lot suspended a few inches from the ground.

"Oh, thank God. That was almost—"

I was halfway through exhaling when a much bigger glass jar containing chia seeds crashed to the floor and exploded everywhere.

I immediately grabbed Penny, who was barefoot and inching her way closer to get a better look at the damage.

"I'm sorry," Charlie said. "I had it, but then…" I followed his gaze to the empty doorway, but Lena had vanished. Penny was convinced the fifteen-year-old had the Gift of invisibility, and while I knew that wasn't the case, I couldn't tell you if she'd retreated outside, or if she'd slipped upstairs while we were all watching the commotion.

"It's fine. I have tons more in the storeroom," I assured him.

"We'll clean it up," Brandon said as he dropped the telekinesis and grabbed a pair of brooms, handing one to his brother.

"I can help too," Mateo offered from the hallway, having no doubt heard the crash. The twelve-year-old took a step towards the dustpan before I saw his bare feet on the now-speckled white floor.

"Mateo, you're not wearing shoes!" I warned, harsher than I intended. "This floor is terrible for spotting glass, and the boys are already taking care of it." I tried to let him know I was trying to protect him, that I wasn't mad, but he wasn't used to me yet. He'd been at Rosehill a little over a month, after bouncing around multiple foster homes, and that was more words than we got from him most days. While Charlie's long hair was a fashion statement, Mateo's was so he had something to hide behind.

"I'll get shoes." He turned to leave, but Charlie stopped him.

"Don't bother, we're almost done." He looked guilty and ashamed, which was the outcome I'd been expecting, but that didn't make it any easier.

"You were doing an excellent job today, Charlie. I was very impressed." I gave him an encouraging smile.

He nodded, then got back to the mess while I brought Penny to get shoes.

The kitchen was spotless by the time we returned, with even the counters sparkling, except for the addition of a rather large aluminum tray filled with lasagna noodles and meat sauce.

"Perfect timing," Chris said, coming out of the walk-in fridge with a head of lettuce, wearing his *Kiss the Chef* apron. "I was looking for someone to help me add the finishing touches to the lasagna." He was Michelin-starred and aspiring chefs would kill to train under him, but he spent his vacation days here, making kid-approved classics with underqualified sous chefs.

"You mean the cheese?" Penny's eyes got wide as she looked up at me with wonder, wordlessly asking if she could do the honors.

"As long as you've washed your hands," I assured her before taking out the plates and cutlery I would need to set the table for dinner.

"You put some underneath too, right?" Penny verified after she moved the bench to the sink and started scrubbing the dirt from the garden out of her fingernails.

"Why, was I supposed to?" Chris teased, but quickly reassured Penny when she looked at the dish with horror. "Ricotta *and* mozzarella," he assured her.

"Thank goodness." She smiled, then poured an entire bag of shredded cheese onto the lasagna, tiny handful by tiny handful.

We made a garden salad while the lasagna cooked, before everyone trickled into the dining room. I tried to get everyone together for lunch as well, but dinner was non-negotiable. Unless you were sick or away, you either ate with everyone, or… it wasn't like I would make anyone starve, but there was no going off to eat on your own. Even before Rosehill's completion, it was a rule I put in place with the construction crews and household staff. It seemed silly to keep up with old and stuffy traditions in the new world, with no one watching. Our friends nearly fainted when they came for a visit and sat down to an evening meal with the maids, butlers, and groomsmen all together, but everyone working at Rosehill quickly became family anyhow.

These days, it was moody teenagers I had to convince to leave their phones behind, rather than busy employees concerned with decorum. Charlie, Brandon, Jackie, and Penny sat down first and got along like siblings, catching up on their days and teasing each other as my brothers and sisters had done with me centuries ago.

Once the lasagna was ready, Chris put it on the table and took the seat next to Ben. They looked like brothers, an older version of Brandon and Charlie, only there was no relation, and Ben, though he looked a touch younger, was more like a grandfather, age-wise. They talked about cars and sports, two things I knew very little about. I understood the rules to everything one of my kids or students played, thanks to all the Sunday games I cheered them on at, but the only athletes I knew from the twenty-first century were the odd few who graduated from Rosehill, or happened to be Gifted.

Lena didn't trust us yet, but she'd quickly figured out that the best way to avoid suspicion was to play her part and pretend she did. It broke my heart to watch her do it, and to know there was a school somewhere, like Rosehill, where they trained little girls to become heartless killing machines. Luckily, I watched Lena in the moments she thought no one was looking and caught glimpses of the heart she kept hidden. Mostly with animals on the grounds who would never reveal her secrets. At least not to me.

"I made the cheese part of the lasagna," Penny told everyone.

"That's the best part," Jackie assured her. "It smells amazing."

"I made sure it was bubbling before Chris took it out, because I know you don't like cold cheese, see?" Penny leaned over the table to show Brandon how browned it was, because he only liked melted cheese. She dropped her doll in the process and Lena, without saying a word, got the doll from the floor and put it back on Penny's chair before she could notice. But I did.

"How was your day?" I asked Mateo, the only other person who was eating in silence. He always sat as far removed from the rest of us as he could and shoveled down his food as fast as humanly possible before asking to be excused.

"Okay." He shrugged.

"I heard you're acing math. At a college level. We might need to hire a new teacher next semester."

If I thought praising the twelve-year-old's skills would help get him out of his shell, I was dead wrong. The glare he gave me would have made me recoil if there wasn't so much hurt behind his brown eyes.

"Math is easy." He dismissed the compliment. "I don't need a teacher."

I had so many questions about his aversion to praise, but he was already on his last bite. He stood up the moment the food was in his mouth and tried to swallow so he could ask to be excused.

"We're making brownies for dessert. You can crush the nuts to put on top," Penny offered before he got the words out.

Mateo looked to Penny, then to the rest of us, who were all waiting for his reaction. It was easy to retreat to an empty room when you wanted to be alone, but Penny made it infinitely harder when she asked you to do something with her.

"I'm not hungry tonight, but maybe another time," he told her apologetically before turning to me. "May I be excused?"

The other kids sometimes asked that question as they ran out the door whenever something exciting happened, but as much as Mateo wanted to be on his own, he never left until I dismissed him.

"Of course. The brownies will be on the counter if you change your mind." I smiled until he turned away, wishing I could figure out how to reach him.

"Give him time." Ben came and put his hand on mine while I absentmindedly watched Jackie, Penny, and Chris making brownies.

"He's only been here a few weeks," I agreed, but Ben's smile told me he knew I was still worried.

"It takes at least a few months to get used to your over-bearing mothering." He shrugged.

"I can't tell if you're teasing or not," I warned as the house phone rang.

I went over to answer it, but Jackie moved faster than was safe for someone who couldn't see where she was going and beat me to it.

"Rosehill Academy, how may I help you?" The seventeen-year-old greeted in her version of my British accent, as if prospective students ever called that number. We didn't adver-tise, so most of our student body came from referrals, or we recruited them. "Are you on your way?"

Jackie dropped the accent, and I could tell from her smile that it was Tristan on the other end, even before she asked a bunch of follow-up questions about Alison and their trip.

"Tristan got used to it," Ben pointed out, stopping me from eavesdropping further. "And I didn't mean it like your constant care and attention is what's stopping Mateo from joining in."

"It just doesn't help?"

"He needs time to understand that he's safe here, that you won't send him away, and no matter how many times he turns you down, you will still be there, ready to welcome him with open arms once he's ready. It's scary when you've been hurt in the past, but time proves it's real," he explained.

"Then I'll keep doing what I'm doing." I smiled, but I wasn't sure if we were still just talking about Mateo, or if Ben was implying some similarities between me and the boy who was hesitant to accept my love.

"Sure, Delia's right here," Jackie said with an exaggerated sigh, handing me the phone.

"How are you? How's Alison?" I asked, nodding when Ben motioned to say he was going to take care of things outside. He'd arrived less than a century ago and worked his way up from the recruiter to teacher to my right-hand man. I was perhaps too reliant upon him, because I couldn't run Rosehill without him at this point.

"We're... okay." Tristan considered my question before answering. "Finally got on the road, so we should be at the airfield soon."

"Are you sure you want to go straight to California tonight? Rosehill is on your way to the airfield. You could spend a few days here and calm your nerves a bit before facing her family." Not to mention my own nerves. That he'd come back to life did not negate the fact that he'd died on me. There was a weight in my chest that wouldn't go away until I saw he was okay.

"Alison hasn't seen them since this all started, which might only be a couple of weeks, but it feels like a lifetime. Do we still have people with them?"

"Of course. Until the threat is over, we will keep an eye on the Carmichaels. But they're all welcome here," I reminded him.

"I'll keep that in mind."

"For as long as they need," I added. I knew Tristan was rolling his eyes at my 'overbearing mothering', but I couldn't help it even if I tried. "I believe Jen is working in San Francisco for the summer, so if you need anything while you're there, I'm sure she and Peter would be happy to help."

"You have friends everywhere, don't you?" he called me on it. He'd met the two of them a few years ago, but had Jen left Rose-hill and settled on an island commune decades before I found Tristan. "We'll reach out if we need anything, but Alison's pretty eager to see her family, and she promised she would spend her time at the hotel or the hospital, so we won't be doing social calls."

"When the world stops making sense, you need your family more than ever. Will you let me know when you get there?"

"Of course." I could hear the smile in his voice. I knew it was a sad one, because he'd lost his biological family, but I was enough of a nagging, worrying mother that he never had to feel like he was on his own.

"Safe travels," was as close as I was going to get to telling him to be careful and drive safe.

"Always," he assured me before hanging up.

CHAPTER TWO

ALISON

Tristan ran his hand through his dark, messy hair before putting it back on the steering wheel. We were off to an airfield in the middle of nowhere because Tristan knew a pilot who could fly us to California under the radar. I would have felt safer on a commercial airline, but I had to get to my family.

There were a million thoughts running through my mind as I stared out the window, pretending I hadn't been listening in on his call. Now that we were driving away from the craziness of the past month, part of me wanted to forget all of it and start fresh in California as if I didn't know that I was a First Lifer with people trying to kidnap me so they could study my blood. Unfortunately, playing pretend wouldn't be much help. Not when I was the problem, with my rare Gift a built-in, very permanent reminder. No matter where I went, random objects I touched would show me their darkest, most traumatic memories. Every Gifted would temporarily lose their Gifts. And, worst of all, every person who got close to me would get sick, losing more and more of their health until there was nearly nothing left, like I'd been doing to my sister for over a decade.

Until I figured out how to control my particular 'Gift',

Tristan was the only person I was touching, and that was because he was the one who initiated it and refused to listen when I told him I would never touch anyone – or anything – ever again. He insisted we would figure it all out together, but to be honest, I mostly agreed with the people who'd kidnapped me. They believed that because of the part of my Gift that took away other people's Gifts, my blood could somehow turn Gifted back into regular humans. I probably would have stayed with them and helped them accomplish their goals if they didn't insist on administering it to all Gifted, whether they wanted it or not. Because given the choice, I would gladly get rid of my so-called 'Gift'.

"You're a million miles away." Tristan reached over the console to hold my hand. The sparks I felt when our skin connected used to give me butterflies, but now I knew it was just the remnants of his Gift that I was sucking away from him, however unintentionally. He didn't let go, but I knew he felt the sparks as well. Instead, he rubbed his thumb against my skin in a soothing back-and-forth manner. I loved him for showing me he wasn't afraid, and that touching me was worth it, but I was terrified of what could happen if we were attacked again while he was so vulnerable.

I could not watch him die a second time.

"Just processing." I gave him a smile, which he returned, before I went back to staring out the window.

"You are taking it a lot better than I did," he shared, getting my attention away from the trees.

"When you found out you were semi-immortal?"

I was fully aware that he was trying to distract me, but I welcomed the diversion. I'd been wanting to ask about his past since the moment I found out he was Gifted. Usually, when you die, you're dead, but if you're Gifted, you wake up with a supernatural ability and don't stay dead until you accomplish some kind of purpose. But how would you figure that out without someone there to tell you? All I knew for Tristan was that the doctors wanted to amputate his leg as a last-ditch attempt to stop the spread of his cancer, but he died before the surgery could take place. He'd never mentioned 'waking up'.

"Being a First Lifer – and being hunted for it – sucks," Tristan began, so as not to take away from my horrific experience. I'd drowned when I was younger, and it took just long enough for my dad's CPR to work that my Gift got activated, even if I didn't fully die. "But if you're not a First Lifer, then you don't find out you're Gifted until after you've died. When you wake up. If you're lucky, you stumble onto another Gifted who can explain everything to you before you get the chance to freak out."

"Is that what happened to you?"

"Not quite. The dying part wasn't bad. I was so tired of fighting that I wasn't even afraid of what came next. They kept giving me morphine to make me comfortable, and I drifted in and out with last goodbyes from the people I loved, and then it was over." He kept his eyes on the road, but I couldn't tell if he was seeing it, or if he was lost in his thoughts. I wanted to ask him what dying was like, but a shadow crossed his face. "Until I woke up." He swallowed. "I was in one of those…"

"A coffin?" I suggested.

"No. I guess you would call it a drawer? One of those things in morgues that only opens from the outside." I understood he knew the last part from experience, which made me reconsider whether I wanted to hear the rest of the story.

"I guess I'm lucky someone I trusted figured it out and sent me to Grace, who tried to teach me how to use it." Although it wasn't so lucky for either of them. Dr. Richards died alone after being tortured for information on me, and Grace barely survived a violent attack from the same people.

I took a deep breath and brought my focus back to Tristan.

"My luck was that it only took an hour of banging and

screaming before someone heard and let me out." He forced a smile, but there was nothing lucky about it, only less terrible than it could have been. "Unfortunately, it was the employee who'd signed for my body and just received hundreds of bookmarks with my face on them. He did not react well to seeing me alive."

"I am so sorry you went through that." I could only imagine how terrible that must have been for him. For both of them.

"I was confused and terrified, but the guy literally died."

"You killed him?!?" I was shocked, and the words came out before I could stop myself.

"Technically. But that was when I discovered my Gift. Not that I understood it at the time. I bent over him and tried to do CPR, but when I did my first compression, shocks of electricity travelled from my hands into him and restarted his heart. I called 911 and stayed with him until I heard the sirens, then I ran off into the night. It took me forever to slow down and realize no one was coming after me. I guess no one believed the guy, and the funeral director didn't want to admit they'd lost a body. But it begs the question of what they cremated for my mom's urn."

"You went home?" I asked delicately. I knew he hadn't spoken to most of his family in years, but I could only imagine how someone would react to finding their dead son on their doorstep.

"Eventually. I saw the pile of booklets from my funeral. Then I watched my parents sift through casseroles and cards through the living room window. I wanted, more than anything, to rush in and tell them I was okay, that there had been some crazy mistake and they didn't have to be sad anymore… but even if I didn't understand it, I knew that I'd died. I'd seen enough horror movies to know no good could come from me coming back to life, so I was going to walk away and leave them alone, but Serena, my little sister, was crying on our backyard swing, looking so lost and scared, until she spotted me. Her face just lit up and… I couldn't leave her."

"You became her imaginary friend." I knew it wasn't nearly that simple, but I got a hopeful smile as he gave the back of my hand a kiss.

"I stayed close by and kept an eye on her, but I was mostly wandering the streets until Delia found me. The guy who found me hadn't let everyone calling him crazy stop him from telling people he saw a dead body come back to life, and eventually, it got back to Rosehill. Delia took me in and taught me what Gifted are, as well as how to control my Gift. I still snuck out to watch Serena play, or popped over for a chat when she was alone in the backyard, but as time went on… imaginary friends aren't so common once you hit high school."

"She was the only one you visited? Not your other sister?" I knew he had two of them, but he only ever talked about the older one.

"Serena was the only one I let see me. My parents would have freaked out and Izzie was afraid of me even when I was still alive." I gave him a confused look, so he explained. "She was born when I was in remission, like a fresh start for the family, but by the time she could walk, I was constantly hooked up to machines with loud beeping and tubes going everywhere… it was just best if I didn't cause her any more nightmares. I tried to stay away from Serena too, especially once she got older, but by then she knew to look for me, so eventually…"

"She asked you to stop coming, and you found me." I tried to add a happy spin to it, but I was painfully aware of how much trouble I'd brought into his life in such a short period. He'd come to Boston for a change of scenery after his sister told him it was better if he stayed away from her, and I immediately put his life in danger and asked him to stay away from me, before he saved my life and I watched him die. Though not in that order.

"My heart broke, and you put it back together," he agreed.

"I can't imagine—"

I had paused to let out a breath and gather my thoughts for something reassuring to say. Instead, I grabbed on to his arm and yelled, "Tristan!" in case he hadn't seen the pick-up that swerved out of nowhere and came to a grinding halt in the middle of the road, maybe twenty feet ahead of us.

I assumed the driver had fallen asleep, and I didn't want Tristan to smash into them, but he was more on the ball than I was, even before the people got out and faced us with a determination I found terrifying. Instead of stopping, Tristan had swerved into the field and drove as far as he could until it got too thick for us to keep going. He covered me a second before they launched something at us that shattered both windshields, raining glass everywhere.

"Run," Tristan commanded, opening my door so I could get out.

My brain was still trying to process what was going on, but luckily, my body was getting used to the adrenaline rush. We ventured through the field toward a wooded area. I made sure not to look back, but all I could think of was the truck's occupants, and how they'd looked like they wanted to kill me.

I slipped on a muddy slope once we got into the trees, scrambling to get up because I knew they were right behind us, even if I could no longer hear them over the rumble of the nearby river.

"Are you okay?" Tristan asked in a whisper when he slid down and joined me.

"I'm fine," I said, but he already had me back on my feet and we were running again, though this time he held on to my hand.

We headed for the river, which was good since they wouldn't be able to hear our footsteps, or my heartbeat that was drumming in my ears, but I didn't like the idea of not being able to hear how close they were.

We followed it a couple hundred feet before we got to a clearing. I'd been hearing the river since the tall grass of the field, but this was the first time I saw it flowing about thirty feet below us. My stomach churned as I stepped back from the edge. I was not a fan of heights and felt that anyone who went cliff diving had something seriously wrong with their brain chemistry. And a death wish.

"Shouldn't we be moving? In the cover of the trees?" I suggested. We were completely exposed, and I did not want a closer look at whatever burst the windshield.

"Do you trust me?" Tristan asked, taking my other hand in his.

"Yes..." This wasn't the first time he'd asked, though I'd trusted him a lot more when it was a question of where we were going on a date. His face was determined, but I could tell I wouldn't like it.

"On three, we're going to jump."

"Into the river?" I whispered it, more because I was hoping I'd misunderstood than because I thought anyone would overhear us.

"I won't let go," he promised. "One, two, three..."

And we jumped.

***

Find out what happens next in
Second Chance

9 781989 950579